BRICKS AND MURDER

SEATTLE SLAYERS
BOOK 2

KEN BEBELLE

JULIA VEE

Sixth
MOON

CONTENTS

PROLOGUE

Somewhere in the Wilds

TYEE

The smell of death was always the same. A thick, sweet scent that hit Tyee in the center of his chest and pulled at him like a magnet. Even here in the Wilds, beyond the Sentinel stones, where the flora grew to riotous proportions, the fresh scent of death pierced the rich aromas of earth and life like a beacon in fog. Mixed in with the intoxicating mix of life and death was the scent of one particular vampire that Tyee had been tracking for the better part of a day already. The scent was getting stronger. They were close.

Tyee moved through the temperate rainforest, his feet silent on the soft earth. He slipped around massive pines and ferns with clutching, poison-tipped fronds. The scent drew him closer to his target and his sense of unease grew as he closed the distance.

As the True Born son of the Night Queen, Tyee enjoyed a degree of notoriety that he relished. There were those in his mother's court who believed his human needs to be a weakness, but Tyee knew otherwise. If fresh blood was lacking, not only could he sustain himself on food and water, but he actually enjoyed it. The taste of this morning's coffee was a faint memory on his lips and he was looking forward to another later today. Once this was sorted out.

Leaves rustled to Tyee's right and he crouched, hiding himself and going completely still. Birdsong and a light breeze played through the trees. Underneath the frenzied aromas of the Wilds, Tyee caught the sharp tang of pine sap, a freshly felled tree, and the loamy smell of turned dirt. A large tree, then. The sound of light footsteps overtook him and carried on ahead. Tyee smiled and rose, his long legs striding out as he hurried to catch up.

The figure wore dark, fitted clothing, with finely tooled leather guards at the shins and forearms. The dark clothing only served to accentuate generous hips as the woman darted from shadow to shadow. Under a dark balaclava, a tight braid of golden hair had worked loose, hanging out at the back of her neck. A compact crossbow was fitted across her back, the weapon tied down and muffled to eliminate noise.

Tyee approached on cat's paws and brought his hand up to grab the woman by the neck. As his fingers brushed the fabric of the balaclava the woman fell into a forward roll and Tyee's fingers swiped through empty air.

The woman spun as she came up. The crossbow seemed to jump to her hands and her nimble fingers drew the crank in an easy motion. Eloise's bright eyes were like stars hidden in the slits of the dark fabric around her head.

Tyee drew up and raised his hands. "Peace, *ma chère*."

Eloise stood and lowered her weapon. "Mon prince! I could have shot you!"

Tyee closed the distance between them. He smiled as he

tucked the loose braid back under the balaclava. "I doubt it, but next time, you're welcome to try."

Eloise shipped her weapon, and stowed the bolt back onto her thigh, exasperation clear on her face. "Are we close, at least? The faster we find Conti the faster we get home."

Tyee's eyebrow twitched. Arturo Conti was a somewhat reliable informant, if a bit of a hassle to handle. As a perennial disappointment from a high-ranking vampire clan, he had the unique combination of access to closed doors and the benefit of being ignored by those who thought him useless. Tyee kept Conti supplied with pretty attendants and party invitations. Conti gave Tyee what he thought was harmless gossip, which Tyee then sifted through like a wizened prospector.

It was not uncommon for Conti to go missing for days. Odds are they would find him blood drunk under a tree. But the Night Queen had thought otherwise and sent Tyee to find the wayward vampire and bring him in from the dark.

Tyee knew to listen carefully when his mother spoke. She had not risen to power due to her ethereal and deadly beauty. She had a keen mind that worked on a staggering time scale. By the time her enemies realized she had out played them, the Night Queen had already moved onto her next targets. Tyee's mother was a primordial shark, ever moving, ever hunting, never quiescent.

This time, his mother had convinced him with only one word. A name. O'Malley.

Pierce Yang, king of the vampires and leaders of the Shadow's Den, was the balance on the scales of power to Tyee's mother. He ruled the Den with brutal strength, as opposed to the Night Queen's quiet subterfuge. But above all else, Yang could be relied upon to follow the law. And Tyee's sources had already informed him of the Vampire King's moves.

Keegan O'Malley was a different story. In the short time he'd been in Seattle, O'Malley had managed not only to make a name for himself, but to also pull a large number of vampires to his banner.

At first, Tyee had brushed it off, thinking O'Malley was merely rounding up feral rogues and using them as attack dogs. But lately O'Malley had been spotted with a growing number of mature vampires. A number that had caught his and his mother's attention. O'Malley was growing a new power base, and Tyee didn't know where it was coming from.

Tyee hated it when he didn't know something.

As the Night Queen's Whispermaster, it was his job, his pride even, to know what others only thought they knew. Tyee took rare joy in not only the knowing, but having the knowledge before anyone else. Somehow O'Malley was making a move, and he'd managed to do it in a blind spot that Tyee hadn't even known existed.

The very thought chafed at him.

The scent of death and blood grew thicker, more present. They were close now. A low hum came from ahead of them. He drew Eloise to his side and silenced her with a look. Tyee moved forward and pushed aside a large fern frond.

Fat flies covered the body in a thick carpet of buzzing wings. The shifter had been dead at least a few days, his thick pelt brittle as twigs with desiccation. A thick pine tree lay on its side, the roots ripped from the earth. Two parallel furrows had been torn through the bark of the tree. Eloise stepped around Tyee and covered her nose with her hand.

"What--"

"Werebison." Tyee knelt and pointed out the thick ruff of hair around the neck and shoulders, and the horns at the temples. One of the horns had broken off, leaving a bloody stump that protruded from the skin. Liquid, bovine eyes, too large for a human skull, stared blindly into the violet sky above them. Whatever had killed the shifter had caught him mid-change, and managed to bring down a charging werebison in half form. No easy task.

Eloise prowled to the other side of the body. "This makes no sense. The shifters at the Ranch are non-combatants. The whole point of living at the Ranch is to avoid...this." She gestured helplessly to the corpse.

Tyee leaned down, ignoring the buzzing insects, until his face was within an inch of the werebison's neck. He inhaled deeply, pushing his senses past the rot and decay, the blood and--

He sat up and cursed to himself. "What's missing?"

Eloise scanned the body, her brows furrowed. Her face cleared and then fell in dismay. "No."

Tyee nodded, holding tight to the fury in his chest. There was no werebison blood in or around the body. A vampire had drained the shifter dry. A vampire whose scent was all over the werebison's dead body. "I'm going to stake Conti myself when I find him."

1

THE DOJO

The muggy summer heat sat thick and heavy in the air and sweat drenched the back of my shirt as I fought in the courtyard. It didn't help that my opponent was my sensei, Kotori the Fox, and that she was three times faster than I was. Every time she smacked me with her staff I would have a bruise there for days.

And yet, I wouldn't trade a second of it. The thwack of bamboo bo staffs striking against each other, the twist of bodies and grunts of exertion felt like home.

When I'd been a kid in Boston, I'd played a lot of basketball and there was something about the squeak of shoes on the gym floor and the swish of the net and the thump of basketballs that always sounded right. Now I was a Slayer initiate in a city dripping with vampires and shifters and fae and the sounds of fighting, in or out of the Dojo, was the soundtrack that made me feel good. Made me feel strong.

And I needed that. Being a Slayer made me a target. I didn't carry the Midnight Rose yet but I'd earned my ink, exsanguinating my first vampire last month. My inking ceremony was tonight and I needed to burn off my nervous energy. Kotori had been more than willing to help.

Earning the Midnight Rose was why I joined the Slayers, part of my plan to save my mom from further decline. The Rose was the only way I knew to transport vampire blood across the Veil. Once I had it, my mom would be saved.

But I had been kidding myself. I'd almost washed out of the Trials on my way to becoming a Slayer initiate and only then did I face the truth—that I'd been doing it all along to live up to my dad's ideals. To step into his shoes and be as great, if not greater than Gabriel Lim, the Breaker of Seattle.

I still wanted that, but now it was tempered by something else—the loyalty I felt to my fellow Slayers. Even my sensei who was currently beating me with a stick.

Kotori's staff found my shin with a crack. I grunted at the pain and danced back a step. She moved smoothly into the opening, a swirling mass of brilliant red leather, the other end of her staff coming around at somewhere in the vicinity of the speed of sound. It didn't matter that I was a full head taller than Kotori, the petite woman could always get inside my longer reach.

In addition to trying to minimize the severity of my beating, Kotori had given me another task while she pounded me into the mat. After my last outing in the Trials, where I had nearly brought down an entire building on my own head, Kotori had deemed that I was in dire need of some finesse.

"Your magic can be an earthquake, but how often do you need an earthquake, *neh*? Any fool can smash a building to rubble." She'd rapped me on the head for emphasis. "But my kohai will master her control and not. Endanger. Her. Fellow. Slayers."

Bop, bop, bop, went her knuckles on my forehead.

So as I backed away, I focused my vision on the collection of three polished wooden bangles gracing Kotori's left forearm.

The bangles jingled as she brought her staff towards my shoulder. Last week had been the easy level. Kotori had precut the bangles, creating an obvious weak point for me to find and exploit. Although finding it while being chased around the mat had been difficult.

I brought my own staff up, barely in time, and caught Kotori's blow with a high block. The impact numbed my fingers and I strained to keep a grip on the bamboo. Dropping your weapon in Kotori's presence was not a good idea. I jabbed at Kotori's neck. The weighted staff passed through empty air as my sensei back flipped away from me, as graceful as a cat. Or a fox.

With a hair's breadth of breathing room, my magic kindled, outlining Kotori in a web of glowing green lines. I took a risk and narrowed my vision down to the wooden rings on her arm. Wherever Kotori was getting the rings made, the craftsmanship was excellent, nearly solid rings of green around her arm.

Nearly.

It was time to go on the offensive. I launched myself at Kotori, ignoring Cordelia's cheer from the sidelines. My staff came around in a low, wide arc, aimed at taking out her legs. Kotori jumped and tucked her legs out of harm's way.

In the split second she hung in the air I threw my magic forward and wormed it into the wooden bracelets. My power crawled up Kotori's arm like a greedy child and sank into the finely polished wood, soaking into the fine pores and grain. It sought out the microscopic fracture lines hidden to the naked eye.

Finding the flaws was the easy part. My magic did this on its own, with little to no effort. The next part, though, would cost me. I gritted my teeth, already anticipating the cost.

Pop! The first bracelet fell off Kotori's arm, neatly sheared in half. My sensei twisted in the air, her back arching, her center of gravity shifting as if by sheer will.

In the distant corners of my perception, the recoil from my magic built like a wave just moments from cresting. I shook off the sensation and pushed forward. My magic leapt to the next target.

Pop! The second bracelet splintered into tiny fragments. A ragged cheer went up from our spectators. Kotori fell to the mat, her crimson cloak swirling as she came down. I strained to reach the last bracelet.

The recoil swelled until it filled all the space behind Kotori like a storm ready to burst. My eyes flicked to the side. My mentor's nose twitched, a movement I'd learned to associate with her chronic disappointment.

Blood red leather filled my vision and my magic locked onto Kotori's cloak, an undulating wave of green light. I ignored it and pushed harder, bringing my focus back to the final bangle. Kotori's impending strike hovered over my head.

My vision blurred and the red leather cloak with white fur trim broke apart, dissolving like wet paint in rain. The cloak became a fan of crimson tails, the fur glossy and smooth, and tipped with arctic white. The shock broke my concentration and my magic snapped back to me. Kotori's staff slammed into my shoulder and rocked me back, stars blossoming before my eyes.

The recoil from my magic slammed into me and I flinched away from the pain and nausea but it was useless, like trying to evade your own shadow. My stomach turned upside down and I dry-heaved. I gave up on grace and simply fell to the mat to avoid Kotori's follow-up strike.

With a grunt of annoyance Kotori elbowed me in the ribs, pushing me into the fall. I landed with a jolt that rang my ears and knocked the breath out of my lungs. I gasped, trying to catch my breath, stuck between the effects of both the recoil and the impact. Long moments later, I came to my senses and found my mentor's staff aimed at my nose.

Kotori's lip curled. "And what did that get you, *neh*?"

I tried to control my breathing, to speak as evenly as she did. It still ended up coming out between panting gasps. "Two out of three isn't bad."

She rapped the end of her staff against my head. Ow. "So. You are dead, and you did not accomplish your mission. A failure on both counts, then."

She lifted her arm. The last bangle was still intact. "Your fear of your recoil is your weakness. Do not run from it, it is a natural consequence of your magic. If you wish to avoid the recoil, then renounce your magic. Are you a Breaker or not? "

I hated that she was right.

The recoil hurt and even worse, it left me vulnerable. I also had trouble fighting at the same time as Breaking. Either I had to learn to fight without using my Breaker magic, or I had to be able to Break things without hesitating. Recoil or not.

Kotori stepped back and I rubbed my head. I didn't think I would have a lump there tomorrow. Maybe. As I rolled back onto my feet, Kotori flicked her fingers at me in a dismissive gesture. "Go work on the mat. I will spar with Wen so I can get my own workout in."

I was insulted and relieved at the same time, which was par for the course when I dealt with my feral sensei. I bowed to her and racked my bo staff on my way to the mats.

Truthfully, Wen was a better hand-to-hand fighter than I was. He had an economy of movement that made his sparring look effortless. Even when fighting the Fox, Wen didn't seem to break a sweat. Not that he beat her. None of us ever beat her. As part of my Trials, I had rapidly concluded that she would crush me but she didn't want to actually kill me and I'd fought accordingly. That was the only way I'd gotten even a scratch on her.

I wasn't so foolish as to repeat that.

A soft puff of air brushed my hair as Wen stepped by. And

by stepped, I mean in that ethereal way he moved, as if traversing an invisible staircase. It would have been even cooler if Wen had long flowing hair to go with his gray monk's robes, but he shaved his head to spotless perfection daily.

My floor routines beckoned, but I couldn't help stopping to watch Wen spar with Kotori.

Wen wasn't tall, but with his robes and musculature, he looked like a giant next to Kotori. They made a striking tableau, the slight Fox in red, and the big monk in gray. All we needed was rain and some mood music.

Their staffs struck against each other in a staccato of hits the human eye could barely follow. That made sense since Kotori wasn't human. But Wen was. His staff speeds were the envy of the rest of the initiates. I'd asked him about it, assuming there was some ten thousand hours type of reason for his skill.

"I know where the next strike will go so I just try to get there," Wen explained.

As far as I could tell, Wen had decades of training *and* his magic here in the Veil gave him a preternatural sense of what would happen next–like fighting clairvoyance. It seemed extremely useful to me, especially for a Slayer.

Behind me, Ulf Skardeson of the Reach, stumbled and then grunted with annoyance as Bashir whacked him on the ribs. "Why this stick? Why not let me train with my axe? Or a sword, I ask you?" Ulf complained.

Bashir laughed. "Sometimes all you have is a stick. What then? You must master all the weapons at your disposal."

"Bah." Ulf shook his head, his long red braids moving in emphasis with his annoyance. He set his bo staff next to mine and came to stand next to me. He slapped my back with what for him was probably a companionable tap but practically knocked me forward.

Bashir gave a sharp whistle, and a swirl of leaves circled

around Cordelia. With a cheerful smile, she waved at Bashir and he tossed her a bo staff.

Cordelia, perfect at everything, leapt in the air and caught the staff in one smooth motion. She launched into a front roll with the staff to land in front of Bashir. Bashir's handsome face split into a broad grin, white teeth flashing against his dark beard. She was his favorite and it was easy to see why. Cordelia was a natural, and she was good-natured to boot.

Somehow, her fae robes didn't get a smudge of dirt on them. I wondered if they were spelled to repel dirt. It would explain how Cordelia managed to stay so clean even after rolling in the mud. I always came out of these workouts a hot sweaty mess, my samue jacket usually sporting a rip or tear.

Cordelia had taken a shine to me at the first Trial and I'd never understood why. I was a grubby street fighter who favored hammers for my weapon of choice. Cordelia harkened from a noble fae family and wielded a milky sword that gleamed like moonlight. She'd earned my loyalty and my friendship, and I'd learned to ignore her critiques of my messy fighting style.

The only time I'd ever seen her smile fade was when she dealt with the mountain fae. Like our first encounter with Ulf and his brothers.

I'd grown fond of Ulf, which was a far cry from how we'd started out. His former sworn brother, Harald Stenson, was a prince of the mountain fae tribe Ulf hailed from. Harald had taken an instant dislike to me in the first Trials to become a Slayer. The battle lines had been drawn that day, with me and Cordelia on one side, and the mountain fae on the other.

Then the Trials escalated. We were forced to put aside old blood feuds, petty grievances, and just plain annoyance to work together and survive those Trials. Ulf and I had made it out of the Box. His sworn brotherhood with Harald had not survived.

Ulf and Cordelia had never explained to me what

happened on their Trial together but they had reached an uneasy truce, with the millennia old blood feud no longer at the forefront of their dealings. They were Slayers now, and their fae politics had taken a back seat. At least, that was how it looked to me.

I was still relatively new to the Veil. This intersection of Tarim magic and powerful factions like the fae, the two vampire courts, the various churches, and the Slayers often confused me. But I tried to keep it simple, like cleaving to my identity as a Slayer. Sometimes things got messy for me, like my interactions with Tyee Wilder, the Night Prince. He was a vampire that I was better off avoiding but couldn't help thinking about. I appreciated that Slayer training kept me busy. Busy enough to avoid wandering by the Pleasure District to bump into Tyee.

Especially after tonight.

We were getting our ink. I would be a Slayer, like my father before me. Cordelia, Wen, and Ulf would be by my side. If that meant I had to avoid a certain flirtatious vampire prince, it was worth it.

"We should go celebrate tonight." I said to Ulf.

"Aye." Ulf was always up for a party.

"Anywhere you want to go?" I asked.

"Why not here?"

"Sure. Here is fine with me."

I was actually surprised he didn't want to go to The Rose and Horn pub. He was fond of the ale, which they served in enormous mugs, and I was fond of the meat pies. There were cheese platters for Cordelia and even salads for Wen. Overall, we'd spent our fair share of time grabbing meals out at The Rose and Horn.

Ulf bunked here at the Dojo. Wen did as well, so they didn't have kitchens. Cordelia kept where she lived under wraps but I also gathered that she didn't cook much. As for me, I kept my cozy studio apartment in the old international district, or risked my landlady's displeasure. It turned out that my baking was a good side hustle as well and the rest of them often bought my meals at the pub since I kept them supplied with baked goods.

Also, I liked having that bit of personal space. It was me, my pigeons, and my side hustle projects, which was just the way I liked it. Slayers was too consuming otherwise and I kept my space to remind myself that I still had to follow through on my promise to my dad. It meant becoming a Slayer but betraying the geas that kept Slayer secrets. Away from Slayers, I could look at that picture of my family and remember that my work wasn't done. Soon.

"Yield." Kotori had maneuvered Wen to the wall, her staff pressing into his neck.

Wen had lasted three times longer than I had. While Kotori often expressed her irritation at my candidacy, I could tell she approved of Wen's addition to the ranks. That she thought he was what Slayers needed more of.

I wanted to be like that, but earning Kotori's approval seemed impossible, so I aimed to avoid her wrath.

Kotori released Wen and he bowed to her. She bowed back and gave him a punch on the bicep. I'd never seen her do that with anyone other than Bashir. I guess after our ink, we would all be equals, but some of us were more equal than others.

Ulf gave Wen a fist bump and then we moved through some stretching routines together and I asked Wen if he had a preference for celebration festivities.

Wen's eyebrows drew down and he frowned. "I wanted to tell you all together."

"Tell us what?"

"I will not be getting the ink."

"What? Why not?"

Wen looked at me, his dark eyes solemn. "Roxy, you should ask more questions about the effects of the ink."

His words hit me like a punch in the gut.

All of us were supposed to get our ink tonight. We'd survived the Trials together and it had made us stronger. And now Wen was telling us that he didn't want the ink.

It was also strange that he should direct that only at me and not Ulf. I hadn't thought about the effects of the ink at all. We all had the scars of our last interaction with the Tarim crystal. When I cut myself on the crystal, it had drunk from me, then healed me. Until that ceremony, I'd always thought of the crystal as inert. But now I knew better.

And Wen was telling me the ink was why he wasn't going to be Slayer.

Now I had to ask myself, did I want to know?

Would I do it anyway?

I WENT HOME for a shower and to get a meal in before the ceremony this evening. Normally I'd be weary after a long workout session but tonight I took the stairs two at a time to my apartment.

A faint blur of light hovered in my doorway though.

"Hi, Ernest."

The light coalesced into more form and substance. Ernest could manifest pretty solidly now. Apparently my feeding him had something to do with that. But he'd saved my bacon at the Box and I was happy to always leave an offering for him.

"Slayer," He mouthed.

That never got old. Ernest had faith in me before I'd even passed the Trials. "Yeah, and I get my ink tonight!"

We grinned at each other and I dashed inside to grab a bowl of rice for Ernest. On my kitchen counter was a small glass jar. I picked it up and inspected it. Pork floss. This had to be from Mrs. Chu. I debated showering first or eating first and food won out. I heated myself some congee, pulled out some pickled turnips and dumped a heap of pork floss on top. The savory fried pork with the cool pickles was so satisfying and for a minute I just blissed out, happy to fill my body with protein, fat, and carbs.

Two sharp raps on my door. "Roxy."

It was Mrs. Chu.

I stopped chewing and concentrated on releasing my locks, my magic opening the series of charmed locks in a rapid fire release. When I used my magic for small tasks like this, the recoil was barely noticeable.

Mrs. Chu came in, decked out in a green velour tracksuit with white stripes. Her face brightened when she saw me eating. "Oh good, you're trying the pork floss."

I nodded. "It's great! Thanks so much."

She sniffed. "You need the protein."

I needed *any* calories. I'd always been on the lean side and the work at the Dojo coupled with long patrol shifts meant I'd honed down to a form rippling with tight muscle. It also meant I was a furnace for calories and had to constantly eat. Which meant I cooked a lot of batches of stuff that would be portable.

The pork floss Mrs. Chu had given me would be great in onigiri. She was so thoughtful. I'd really lucked out having this gracious woman take me into her home.

"Could I send a pigeon to Bev?"

I swallowed the last of the congee and stood. "Sure, let's go out on the balcony."

Noodle and Dumpling stepped up their cooing when they saw Mrs. Chu. She cared for them often when I was out on patrol and I suspect she snuck them extra treats.

She chatted with Noodle as she tucked a note into the capsule. With a gentle lift, Noodle was off to the Wilds.

"You expecting a return message from Bev?" I asked.

Mrs. Chu shrugged. "Bev missed our Market day, which

isn't like her. Her farm produces a lot of essential oils and herbs that do well at Market. So Malia and I picked up some provisions for her. I just asked if she needed anything else before I come down for mahjong night this week."

Ah yes, their mahjong night was regular as clockwork. Sometimes I lost track of the days and wandered up there and always regretted it. The scrutiny of four aunties was too much for me. Bev Peterson owned the River Rock Farm and enjoyed her privacy. She came out from the Wilds twice a week, once for Market and once for mahjong. But I guess it was her turn to host this week.

"I'm going to be gone tonight, Mrs. Chu."

"That's fine. I can come up and check for Noodle's return."

I beamed at her. "I get my ink tonight!"

She patted my shoulder. "Congratulations. I know how hard you've worked for this."

I wrapped my arms around her and gave her a quick squeeze. "Thanks for helping me through it all."

I'd made it at last. And soon I would have the ink that proclaimed to all of Seattle that I was a Slayer.

2

INK

This was it.

I was finally getting my ink tonight.

I wondered who would come for this. When Cordelia, Wen, Ulf and I had passed the Trials, all of the Seven Freaks of Seattle had come for our initiation. It had been unlike anything I could have imagined. We'd taken an oath to never speak of it but whenever I looked down at the scars on my right hand, the way the faint lines crisscrossed over my knuckles, I wished I could talk about it with Mrs. Chu, my wolf shifter landlady surrogate aunty.

But now Wen had planted a seed of doubt in my head. What did he know that I didn't about the ink?

There was only one person I could ask about it, but the problem was I seldom got answers from him. Or full answers anyway.

I left the sparring area behind and sought out my uncle. He often retreated to the Armory, his Maker magic sparking so bright I could spot it from the other end of the hallway. This part of the Dojo was old, the pine aged with a golden patina. The dim twilight streamed in through the slatted windows and shoji panels. As always when I walked these hallowed halls, I felt a sense of connection to my father. He'd walked them once too and now I was here.

I knocked on the wide double doors of the Armory.

"Come in."

The deep timber of Samuel's voice was so achingly familiar, but that patient tone was uniquely his. My father had never been patient.

Weapons of all shapes and sizes were racked up on the walls. For obvious reasons, most of them featured extremely sharp blades. That was more useful for a decap.

But on the rosewood table before Samuel lay several glowing shards of the Tarim crystal. Samuel augmented these into specialty weapons for things like exsanguination. Or my father's spear that was still deep in the bowels of The Box. Thinking about that still brought a pang of loss. Samuel had given me that spear and I'd managed to hold onto it for less than two days.

"Roxy, I'm glad you came to get me."

His broad face creased into a rare smile. The family resemblance between us was so strong it had been laughable to think that Samuel had initially tried to hide it when I was going through the Trials. Standing together, anyone could see we had the same angled jawline, the sharp cheekbones, and arched brows that framed our faces. We were both tall and strong, and while I was on the lean side, Samuel had shoulders like a linebacker. He should have had gray in his long black hair, but the Veil had kept him looking young. His eyes though had the battle-hardened weariness of decades.

His smile gave me a warm flush of happiness because he wasn't a person that dispensed much praise. I'd thought he would be my inside line to getting into Slayers but instead he had been so relentlessly determined to appear neutral he'd almost let Aislinn and Kotori boot me out of the Trials.

I was glad that was behind us now. He was proud of me for getting this far and sometimes I thought my dad might be too.

I leaned forward and tapped the wood next to the closest crystal shard.

"For my ink tonight, is there more you can tell me?"

"What do you mean?"

"Are there any side effects?"

Samuel frowned, his right hand absently going to the back of his neck where his ink lay.

I'd never fully understood why Slayers had their ink on the nape of their necks but after Wen's admonition, I realized I should try to figure it out now.

Samuel wore his hair long, so his ink wasn't visible. But Kotori often sported an undershave which showed off the Slayer's ink on her nape. A shimmering outline of two raised arms, one hand clenched over the fist of the other. Shifters could heal virtually anything. For a tattoo to be permanent on Kotori should have been my first clue that the ink was something special.

He dropped his hand and then reached for one of the shards of crystal on the table. He held it up and it gleamed with an inner fire that had nothing to do with the fairy lights strung around the ceiling.

"Do you remember your initiation?"

"Sure."

"Have you been back in the crystal chamber since then?"

I shook my head. It was pretty much off limits to us grunts. As far as I knew, only Tanner and the Seven Freaks had access.

Samuel's lips thinned. "Of course not. I didn't think."

He picked up a second shard, a bit longer than the first. He struck them together and instead of the dull clack I expected, the shards clanged like two chimes. The surprise must have shown on my face.

Samuel gestured to the shards. "Close your eyes and listen."

He struck them again and I obeyed, squeezing my eyes tight. The sound of the crystal was light but piercing. I waited and though seconds had passed since Samuel had hit the crystals, I could hear the faintest jangle still, like an afterimage smudged into my brain.

"Okay, why does it sound like that?"

Samuel shrugged. "We don't know. But after the ink, it's stronger."

Weird, but why did that trouble Wen? Maybe I was coming at this the wrong way. "What's the ink made of?"

"We grind the crystal and then mix it with akkorokamui ink."

The akkorokamui were the giant octopi of Ainu legend. When the Drowning happened and when the Tarim crystal pyramids rose, many creatures emerged from the deep of the Pacific Ocean. The akkorokamui were one of them. Maybe mixing Tarim crystal and megafauna ink led to volatile results. Perhaps that was why Wen was concerned?

Wen had the most measured and calm approach to life of anyone I'd ever met. I couldn't see him being alarmed on speculative grounds though.

I held out my hand and Samuel obliged, dropping one of the crystals into them. I traced the sharp edges, the scars on my knuckles reminding me of that surreal initiation experience. I'd bled on the crystal and my blood had been absorbed by the surface immediately. As if it had drunk it. But it had healed my skin instantly and I thought about the minuscule bits of crystal that were embedded in my scars now. That was how it sparked when we met other Slayers and greeted each other.

"When you say it's stronger after ink, what do you mean?"

My uncle frowned, his thick eyebrows drawing together in concentration as he struggled to form an answer. Finally he responded, "It's like you expect to hear more, and while you wait the feeling is stretched out and you want to hear the next note of song but don't."

That was totally not what I was expecting.

It sounded like longing.

Did I want more of that embedded into the nape of my neck?

Samuel set the two crystals down on the rosewood table, giving them a slight roll as he did so. They should have sounded like dice clacking together. Instead, they gave off the soft ping like my Tibetan singing bowl.

Samuel reached out both arms and set his hands down firmly on my shoulders. "I'm proud of you, Roxy. I know it was hard getting here."

Tears stung the back of my eyes and I swallowed hard. "Thanks. That means a lot to hear you say it."

It really did.

In that moment I knew without a doubt that I would be getting the ink, weird sounds or not.

I FOUND Ulf and Cordelia in the courtyard just inside the gates to the Dojo. Above us, the sky of the Twilight was an unbroken canvas of violet clouds. To the south, the moon was a bare hint of light behind the Veil. A ring of torches had been set up, along with several benches. Cordelia smiled at me when I entered the ring but didn't take her attention from the tall and coldly beautiful fae before her.

Aislinn. As one of the Freaks of Seattle, she was one of the governing members of the Slayers. As I understood it, she was also one of our most powerful magic users. Perhaps she was giving her fellow fae some pointers for the night. Cordelia certainly seemed to be paying close attention.

Ulf sat on the far bench, where he was trying valiantly to

fend off Altan's attempts to push a jug of something that I could smell to be alcoholic, even from ten feet away. Actually it smelled quite nice, and I made my way to join them. If nothing else I could swap recipes with Altan.

Before I crossed the center, someone called my name from the darkness. I turned to see my charge, Finnegan running across the courtyard. As he got close, I could see sweat beaded on his pale freckled skin, his strawberry hair muted in the torchlight. Finn's eyes looked hazel at first glance but once I'd spotted the tips of his ears, I could see his fae heritage more clearly and the gold glints in his eyes became more obvious to me. When we left the Dojo though, he always wore slouchy knit hats to cover those ears.

The kid was finally putting on some weight. Not quite muscle exactly, but Finn no longer looked like a stiff wind would knock him down. He was still a teen, so I expected that if he kept eating like he was one of the stablemaster's prized thoroughbreds, he would eventually get some heft.

Goddess knows that I worked him hard to improve his hand to hand fighting. Mostly evasive and knife work. He could call lightning but that tapped him out fast and he couldn't rely solely on magic to do his work.

"Roxy, Aislinn says I can't watch you get your ink tonight."

I tapped my knuckles against his, the sparks of orange lit up between us. He grinned and I did too. Finn and I had been paired up by Kotori a couple of months ago and our crazy misadventure with the Aurora Troll had led to my first score.

"I'll come when you get yours."

He leaned in and startled me with a quick hug, wrapping his thin arms around my waist. "Congratulations, Roxy."

I patted his back. "Thanks, kid. You better get back to work before Kotori catches you."

Finn laughed and let go of me. He glanced around the

courtyard, and looked relieved the Fox wasn't around before he dashed off.

I looked back at the doors to the Dojo and Tanner Matsui emerged from the murky darkness, his armor glittering as he stepped into the ring of firelight.

"Roxy. Just the person I wanted to see."

Tanner's smile was just as dazzling from up close, but it was hard to decide if his statement was inviting, or menacing. "Sir?"

Impossibly, the smile widened. "Please, call me Tanner."

He dropped his voice to a conspiratorial whisper. "I know everyone looks to me as the leader of the Slayers, but I feel more comfortable knowing we're all friends. Congratulations, by the way. Your Trials were the most entertaining I've seen in some time."

As he spoke I found it hard to keep my eyes off his gear. We were only here for the Inking, but Tanner was kitted out like he was going to wade into a peril all by himself. His armor gleamed, and the oiled joints at the shoulders moved with buttery smoothness. The hilt of his sword was crusted with gems that caught the flickering light. He had to be wearing enough gear to pay my rent for years. Heck, he could probably buy my whole building just by knocking a few gems off the sword.

"Yes, sir. I mean, Tanner." His name felt awkward and wrong as I said it.

He cuffed me across the shoulder. "That's the spirit!"

I nearly staggered. Where I was long and lean, Tanner was built like a bomb shelter, nearly as tall as I was, and covered in dense muscle. Of course, he had to be strong if he was going to fight, much less walk around in his armor.

If he noticed me wavering he didn't mention it. "I know you're eager to get out there. Your father did the Slayers proud in the short time he had with us. Your uncle, too, is one of our most valuable assets."

My dad had been known as the Breaker of Seattle. I knew his name carried some notoriety with it, and it was nice to hear Tanner being complimentary. My uncle had hinted that he and my dad hadn't left on the best of terms. It was a relief to hear that Tanner thought well of my dad.

"...non-combatant. What do you think?"

I blinked. I'd gotten lost in my own memories and lost track of the conversation. "I'm sorry, what was that?"

Tanner said, "I don't need a commitment from you now, Roxy. But I think a leadership role in the Slayers would fit you well. Come with me tomorrow, and you'll see what it's like. How does that sound?"

I wasn't sure what I was agreeing to, but it didn't seem like it could be all that bad. And maybe a day out with Tanner meant one less day getting beaten up by Kotori.

"Sure," I said. "Sounds good."

"Great! We'll meet here at the tenth chime."

He shook my hand before begging off and walking back out into the darkness beyond the torches. Was he not going to be here for the Inking?

Ulf and Cordelia appeared at my side.

Cordelia poked me in the ribs. "Teacher's pet, I see."

I scowled but Cordelia's tone was light.

Ulf scratched at his beard. "It is an honor, is it not, to have gained such attention?"

I rubbed my poor shoulder, beaten up twice in the same day. Tanner seemed to have taken some interest in my career with the Slayers. That was a good thing, right?

I gestured up to the torches. "We doing the inking here?"

Cordelia nodded. "Yes, Aislinn tasked us with setting up the torches and helping Aanya set out the akkorokamui ink and needles."

That reminded me of my discussion with Samuel. "Do you

guys ever feel or hear anything weird around the Tarim crystal since our initial ceremony?"

Ulf scratched his beard. "No."

Cordelia shook her head. "I have no idea what you mean."

"It's nothing. Just something Wen got me curious about."

At the mention of Wen's name, Cordelia's face dimmed. "I wish he was doing this with us tonight."

"Me too."

Ulf gave me a hearty slap on the back. "He will still be here at the Dojo to celebrate with us after."

Trust Ulf to focus on the important part–the celebrating.

Cordelia and Ulf left to get the squid ink. Soon it would be the three of us kneeling before Aanya while she inked us. Instead of the menacing balachita she normally favored, she would be wielding the silver needles that pierced our skin. I rubbed the back of my neck, my skin slightly tacky with Seattle humidity.

Aislinn's voice came from behind one of the shoji screens. "Just in time to avoid all the work, I see."

I whirled to face her.

Aislinn's voice was like her expression, icy and remote. Her eyes were golden shards of light that should have been warm like Cordelia's but instead scored me with her disdain. She'd made it clear to me early on that she thought being my father's daughter was a hindrance rather than a help.

It was true that I had barely survived The Box, but I thought I'd acquitted myself well in the last few months since the Trials. I'd been the first to exsanguinate a vampire of the four of us. Granted, it hadn't been planned, but a score was a score. Also true, I couldn't beat her or Kotori at hand-to-hand combat yet but since Aislinn was centuries old and Kotori was a kitsune, I felt like I was still able to hold my own, all things considered.

I was getting my ink tonight. So I wasn't going to get defensive.

"Is there something else I can help out with?" I asked.

Her lips twisted into a mirthless smile. "Tanner tells me he'll be bringing you to the Tarim Temple."

"Uh, I'm not sure where we are going."

"Don't play dumb with me. It doesn't suit you."

Heat flushed my face despite the cooling evening air. I didn't want to argue with her but I really didn't know what she was talking about. I also resented that she'd neatly cornered me into having to defend myself by in essence arguing that I wasn't playing dumb but was actually dumb. Annoyance made my words sharp.

"What is your problem with me?"

"You have no business going to the Temple as a Slayer representative!"

"Why not? I'm a Slayer."

"You're an infant."

Anger boiled up in my chest at her tone. I was young, but Aislinn's dismissive condescension was humiliating. I had absolutely no idea what Tanner had been talking about earlier or whether he was actually taking me to the Tarim Temple, but now I was going to double down just to spite Aislinn.

I gestured with a wide sweep to the ring of torches. "Tonight this infant is getting her ink. Tomorrow, this infant is going to the Tarim Temple. Deal with it."

I pivoted on my heel and stalked away. I would be the best Slayer representative the Veil had ever seen if it killed me.

3

TRUE

Thankfully Cordelia and Ulf had distracted me from my earlier confrontation with Aislinn. Now the three of us knelt in the torchlight while Aanya ground the blocks of dried akkorokamui ink with the crystal powder.

It smelled like smoke and brine, and I shivered in anticipation.

Tanner gave us all a perfunctory congratulation and then returned inside. Aislinn, Kotori, and Bashir were on shifts tonight. Thankfully that left Uncle Samuel and Altan off to the shadows handing the wine jug back and forth. Altan let out the occasional cackle and I suspected he was sharing some kind of ribald story with my Uncle. As usual.

To my delight, Akhil had come out from the Farm and would perform the ceremony. His ink black curls framed a clean shaven jaw. He wore a white linen shirt and wool vest that made him look more like a poet than a Slayer. As always, the stablemaster projected an aura of calm, which I greatly needed.

"We wear it here behind our fifth chakra to remind us to speak true, slay true, and be true."

Cordelia, Ulf, and I stood shoulder to shoulder, facing Akhil.

Akhil continued, "Slayers work as one. Tanner is the head of the Slayers, and when one of the Seven gives an order, we speak with Tanner's authority."

Aanya paced behind us, her hand trailing across our backs. Whatever she was looking for, she paused when her hand brushed across the center of my back. She drew in a breath and stopped.

Akhil stopped talking and took a half step away from us. If he had any idea of what Aanya was doing, he gave no indication. Sweat broke out along my hairline as Aanya traced her hand up and down my spine, muttering to herself.

"Um--"

Aanya cut me off. "Ssh. I need to concentrate."

Her strong fingers pushed into my back. I couldn't help it. I twisted to see what she was doing, only to get whacked on the back of my head.

"Stop moving."

Cordelia made bug eyes at me and mouthed a question at me. I shrugged, which only got me another slap from Aanya.

Aanya's fingers finally stopped in the center of my back, behind my heart. She pressed in and the sensation seemed to light up my limbs, sending a feeling of warmth down to my hands and feet.

The elder Slayer gave a satisfied grunt. "Hmm. Truly your father's daughter, then."

Her tone of voice made the statement ominous. "And that means...?"

Aanya pulled her hand from my back. "Quiet girl, your elders need to discuss."

They moved off a dozen paces and spoke in hushed voices with Samuel and Altan. The three of us stayed rooted to our spots but Cordelia managed to cuff me on the shoulder.

Ow. Always the same shoulder! I glared at her, but both she and Ulf had worried looks on their faces.

"I'm sure everything is fine," I whispered.

Ulf's voice was a quiet rumble. "I do not believe you have reason to believe that."

Wow, with friends like these I was going to go far. Before I could come back with a clever retort Akhil and Aanya returned to us. Aanya had a strange gleam in her eyes and seemed to be holding back a smile. Akhil however, held himself with even more of his trademark calm reserve.

His hands unfolded, long fingers graceful and softly glowing. "Roxy, why don't we start with you?"

"You're not going to tell me what's going on?"

Aanya released the grin she'd been holding. She was missing one of her top teeth, and her smile made her look like a little kid. It was adorable. "You're going to make Bashir inordinately happy, that's what. Everyone knows he's pushing hard for you to take your father's place. You're taking another step towards that today."

I knew all this. Getting my ink wasn't a surprise, unless you considered how narrowly I'd completed the Trials in the first place. But Aanya's manic grin made me think this was about something else.

Akhil sighed. "Your father was unique, Roxy, and it seems you share some of his more... memorable qualities."

Aanya blurted into Akhil's silence. "You're getting inked twice tonight, girl."

She nearly cackled at the look on my face. "It's a testament to how strong you could be. Oh, but Aislinn is going to have a fit when she hears about this!"

Akhil held up his hands. "If we could please keep our focus? Aanya, if you would?"

The spry woman bustled up behind me and tapped my shoulders, pushing me to my knees. She then moved to kneel in front of me and cupped my face in her hands. She smiled again, her dark skin wrinkling around her eyes.

"Keep your eyes on me, Roxy."

Akhil moved to stand behind me.

"The ink we wear at our fifth chakra is our reminder to speak true, and slay true."

Akhil's power blossomed at my back. Aanya's eyes squinted at the sudden glare of light and heat pushed into me like a physical weight. Aanya grabbed my chin and kept me from turning my head. "Eyes front!"

Akhil said, "This may sting a bit."

Pain like a white-hot blade seared across the back of my neck. I gasped and nearly bucked against it but between the two Slayers they held me down. Cordelia might have cried out, or it might have been me. I wasn't sure.

The pain inched its way down to the base of my neck. I discovered the enticing aroma of my own burning flesh and my stomach clenched. Thank the moon I hadn't eaten first. Bile shot up my throat and stung my nose and eyes.

Aanya's strong hands held me tight. "Breathe, girl. Focus. Ride it out. You can do it."

After a subjective eternity the starlight behind my head faded and the electrifying pain in my neck faded to mere cheese graters.

Of course, it wasn't over yet.

I heard Akhil's feet shifting. "Ink worn at the fourth chakra indicates the potential to do great and terrible things. Your father did both. The ink pushes you to strike a balance with the natural world. Your magic, your father's magic, changes the world, Roxy, in ways you have yet to learn."

The mention of my dad's name was enough to make me nearly forget the burning pain and the sweet stench of my cooked flesh.

Akhil's voice deepened, gaining a rough hoarseness. "I

should have done this for Gabriel. If I had, perhaps your father might still be with us."

Tears pricked at the back of my eyes when I heard the catch in Akhil's voice. Aanya's eyes shone with unshed tears and I understood that she was seeing my dad in me. I would live up to his name. I would make him proud of me.

I looked up at Uncle Samuel. His big body was utterly still, and the jug dangled from his left hand. He took a step into the ring of torchlight and under the flickering light, I saw his eyes. They were wet with tears. "Gabe's still with us. Even now."

A rush of emotion washed over me and I could hear the echoes of Dad's voice. "Just like we practiced, Roxybear."

I nodded at Samuel and settled my weight. Aanya grabbed my wrists and I did the same to hers. We locked our arms and my heartbeat ticked up. Aanya nodded, a quick, decisive movement. I took a deep, cleansing breath and willed my limbs to relax, visualized my magic gathering within me.

"Do it."

Akhil's light flashed as bright as a star and bleached out my vision.

I woke and found myself on my back, staring up into Aanya's dark eyes.

"You made it."

I appreciated that she made it a statement, rather than a question.

She helped me sit, slowly, and brought a canteen to my lips. I sipped slowly, washing the sour taste of bile and adrenaline out of my mouth. Half of the torches were out and the shadows had grown bold, creeping back into our circle to blot out our vision.

On the other side of the clearing I saw what looked like

Ulf's blocky form bent over Cordelia, who appeared, impossibly, to be heaving her guts out in very unladylike fashion. Even more impossibly, Ulf appeared to be holding her hair for her.

Impossible. It had to be a trick of the shadows and my pain-hazed imagination.

I'd done it. I'd gotten my ink. My hand crept up to my neck but I flinched away as soon as my fingers brushed the edge. "Ow!"

Aanya laughed, her dark eyes sparkling. "Too soon, young one. Too soon. Give it time. It will heal and make you stronger for it."

I knew the other Slayers used their ink to their advantage when fighting, but I didn't understand how just yet. Aanya saw the question in my eyes.

She tapped her fingers at the base of her throat, where her own ink sat on the back of her neck. "Our power comes from here, so the reflection, the recoil, is here as well. The ink provides a path for the power, helps you dissipate the recoil so that it doesn't hit you all at once."

Memories of my recoil socking me in the gut nearly made me wince with pain. "So, it gives it a soft landing."

Aanya shook her head. "Not on its own. You are still in control of your magic. This just lets you direct the recoil."

She held out one hand, as if aiming to throw a rock. "You see the recoil coming. You guide it back. It is coming anyway, so you give it a path. A path that uses your ink."

Aanya closed her hand in a fist and then opened it, splaying her fingers in an elegant gesture. "Poof."

"Poof?"

She grinned. "Poof. Perhaps one of the others can teach you better than I can."

I looked around for my uncle, but neither he nor Altan were in the courtyard. My shoulders sagged. It would have been really nice to be able to see Samuel, to just see the broad bones of his cheeks and jaw that reminded me so painfully of my dad.

Akhil appeared at my side on silent feet. If I hadn't been so spent I would have jumped when he appeared next to me. He crouched next to me and offered me a battered tin the size of his palm. "A balm for the tattoo. Keep the areas clean and apply this twice a day. It will help with the pain. Luckily, due to the Tarim crystal the healing process is quite a bit faster than normal."

"Thank you."

I opened the tin and sniffed. It smelled herbal and minty.

Akhil reached over and popped the top off the tin and scooped out a bit of the ointment. He gestured to me to lean forward, and his strong fingers massaged the ointment onto my new tattoos. First the nape of my neck, then Akhil pulled back the collar of my shirt and gave a quick sweep of the balm onto my spine between my shoulder blades. The balm had an immediate cooling effect and I could feel it almost like an icy spiral beneath my skin. Beneath the new symbol that marked me forever as a Slayer.

I sealed the tin. "Do you know where Samuel went?"

Akhil sighed. "It's always hard to watch this ceremony. It's worse when it's someone you really worry about."

I digested that for a moment.

"What is he worried about?"

"Whether the things that drove your Dad are the same things that drive you."

I frowned. "I'm not my dad. And I'm pretty sure that I never really knew what my dad was like before. Here, I mean. After he got sick...he really changed. I had so many questions I wanted to ask, so many things I still didn't know."

"Your father was a man in conflict with himself, even when he was younger. Like his magic, he could be unpredictable."

Akhil paused, as if choosing his words while he spoke of the dead. "Roxy, your dad was a good Slayer. His methods were unorthodox, but he always upheld the Slayer vows."

Akhil stood up and then held out his hand to me. I took it and with great effort, hoisted myself vertical. My back already felt better. "Your father and uncle were a matched set. The Maker and the Breaker. When they were together..."

Akhil paused and a joyous light flashed across his eyes. "...when they fought together, it was glorious."

His eyes darkened. "When they drifted apart, things started to go wrong, and nothing we did seemed to be able to mend the rift between them."

Aanya held my hand. "Your uncle sees his brother in you, and that brings him both joy and fear."

A cold weight that had nothing to do with the damp night air settled into my chest. Dad had loved to regale me with stories of his exploits behind the Veil. His war stories, he'd called them. Whenever I'd asked him about how he'd decided to leave, he'd always found a way to dodge the question. After he'd picked up drinking, I'd stopped asking him at all. I suddenly wished that I'd pressed him on it, despite the cost.

I looked back and forth between Akhil and Aanya. "What do you see?"

The two of them shared a look and their eyes spoke volumes. Finally Akhil said, "We see promise, Roxy. And we hope that's a good thing."

4

HOME

Fairy lights swirled across the ceiling of my apartment and I tested out my latest batch of shine. Made from tart dryad apples and sweetened with fireweed honey, this one was a winner. I set out the jam jars I had been collecting and went to work filling them. I had worked out a good barter system for this liquor and it equaled nice fatback bacon in my larder. Of course, I also saved a jar for Mrs. Chu and her mahjong buddies. They were all shifters so the alcohol didn't do much for them but they enjoyed the taste.

I touched the back of my neck again. I'd applied the balm again this morning. The ointment quieted my aggravated nerves. Only the faintest trace of coolness reminded me the ink was there. My Slayer ink. It seemed fitting now that I had the scars of a rogue vampire on the front of my neck and the Slayer mark on the back. I was truly a warrior of the Twilight Veil now.

My side hustle tasks completed, I went to check on my homing pigeons, Noodle and Dumpling. Today they were getting a mix of seeds I had sourced for them. When they were out and about, I figured they ate bugs.

My apartment was an ancient building that had survived the Drowning and aside from its apparent sturdiness, I was extremely fond of the balconies. I know my neighbors Jimmy and his husband Henry liked to dine out on their balcony but Mrs. Chu had indulged me so I had enclosed mine with fine gauge wire for when I let my pigeons out of their dovecote. The perpetual purple haze of the Twilight cast Dumpling's white feathers almost lavender. I gave her broad chest a gentle stroke, and reached down to change out the papers lining the dovecote.

Something gold caught my eye. I leaned forward to get a closer look.

It was a gold feather stuck in the edge of the base. I pulled it out and examined it.

That was strange. While Dumpling was largely white, Noodle was a gray pigeon, striped with charcoal markings and the classic iridescent green neck. Neither of the pigeons had gold feathers.

I looked at Noodle. He stared back at me, his beady eyes watchful. Like he was waiting for something.

"Right, I've got your seed mix right here."

They pecked at their seeds while I tidied. My notes to Ava and Jasper were fine for updates but did nothing to fill the loneliness of being away from them. I missed them so much that sometimes it hollowed me out. Sending silver home was great, and I knew the treatments helped make Mom more comfortable, but they weren't a cure. I wanted more. I wanted them to be here, or me to be there, and us to all be together. I wanted us to have a big meal together. I wanted my mom to be better.

So much of my life in Boston had been about getting them fed, and off to school. They were the brains. I was the...well, not brawn exactly. But I was the doer. And it was serving me well here in Seattle. For a moment I pictured them all in my little tiny apartment here, with my Uncle Samuel coming over to join us, and Mrs. Chu ladling out soup. That seemed pretty perfect. Also, pretty impossible.

For now, I had to content myself with the short notes we exchanged.

"I got my ink. Miss you all."

After sending Dumpling off, I headed upstairs with a jar of the shine for Mrs. Chu. As usual, she yanked open the door before I could knock. Her werewolf senses could detect me coming from a mile away.

"Come in, come in. I'm just packing." She turned from the door and hurried to her kitchen.

Instead of her usual velour tracksuit, today she had on black cargo pants, a black long sleeve crew neck, and a beige fishing vest. She looked like she was ready to go on an expedition.

A giant green canvas rucksack sat on the tile floor of her kitchen. A row of wrapped parcels in various shapes sat on the counter and Mrs. Chu was stacking them inside the rucksack like an expert grocer.

I placed the jar of apple pie shine on the counter. Mrs. Chu popped up and her eyes glowed with pleasure as she hefted the jar.

"This will be good while I'm on the road." She tucked the jar into the side pouch of the rucksack.

"Where are you headed?"

"It's Bev's turn to host mahjong this week so I'm off to the Ranch."

"Why are you bringing so much stuff?"

"Bev missed market last time, so I picked up some provisions for her."

Then I remembered why she'd asked to send a pigeon. "Oh yeah. Did Noodle come back with a message from Bev?"

Mrs. Chu shook her head. "Noodle came back and the capsule was empty but no return note."

That was odd.

Mrs. Chu cinched up her bag. "Bev must be so distracted with the harvest that she was too busy to make a list for me. No matter, I'll see her shortly."

My eyebrows shot up. That rucksack looked like it weighed two hundred pounds. Werewolves were strong in their human form, but sometimes I forgot that while Mrs. Chu looked like a human woman in her sixties, she was as strong as an ox and could likely bench press said ox.

Mrs. Chu reached into her fridge and pulled out a large ceramic bowl painted with pink flowers. "Here. Drink this."

I accepted the bowl. It was a good trade, moonshine for some Mrs. Chu's chicken soup. To keep things interesting, sometimes the soup had treats like pork hock. She said I needed the collagen. She wasn't wrong.

"Walk me to the station."

"Sure." I didn't have to meet Tanner until 10 chimes.

As we exited the building a beat of sound brushed my ear and I ducked. The rush of wings passed overhead.

"Whoa! What was that?"

Mrs. Chu tilted her head and sniffed. "Unusual. Fiery feathers. Smelled like hot stone and smoke."

Weird. But the Veil was filled with weird things.

We headed out to the closest station where Mrs. Chu could catch a wagon to make the crossing through the Wilds and to River Rock Farm. My legs were a lot longer than hers, but I had to hustle to keep up with her.

"You smell different."

Whatever I thought she wanted to talk to me about, I did not think she would lead with that.

"How do you mean?"

"You smell like the Slayers now, but more intense."

I thought about my ink. Maybe it was the squid. Which raised a new concern. "Do I smell fishy?"

Mrs. Chu snorted. "No."

I rubbed the back of my neck. It was still cool from the ointment. I felt an answering tingle in my scarred knuckles. Was it the Tarim crystal? Could shifters like Mrs. Chu smell the crystal?

"Can you smell crystal?"

Mrs. Chu laughed, a dry wheeze of amusement. "Look around us. The Tarim surrounds us with their magic. I'm no crystal bloodhound."

"Then why do you say I smell like the Slayers?"

Her eyes flattened. "They live together, humans, shifters, and fae. They fight together, they bleed together. They smell of each other, sweat, and stale vamp blood."

Oh.

If this is what I smelled like to a shifter, what did I smell like to a vamp?

We didn't say anything more until she got to the station. I told her to have fun with the mahjong ladies and loped off to meet Tanner.

5

THE THIN LINE

The emergence of the Tarim pyramids had coincided with the Drowning of Seattle, and it was generally understood that the Tarim were responsible for raising the Pacific Ocean to catastrophic heights and destroying the city. The permanent rise in ocean levels meant that many parts of Seattle vanished under the waves and never reappeared. Through these low-lying areas around the hills of Seattle, the Pacific Ocean now intruded into the city like the clutching roots of an invasive seaweed.

Tarim power was mysterious, as were the Tarim themselves. No one really knew for certain why the Tarim had drowned Seattle, or indeed, why they had chosen this particular city. What we did know, is that in the aftermath, the Tarim were the supreme power to fear and bow to, if you chose to live in Seattle.

Since the Tarim came from the ocean, many considered the various tiny tributaries of salt water to be extensions of their influence. The highly superstitious were careful not to speak ill of the Tarim if they were within sight of ocean water, and they crossed these small bodies of water with speed and silence.

I didn't quite believe the Tarim could hear us through the water, but it made a kind of sense to me that their temple was placed where it was. At the mouth of the inlet that separated Queen Hill from the Market, a solid wall of violet fog rose like an unnatural column of shifting colors. As we approached, local activity died off until Tanner and I were the only people for hundreds of yards in any direction. The dark mud of the flats sucked at my boots as Tanner and I stopped before the Veil.

My heart rate went up a few ticks. "Sir? I thought we were going to the Tarim Temple."

Tanner's breath puffed slightly. He was dressed in his ceremonial plate. Not that I thought any less of him for it. If I had armor like that I'd probably wear it just for eating noodles. He pointed at the obstinate wall of purple mist.

"We're in the right place, Roxy. It's behind that."

I'd crossed this barrier once before. Not here, not in Seattle, but on the western edge of Nevada. No one knew who could safely cross the Veil, but it was somehow linked to your genetics. If a close family member could cross safely, you had a good chance. The more distant the family member, the more your chances diminished. With my father and my uncle both crossing safely, I had known my probability was high, and yet my first crossing had still been a clammy, sweaty experience. And not an experience I was keen to repeat.

"They couldn't just spring for guards with weapons? Locked gates and high walls?"

Tanner scratched his chin thoughtfully. "No, they've got all that, too. This is just the first line of defense. I think... I think this is to weed out those without strength of conviction. If you can cross the Veil, it means something to the Tarim."

I scowled. "I crossed in Nevada. That should count for something."

Tanner laughed. "This is their world, kiddo, we're just

playing by their rules. They say we cross the Veil, we cross. Got it?"

I wasn't exactly in a position to argue with my boss. If he said we were going through, then I was sucking it up and we were going through. At the Nevada crossing, the other side of the Veil had been littered with abandoned cars and gear, the detritus of so many who had attempted the crossing and failed. It had taken me a week to screw up my courage to simply place one foot in front of the other and walk myself into the violet mist.

Tanner held out his gauntlet-clad hand. "Ladies first."

I thought of my uncle. I thought of my dad. I held my mom's face firmly in my mind, and I stepped into the fog.

THE SENSATION WAS STRANGE, like dream walking, where the floor clutched at your feet and the very air felt like liquified taffy. I pushed forward, one step, then another, fighting for every inch of progress. The darkness in the Veil was absolute. I kept blinking to make sure my eyes were actually still open. I stretched my arms out in front of me, groping blindly ahead for anything.

I took a deep breath and held it for a count of four, enough time to take two slow steps forward. I let the breath out slowly, gradually, releasing the coiled tension in my chest as I did. Fear like a live wire thrashed in my chest, whipping about like a wounded animal, trying to force me to run. I stilled my legs and took another step.

If I ran, if I let the fear run free, I didn't know if I would be able to stop. Would I lose my way? Would I die, blind and lost within the Veil? Is this what happened to those who were unworthy to cross?

Tanner's baritone appeared just behind me. "You're doing fine, Roxy. Just a few more steps."

Two more careful steps and I felt an odd resistance, like I'd stepped into a sheet of plastic. I pushed through and jerked my hand back. Whatever was through that resistance was hot.

Tanner grunted. "That's it. Just push through."

I pushed again and this time the resistance gave way and I nearly fell forward onto my face. Blinding light seared my eyes and hammered my senses. My hands and knees hit the ground and my only instinct was to cover my eyes with my hands. I curled into a ball and tried to shrink away from the light.

Hands found me and patted along my arm until they got to my shoulder.

Tanner said, "Roxy. Sit. Get up."

Strong hands grabbed my wrists and pulled me to a seated position. "Roxy, close your eyes." Tanner shook me a little.

"Listen, Roxy. Close your eyes. I'm going to pull your hands away."

I whimpered as Tanner moved my hands and heat bathed my face. Dull red light glowed through my eyelids.

Tanner's voice was very close to my ear. "You haven't been here in the Twilight that long, Roxy. You remember this. Your eyes remember."

It went against my every instinct, but I cracked my eyes open. Dazzling sunlight rippled around us, the heat haze distorting the air. The light seemed to come from every surface. The dirt and rocks seemed to glow with light. It was painful, like being struck across the face again and again, but after long moments, my eyes remembered what to do and my pupils contracted.

The world shifted into focus again. Instead of a blurry gray haze, Tanner materialized before me, the sunlight glinting off his armor.

His eyes were closed tight. The two of us were in a narrow

space, maybe ten feet across, bounded on both sides by walls of violet mist that reached straight up. I squinted and looked around us. The earth was baked dry and it looked like the narrow path we were on turned ninety degrees on either side of us.

And then I looked up.

My eyes snapped shut on reflex but I forced them open again so I could drink it in. Dazzling, clear blue sky, complete with a few fluffy clouds drifting across the narrow band I could see between the walls of the Veil. Sunlight hammered into the tight column and burned away all the humidity. I'd only been in the Twilight for less than a year, but I'd nearly forgotten what blue skies looked like.

If we were truly on the other side of the Veil now...

I focused on Tanner's armor and got nothing. My magic was gone. However the Tarim had constructed this place, they had effectively built an anti-magic moat around their Temple.

Tanner's eyes were still closed. "Impressive, right?"

Impressive wasn't quite the word for it. It was scary as hell. The idea that the Tarim had created the Twilight Veil was something that all residents of the Twilight simply accepted. It was the barrier that separated us from the regular world, and granted us access to our magic, to increased health and vitality, and to vampires, shifters, fae, and demons.

I'd never considered that the Tarim might be able to actually use the Veil like this. To weaponize what most people thought of as a simple border between lands. I was willing to bet that most people hadn't considered the possibility.

Tanner turned his face up to the sky but kept his eyes closed. "It feels good, even if I can't see it. It's been a long time, but I can still see it in my mind."

He turned back to me. "And a rather effective vampire deterrent, don't you think?"

Actually, I could think of exactly one vampire who might

not be deterred by the Tarim's moat, assuming he could cross the Veil in the first place. Now didn't seem like the time to mention Tyee, though. "I think it's a pretty effective moat for all of us, sir."

"Nonsense. This is meant to keep out the unworthy. Not us."

Tanner stood and pulled me to my feet. "One more crossing, and we're in the Temple. Let's go."

A SOLITARY, imposing structure, the Tarim Temple rose out of the mud flats like a lost, alien jewel dropped in the dirt, in the middle of a column of darkness, surrounded on all four sides by the Twilight Veil.

Dark mud sucked at my feet again as I followed Tanner out of the Veil and back onto the flats, towards the glowing, angled lines of the Temple. The glowing orange pyramid stood at least four stories high at its peak, and the base spread out what looked like a hundred feet on each side. The slanting walls of the pyramid gave off their own strange light and seemed to repel both dirt and moisture. As we got closer I could make out strange symbols that seemed to float inside the crystal. When I tried to focus on them, they faded, only to appear like ghosts at the edge of my vision.

We stopped at the base of the pyramid. Tanner placed his hands on his hips and simply waited.

"Should we...knock?"

Tanner chuckled. "No, no. Patience, Roxy. They know we're here."

After more than a hundred years of rebuilding, Seattle had finally pulled itself out of the mud. Buildings and roads had been repaired, and we lived in a semblance of our original comfort and civilization. It had all felt so strange when I had first arrived, like stepping back in time. But standing before the

Tarim pyramid, I again felt the initial strangeness, the wrongness, of our existence, living under the invisible, watchful eyes of the Tarim.

Nothing else in Seattle had the clean, precise lines of the pyramid before me. The surface of the crystal was a smooth, unblemished surface. I reached out to it, and when Tanner didn't object, I laid my hand on the surface. The crystal was warm to the touch, and seemed to hum, a barely perceptible vibration that came from deep in the earth.

Or, possibly, deep in the ocean.

The pyramid felt immensely solid, like I was pushing on the side of a battleship. A staggering amount of mass and engineering that would crush me like a gnat if I had the temerity to crawl beneath its boot. I snatched my hand away when I realized that the subtle vibration was being echoed in the new tattoos on my back and neck, making my scars tingle and itch.

Wen's warnings suddenly sounded a lot more dire. Had my uncle experienced this as well?

Tanner didn't see the disgust on my face. "Impressive, isn't it?"

I clenched my fingers, trying to still the vibrations that seemed to linger in my bones. "Yes, very impressive."

He leaned back to look up the smooth expanse of crystal. "I remember coming here for the first time like it was yesterday. Just being here felt...right. Like I had found my place. The Tarim have always helped me when my path became dark. I hope they can do the same for you, Roxy."

A vertical line appeared in the face of the crystal and expanded until it drew a narrow, rectangular outline. The orange glow inside the rectangle dimmed until the shape was a dark hole punched in the side of the pyramid.

Tanner smiled and waved us forward. "You see? Patience."

I stepped forward into the darkness and found a smooth surface just inside the opening. When my foot landed a tingle of sensation sparked in my ink and flowed up to my head. I stopped abruptly. What the –?

Tanner stepped heavily behind me. "Come on, Roxy. Can't keep them waiting."

At least with Kotori I knew what I was in for. That beating was looking pretty good now. I shook off the uncomfortable sensation of being watched and walked into the darkness.

WHATEVER I HAD EXPECTED of the interior of the Temple, I didn't expect this. Once my eyes adjusted to the darker interior I could make out a long corridor that, like the pyramid, seemed to be carved out of a solid piece of Tarim crystal. The hallway was just wide enough for Tanner and I to walk shoulder to shoulder. Despite the narrow confines, Tanner proceeded forward without so much as a backwards glance. I guessed that this was familiar territory for him.

I followed close behind him, but I couldn't help but glance back several times. When we had gotten about twenty feet from the doorway it sealed shut with a thump. My initial panic was only slightly assuaged as the walls of the hallway brightened, lighting our way into the distance. I still felt like a rat in a test maze. Was there a treat or a deadly trap at the end of this maze?

For his part, Tanner seemed wholly unconcerned about our situation. He walked on, shoulders and arms relaxed, even humming a little tune under his breath. I tried to emulate his sense of calm.

It didn't really work.

"What exactly are we doing here, sir?"

Tanner looked back at me. "Please, Roxy."

"Sorry, Tanner." That was going to take some getting used to.

"Crossing Day is nearly upon us. On that day, the Tarim re-seed the crystal chambers for the ruling factions of Seattle."

That definitely didn't sound like anything I'd heard from my dad. "Ruling factions?"

Tanner laughed. "Yes, that's the closest concept the Tarim have for us. We don't really rule Seattle, of course...but communicating with the Tarim can be an interesting experience. They're not human, you know. I don't think anyone knows what they are."

Dad hadn't told me any of this. I had the sensation of being in unexpectedly deep, dark waters. Waters filled with hungry predators. "So how do we communicate with them?"

Tanner waved his arms around us. "That's what we're here for. In their temple we speak with the Tarim Acolytes. They act as intermediaries and translators."

The glow in the walls had gotten steadily brighter and now the hallway started widening until the walls fell away to reveal a sharply angular room with no entrances other than the hallway we came in from. As we crossed inside the hallway behind us disappeared behind a featureless wall of crystal.

I whirled, my heart rate spiking in response.

Our exit had vanished and now we were trapped here.

"Hey!" I raced back to the missing door, my arm raised to pound on the smooth surface when Tanner's gauntleted fist closed around my wrist.

"Roxy. It's fine. The temple walls always do this."

My eyes darted around the room, taking in the smooth walls. "Doesn't it freak you out?"

Tanner shrugged. "By the terms of the Pact, the Tarim Temple is neutral territory. "

That calmed me a little, but it didn't address my concern that the Pact probably didn't prevent the Tarim from doing anything to us.

Tanner released my arm and I pulled myself together. His

eyes traveled around our small confines. "You have a lot to learn, but I know you're the right person for this."

This was all very flattering, but also more than a little unexpected. "Why me? There are plenty of others with more experience than me."

He grimaced. "Yes, plenty of Slayers with experience hacking and slashing their way through perils of rogues. You'll find that the true battles for Seattle's safety don't always involve silver blades or wooden stakes. I need someone who can fight those battles as well."

I was perfectly happy to hack and slash my way through perils of rogues. In fact, I wanted to get better at it. So whatever it was that Tanner was referring to, I was definitely out of my depth here. "What about Samuel?"

Tanner paused, looking thoughtful, and I got the distinct feeling that he was choosing his words carefully. But when he opened his mouth the wall in front of us flashed and a section of the wall disappeared in the light.

Two shadowy figures appeared in the light. I backed up a step, putting my arm out to block Tanner and push him behind me.

Tanner sighed. "Roxy."

Oh. Right.

The shorter figure resolved into a fit and trim older woman with a head of stiffly permed gray curls. Lydia Bjørn, or as she was more commonly known – Grandma.

Today, Grandma's tracksuit of choice was pale blue, the jacket unzipped halfway to reveal a fitted white blouse beneath. I guessed this was Grandma's version of formal wear when visiting the Tarim? Of course, if she shifted into her massive bear form the clothes would be ruined anyway, so perhaps she didn't invest much in expensive clothing.

If Grandma was here then the stocky form behind her had to be Dario. When he stepped into the room he gave me a little wave. I grinned when I saw him. Even when coming to the Tarim Temple, he still showed up wearing his leather vest over his bare chest. It didn't matter that Seattle was a cool, drizzly climate compared to Brazil, he still dressed as if he would be bathed in sunlight. His body rippled with lean corded muscle as he strode across the temple. He was wearing his curly hair a little shorter now, shaved on the sides. New pink scars streaked across the deep brown skin of his shoulders. With his enhanced healing those scars would be gone in a few days, but it meant he was still having problems at the Zoo.

It was really good to see him. After he'd missed the cut during the Trials, he had retreated to the Zoo and we didn't get to see him much. I'd heard from Grandma at mahjong night that Dario had become the Alpha of the Drowned City Pack, which meant he had his hands, or paws rather, full now.

Dario's smile faded and his expression turned to business when he spotted Tanner. His eyes flicked to Grandma, who sighed loudly and lifted her hand in our direction. Dario squared his shoulders and marched up to the leader of the Slayers.

"Could I have a word with you, Councilman Matsui?"

Tanner took half a beat to glance at Grandma and then look Dario up and down before answering. "Of course. My door is always open to the Alpha of the Drowned City pack."

Dario's shoulders relaxed a bit. "I believe one of the vampire clans is moving against the shifters. The Slayers' assistance would help--"

Tanner reached out and clapped Dario on the shoulder. "Ah, well unfortunately Queen Hill is beyond the purview of the Slayers, by the terms of the Pact. But I don't doubt the new alpha's ability to resolve the issue, right?"

Grandma, hidden behind Dario, rolled her eyes like a teenager. She grabbed Dario by the arm and dragged him past us. "What did I tell you? Let's go, junior."

A spark of anger flared in Dario's eyes as he stomped away. He shot me a disgusted look before the far wall melted away to reveal another hidden hallway. The wall reappeared as soon as they were out of the room.

A sick feeling twisted my stomach. Dario had tried to ask the Slayers for help. Tanner had just brushed him off and it felt like a betrayal.

I turned back to Tanner. "Why didn't you hear him out?"

Tanner adjusted his breast plate and brushed back his hair. "Roxy, you'll learn soon that making the Slayers an effective unit is about carefully managing our limited resources."

He waved an arm. "All around us, we have vampires, fae, shifters, demons, possibly demi-gods, and whatever the Tarim really are. Even if we're good at our jobs, we're only human. We are charged with maintaining the Pact within Seattle, and even then, only under certain circumstances. Anything beyond that would strain our few resources and weaken the Slayers Guild."

I frowned.

"Roxy, it's not that I don't appreciate Dario's problem. But the Zoo is beyond the bounds of the Pact. If I send Slayers in there, they're going to face real danger without the protection of the Pact. I won't spend the lives of our Slayers so carelessly."

And I heard what he didn't say – without compensation.

The Guild paid us well and in order for them to do that, they were receiving healthy compensation for their enforcement gigs. The Herbal College for example, paid Slayers handsomely to patrol their downtown campus and their grow farms out in the Wilds. The Herbal College also made money hand over fist for their tinctures and ointments. The Slayer's biggest client was probably the merchant Caravan, which brought much needed supplies through the Veil and into the Market. They paid Slayers handsomely to provide security for its merchants.

The Drowned City pack wasn't wealthy–they couldn't afford us.

Tanner gestured to his armor. "Look at this. I train hard and I'm strong, but my skin still needs armor. I'll never be as fast or as strong as a shifter, Roxy."

This was true. This was why Kotori rubbed my face into the mat at the Dojo on the regular.

"They're shifters, Roxy. They have supernatural strength and healing, and shift into even more powerful half-forms that are perfect for fighting. Dario is incredible. Have you seen his dire wolf form? He would have been an amazing Slayer, but now he is a strong alpha for that pack.

"Dario is very capable and I trust in his ability to lead his pack through their latest difficulty. But the Slayers are a thin line of defense for the humans of Seattle and I need to make sure we're doing what's most important. I need you to help me make sure we're doing our jobs. Are you with me?"

Up until now I hadn't spent much time with Tanner to develop any kind of opinion on him, other than to note my uncle's habit of distancing himself from Tanner. This was different. I'd never seen this kind of zeal from him, and I had never heard this perspective of the Slayers from my dad or Samuel.

My landlady could lift a two hundred pound ruck sack and still run flat out across the city. But my neighbor Jimbo needed spare parts to keep his bike functioning, and his husband Henry just wanted fresh groceries to make the best lasagna possible this side of the Veil. Someone had to cover for people like Jimbo and Henry, and that was the Slayers Guild.

I thought about that time I'd been attacked in the Fangs by the Shadow's Den vampires. How with all my training, I was puny and weak compared to them. How galling it had been that Tyee had saved me.

My jaw clenched at the humiliating memory. "Yes, I'm with you."

Tanner gripped my shoulder with a meaty hand and grinned. "I knew I could count on you."

From the first day of my Trials, my uncle had maintained what he felt was a safe distance from me. He didn't want anyone to think he'd given me any shortcuts to making it through the Trials. It was fair, but tough. And it had been hard.

Before he died, my dad had been a mess. Splitting his time equally between being angry about not being able to help mom, and berating me for not helping her enough. That too, had been hard.

Tanner's patient discussion had been something I rarely received. It was a vote of confidence in me and my abilities that soothed a sore spot in my heart that I had forgotten about. A pain that had been there for so long that I'd grown accustomed to it.

I returned Tanner's grin with a slow smile. "Thanks for explaining."

"Let's go meet the Tarim."

6

THE TARIM TEMPLE

I was surprised to learn the Tarim Acolytes were human... sort of. They still looked mostly human on the outside, anyway. I wasn't sure what I had been expecting, given the mysteries surrounding the Tarim.

As we walked through yet another magically appearing door, Tanner explained that a select few people had been drawn to the Temple at the time of its formation. No one knew why these people had been drawn there, only that they had reported an urgent compulsion to come to the strange new crystal structure that had appeared just off the wreckage of Queen Hill.

"According to records from the time, the pyramid...well, it was less of a pyramid then...it opened up like it did for us and the Acolytes went inside. And then no one heard a peep from the temple for the next ten years."

"Wait, so you're telling me that the Acolytes we're about to meet--?"

"...are the same who entered the temple over one hundred years ago. Yes."

Which was not unsettling in any way at all.

The corridor opened into a large room with a vaulted ceiling. This room felt vast, as if it took up a large part of the footprint of the temple. The ceiling rose high above us, ending just under the peak of the pyramid. Angular staircases led up the walls to delicate terraces that followed the perimeter. These terraces continued up the walls of the pyramid, the last one just below the apex. The highest terrace faced out to translucent exteriors and I could almost see the moon. It made me wonder if the Acolytes climbed those staircases to come moongaze.

From inside the walls of the pyramid were actually quite thin, or at least thinner than I would have expected. The crashing surf was visible through the crystal. Dark, frothing waves beat against the western wall of the pyramid.

And that was when the strangeness of it finally struck me. The waves were completely silent. There wasn't even the sound of the impact of the water on the structure. Somehow the inside of the pyramid was totally sealed from the exterior. I finally registered the clean scent of the air, absent the ever present brine scent I'd gotten used to in Seattle.

Tanner noticed me noticing. "I told you it was impressive. Now, for today I just need you to stay quiet and follow along. If you have any questions I'll try to answer them for you later, alright?"

Tanner stopped in the center of the room. Unlike the smooth walls, the floor had a pebbly texture, as if we were walking around river rock. In the center though the texture gave way to a medallion of orange concentric rings, a fiery mosaic of light. As I stared at it, it seemed to pulse in time with my heartbeat, which was disorienting.

A new door materialized on the far side of the room and two people dressed in shimmering pearlescent robes walked through. Both were of average height and build, and their floor length robes changed color as they walked, one moment white, another step and the robes were the deepest teal. Their faces were obscured by wide hoods pulled low. Similarly, their body shapes were rendered anonymous by the voluminous fabric. I couldn't tell their gender or more importantly whether they carried weapons beneath. My training had helped me hone my ability to assess threats. The appearance of the Tarim and being here in this crystal pyramid had scrambled my instincts. My tiny hind brain told me to run. My logic told me there was nowhere to run to. So I clamped down on my gut reactions and tried to emulate Tanner's breezy calm.

The two walked noiselessly across the room and met us in the middle. I didn't hear any footsteps, either, although their robes did swish across the floor. In one synchronized movement they raised their arms and swept back their hoods, revealing a man and woman of indeterminate ages. They certainly didn't look over a hundred years old. Both their faces were smooth and unblemished and their hair was gray, rough cut to shoulder length. Any pigment that had once been in their skin had faded, and it had a washed out look, like paper left too long to the elements.

With their hoods pulled back, I could see now that they each wore an elaborate pendant necklace. The woman wore one that had the look of mother of pearl, smooth and iridescent. The man had a pendant of orange fire–the Tarim crystals, but polished smooth and round like pebbles with a large centerpiece, a flat disc, shaped like a nautilus.

The woman stepped forward and a wave of orange light washed over her irises. When she spoke, it sounded like a chorus of voices were powering the sound. All the hairs on my body stood on end.

"Greetings, Tanner Matsui of the Slayers Guild. Are you ready to renew the Pact?"

Tanner nodded.

The man took a step forward until he was even with the woman. His eyes also flashed orange, and when he opened his mouth the same eerie chorus came out. "Have you brought your offering?"

Tanner reached under his chest plate and pulled out a small leather pouch on a string around his neck. With two fingers he expanded the pouch and withdrew three slim shards of Tarim crystal.

I clenched my fists and the scars on my knuckles tingled, as if sensitized by the mere presence of the crystal. These were raw shards, unfinished, nothing Tanner had taken from the armory. These had to be from the chambers where we held our initiation. Why was Tanner bringing them back to the Tarim?

The Acolytes moved forward in perfect synchrony and reached for the shards. The woman took one, and the man plucked the other two from Tanner. She tilted her head to the side and brought the shard close to her eye. The man tapped the two shards against each other, producing a high-pitched tone. He tilted his head, mirroring the woman's movement, and held the humming shards next to his ear.

My neck itched but I held my arms still and suffered the sensation as it crawled down my neck and to the spot between my shoulder blades.

The woman said, "The offering is pure."

The man said, "The offering is complete."

Whenever they spoke my new tattoos tingled, a low level pain that felt like I was being shocked with electricity. If Tanner felt any such discomfort he didn't show it.

None of this made any sense to me.

It was known that the Tarim gave crystal to the protectors of Seattle, ostensibly to maintain the peace. But why would Tanner bring some back? That meant the Tarim were getting something from the exchange, right? Or was it merely symbolic? It was baffling. Now that I stood here in the heart of their temple, it finally occurred to me to wonder why the Tarim cared in the first place. The Twilight was a mercenary place, where most everyone tried to get the best deal possible for themselves. Why would the Tarim be any different?

I doubted that only the Slayers returned some crystal to the Tarim. What about everyone else? How much crystal had Dario brought for his offering? Why did the Tarim want the crystal back, and why did they give it to us in the first place?

The Acolytes pocketed the crystals. When they spoke this time the voice alternated between them. The sound echoed off the crystal walls and rang in my ears. "Your offering is accepted, Tanner Matsui. Are you prepared to renew the Pact?"

Tanner gave me a significant look and turned to face them. "Yes, the Slayers and I are prepared to renew the Pact. We vow to uphold the Pact and the peace it represents."

The Acolytes raised their arms in unison, the sleeves falling back to reveal more creepy washed out skin. The floor beneath us rumbled and I tensed. The mosaic on the floor started to flash, and then it spread apart as shards shot upward. The acolytes fell to their knees and pressed their heads to the floor. In a blink, where the mosaic had been now stood a trio of jutting crystal columns taller than all of us.

They looked like what we had back at the Dojo, but deeper in color and they practically vibrated with energy. The ink on the back of my neck and back felt alternatingly hot and cold, like I had gone from the sauna to an ice plunge.

I looked at Tanner in alarm, but other than taking a slightly wider stance, Tanner didn't seem fazed at all by these events. I copied his stance and hoped my face didn't show my panic.

The acolytes stood and spoke in unison, "In the light of the Crystal, you must renew the Pact."

Tanner withdrew a small blade from his sheath, the handle a shimmering mother-of-pearl. I wondered if the Tarim had given it to him. He held out his palm and drew the tip of the blade across it. The blood welled up in his palm and he smeared it on the face of the closest crystal column. The tower of crystal glowed faintly as it accepted his blood. He turned and handed me the blade, handle facing me.

My eyes widened as I realized what he expected me to do.

Nobody told me about this.

Nobody told me about any of this.

I didn't like being put on the spot like this. What was I going to do? It's not like I could refuse my boss, or even question him in front of the Tarim. Resentment rose in my chest but I didn't protest.

I reminded myself I was a Slayer now, and the ink came with responsibilities. I reached for Tanner's blade and he gave me a small nod. I accepted the blade and hoped that Tanner missed my trembling fingers. Kotori's presumptive beating definitely looked better now, but as Tanner had said, the Slayers were the thin line defending the defenseless in Seattle. A little blood to renew the Pact was a small price to protect people like Jimbo and Henry.

I drew the blade lightly across my palm. Tanner certainly knew how to upkeep his blades. The edge slipped across my skin with hardly any resistance. I only registered the hot line of pain when crimson droplets beaded up across the width of my hand. I sucked in a breath and slapped my hand onto the crystal.

In an instant, the crystal tower ignited with brilliant orange light that blasted the room like a bonfire. Under my hand I felt the crystal thrum like an engine. The other two crystals picked up the resonance and the three towers sang a high, clear note that shook the walls of the Temple. My magic flared to life, stronger than I'd ever felt it, crowding my vision with glowing lines of force and stress.

Time seemed to slow. The lines of my magic covered the tower before me, radiating out from under my palm. The lines split as they moved away, dividing into intricate fractals. My power spread until it covered the two neighboring crystals.

Vibrations raced up my arm and stirred something deep in my chest. I took a breath and thundering power trembled under my hand, just beyond my grip. The Acolytes both took a step back, their eyes widening.

Rough hands grabbed my arm and yanked me backwards. The high, clear resonance cut off as sharp as a razor and silence roared in my ears. The power washed away like a whisper in the wind and left me feeling vaguely empty. I blinked.

Three pairs of eyes stared at me.

Tanner moved to block my view of the crystal and the Acolytes. "Roxy? Are you okay?"

He sounded tinny, and distant. His eyes darted back and forth and his fingers gripped painfully into my shoulders. He was sweating despite the relative cool inside the Temple. Why did he look nervous?

The roaring in my ears faded and the world seemed to slip back into normal speed. I released what felt like a long pent up breath. It felt like I'd just awoken from a nap that had been too long, my brain was foggy and slow.

"Tanner? What happened?"

The worry lines around his eyes relaxed. "It's the transfer, I think. It hit me hard, too, the first time I came here."

He turned to the Acolytes. "She's fine, thanks for asking."

Two pairs of eyes backlit with orange fire stared at me. They most definitely did not look concerned for my well being. They looked like they were considering me for dinner.

Tanner turned me towards the far wall and gave me a nudge. His voice dropped to a whisper. "Let's go. Just keep walking."

From behind us, the strange choral voice rang out. "On your life, on your blood. The Pact is renewed."

I couldn't tell which one was speaking, and the echoes of their farewell followed us into the exit.

TANNER RAMBLED as we walked down the hallway. I couldn't tell if he was talking to assure me or himself.

"I should have warned you, the process can take a lot out of you. Last time I brought Aislinn with me and even she had to rest afterwards. I usually sleep it off for the rest of the day."

Now that he was saying it, a heaviness had definitely settled into my limbs, making our little stroll feel like the end of a marathon. Contrary to what Tanner was saying, the experience hadn't been unpleasant. If anything, the power of the crystals had ignited something in my magic, something that I had yet to tap into. I looked forward to trying to tap into that feeling again.

Tanner was the leader of the Slayers. My commander. And yet my gut told me to keep the truth of my experience to myself. For now.

I ran my hand through my hair. "Yeah, I can barely keep my eyes open. That was...something."

Tanner's relaxed ease slid back over him like an old coat. "The important thing is that you bounced back, yeah? Like I said, I knew you'd be a good fit."

The corridor widened again as we approached the antechamber where we had met Grandma and Dario. Two dark shapes were outlined in shadow, backlit by the orange glow of the walls.

The figures resolved into a tall, thin man with dark skin and close cropped hair that was graying at the temples. He wore a dark robe with full sleeves. A pattern of entwined crosses stitched in silver thread traced around the hems of the sleeves. A single silver cross with a narrowed point at the base adorned his chest.

I took an involuntary step back and nearly collided with Tanner when I saw the young woman behind the priest. Marnie had let her hair grow out a little since I'd last seen her outside the Box at the end of our Trials. Her wardrobe still favored black leggings and an excess of knives. She smirked when our eyes met and I cursed myself for taking the step back.

The dark priest smiled, a surprisingly warm expression that didn't match his attire. The smile stopped well short of his eyes. "Tanner! So good to see you." The priest held out his right hand where he wore a large ring of Tarim crystal on his middle finger.

Tanner grabbed the priest's hand and shook. "Cardinal. It's good to see you, too. May I introduce Roxanne Lim? She is one our most recent initiates."

Cardinal, the infamous leader of the Church of the Sharpened Cross, who presided over a growing congregation of zealots devoted to eliminating all vampires. Marnie had to be the most righteous zealot of them all. His eyes flicked briefly to his hand, swallowed in Tanner's huge grasp, before landing on me, somehow with considerably less warmth than when they started. "Ah yes, I've heard so much about you, Ms. Lim."

Marnie's eyes bored into me even as I maintained eye contact with Cardinal. "Well, I hope it was only good stuff."

Cardinal said, "Yes, one should always hope."

The priest's eyes slid off me and back to Tanner. "I know our time here is precious, but if we might have a quick word?" He gestured off to the far side of the room.

"Sure, sure."

Cardinal turned to Marnie. "My dear, why don't you and Ms. Lim get...reacquainted."

He held out his hand and Marnie reached for it without hesitation, bending low to kiss the ring on his finger. "Yes, Cardinal. Your will is my will."

Creepy town.

The grownups moved off to the far corner, leaving me alone with the insane woman who had tried to leave me and Ulf behind to die in a derelict death trap building filled with nightmares. So yes, I might have a few bones to pick with her.

Marnie pulled one of her many knives and began fiddling with her fingernails with the tip of the blade. "It doesn't look like you're any worse for your time in the Box."

"No thanks to you."

Marnie bared her teeth. "I heard Ulf survived as well."

The nerve of this one. "Unlike some people, I don't leave a teammate behind."

Her eyes flashed, cold and hard. "You drank the vampire blood. It doesn't make you virtuous–it makes you weak."

I gave her a tight smile. "I'm strong enough to take you to the ground, any day of the week."

She hissed. "You belong on the ground, with the filth. In the end you'll see. You haven't done Ulf any favors either. He was obviously too weak to survive. You've only given him false hope until his inevitable end. He's going to be eaten by another predator, one that comes around when you aren't there to protect him."

Rage threatened to swamp me, but I shoved it down. Not here, and not now. I clenched my fists and reached for some clarity, the way I did when Kotori was bashing me with a staff.

I would not be caught scuffling with some nutjob in the temple of the Tarim. She was the past, just an inconvenience I had to endure a few moments more until I could leave this place.

I knew a little about the Church of the Sharpened Cross. In a world where vampires were a constant threat, the church offered sanctuary and more importantly for a lot of people, vengeance. If it came to a straight up fight, the Church could put more boots on the ground than we could, but we had them on training. Marnie was one of their exceptions, otherwise most Crossies were just untrained thugs with sharpened stakes and second hand swords.

The problem was that the Church recruited from those who had lost family to rogues. What the Crossies lacked in formal training, they made up for in desperate zeal. There was nothing quite as ferocious as a man who had lost everything, and then promised bloody retribution. If Marnie's story about her past had been true, she was the perfect candidate for the Church. Bereft of her family at an early age, and completely impressionable to their code.

I felt sorry for her.

"You're right, Marnie. The Twilight is a hard place. And one of these days, you're going to need someone to watch your back and no one will be there for you."

She sneered. "My god will be there for me. Who will be there for you? Your damned vampire? You're such a hypocrite. So righteous even as you make deals with the wretched. What would your precious Tanner say if he knew of your dealings with the Night Queen? But, no, go play your little games with the vampires. Enjoy your flirtation with the darkness before it brings you to ruin."

Marnie leaned in close until I could feel her breath. "You have no idea what's happening and it's right under your nose. By the time you understand you won't even matter any more."

She pulled back just as Tanner and Cardinal returned. The two men were all smiles as they clasped hands again. I caught the barest glimpse of something passing between their hands.

Tanner released his grip and his hand came back empty. "We won't keep you from your audience with the Tarim, Cardinal. As always, it was a pleasure and the Slayers look forward to our future endeavors."

Cardinal looked at me and smiled again, the effort perfunctory. His eyes said something else entirely. "Yes, we also look forward to our cooperative efforts."

Marnie gave me a sly wink as she and Cardinal disappeared into the crystal and moved off towards the Tarim Acolytes.

7

MARKET DAY

Tanner assured me that he'd taken me off the roster for two days, which was good because I could barely navigate the stairs to my unit. Ernest floated by, his ghostly form flashing in concern.

"I'm okay. Mostly. Just need to sleep it off."

"What happened?" he mouthed.

"Went to the Tarim temple."

Ernest fluttered in agitation and followed me to my door. He pressed his palms together, holding them under his ear in the universal symbol for sleep. Yes, that was absolutely my plan. He hovered in the corner and I appreciated him watching over me. He'd really saved my butt in the Box and I would never forget it. I had fed the ghost without expectation, but now I always made sure to light the joss sticks for him too. I didn't know how long he would decide to stay on this earthly plane, but I tried to honor his spirit.

My ink was still burning hot and cold and the rest of me felt like I'd been run over by the entire merchant caravan.

I jerked off my boots and tossed them aside, then collapsed face first into my bed. Everything else could wait.

THE CONCRETE MAZE of Boston blurs past me as I barrel down the sidewalk. Cold air burns my lungs and a sharp stitch in my side threatens to crumple me. I pump my arms and force my legs to keep moving, keep running. My sneakers sense my increasing desperation and slither up my legs, nanofibers firming around my ankles, stabilizing my feet as I lean into a hard turn. The sidewalk stretches before me, seemingly endless, now warping and twisting in the distance.

Boston General Hospital teases me with quick glimpses through the distant skyline. Dread fills my chest like ice water as I judge the distance to the hospital. The distance to mom. I pour on the speed, knowing that I am already too late. Ava and Jasper's voices ring in my ears and guilt drags at my feet like sucking mud. My legs keep pumping but the sidewalk crawls under my feet, each step is like climbing a mountain.

Ava cries out, high-pitched and panicked, "Hurry, Roxy! Hurry!"

Jasper shouts, and the sting of fear in his voice twists my stomach. "Roxy! Help!"

The hospital looms ahead, vast doors of smoked glass clad in chrome. Glittering red security lasers scan the approach to the doors. The beams cut across my body as I sprint the final distance. I block out the pain but I can't ignore the scent of my singed clothing, my burnt skin. I stumble and my shoulder slams into the hospital door. The massive sheet of reinforced glass trembles on impact but does not open.

I pound on the glass and my fists leave bloody streaked crescents. I shout, calling for Ava, for Jasper, for my mother. My voice breaks, goes hoarse. The glass shakes but does not move. The doctor appears behind the glass, her eyes severe, solid black orbs that stare down on me in judgment.

"Let me in! I can save her!"

I hammer at the door and the pounding sound is the drumbeat of my heart slamming against my chest. My mother is dying, just beyond my reach. If only I could reach her, I could save her. I need to get inside. My fists fly, my skin breaks, my bones snap.

The sound of pounding fills my ears, swamps my being, and fills the world.

~

THE POUNDING STARTED AGAIN and shook my door in its frame.

"Roxy! Open up!"

I rolled over and pulled my covers up over my head. The nightmare faded but I wasn't ready to wake up.

"Roxy! It's me, Malia!"

My eyes snapped open. Wait, why was Auntie pounding on my door? With a groan I crawled out of the covers and stumbled my way to the door. With a clap of my hands, the myriad of locks and talismans I had in place clicked in unison and my door unlocked.

I yanked open the door and Auntie almost fell in. Given that her shifter form was a mako shark, a graceful predator that cut through the turbulent waters of the Pacific, it said something about how rattled she was.

When not in the ocean, Malia ʻAukai looked like a librarian. Her eyes held ageless wisdom, sparkling bright in her round face. Her skin was smooth and brown, wrinkling only around her smile lines. She caught her inelegant stumble, then straightened out her red floral blouse and gray wool skirt. A large white canvas bag was slung over her shoulder.

Auntie skipped all the formalities. "Jackie and Bev are in trouble"

Part of my body was still futilely beating on the doors of the hospital. It took me a moment to comprehend who she was talking about. "Jackie? Mrs. Chu?"

Auntie huffed, her hands trembling with unspent energy.

She moved into my little living area and began nervously straightening my furniture. She spoke slowly, taking care to enunciate each word. "Yes, your landlady."

I felt like I was trying to catch up from very far away. I had very little idea what Mrs. Chu did in her free time, other than brew delicious soups. "She isn't at home?"

Now Auntie stood and glared at me, her frustration turning to anger. "Why would I be pounding on your door if she was home?"

She had a point. I really had to get my brain up to speed. I backtracked in my mind, going over my last conversation with Mrs. Chu.

"She went to Bev's Ranch."

Auntie's eyes flashed and her skin rippled. I swore her teeth lengthened into razor sharp points. "That was two days ago, Roxy. Yesterday I got one of Bev's pigeons, but with no note. Now Jackie and Bev have missed our trip to Market today."

That statement landed on me like a bomb. "Wait, what? Two days?"

Auntie grabbed me by the shoulders and shook me. "Why can't I get through to you, girl? Jackie should have been back yesterday! Today is our market day. She never misses it! The pigeon from Bev is bad news, I know it!"

Despite months here in the Twilight, habit still had me looking out my window, searching for signs of the sun. All I saw as the brilliant purple of the Twilight Veil that draped all of Seattle in eternal dusk. Auntie had said two days. At a cautious estimate that meant I'd been asleep for at least a day and a half, possibly more.

I'd missed feeding my own pigeons. I'd assumed Tanner had simply meant I'd be tired, not that I'd be dead to the world. The shock of seeing Auntie at my door finally worked through my system, getting my brain in gear. Finally I said, "I'm sorry, I had a rough shift and lost track of time."

"She should have been back yesterday." Malia repeated.

I blinked, my thoughts still muddled. "No note with the pigeon?"

"No! Are you caught up yet?"

"Maybe she decided to stay an extra night at Bev's." My voice trailed off, uncertain.

Auntie shook her head. "I've known Jackie for decades. She's never missed our Market day. In any case, Bev should have been here for Market, too. They just finished the honey harvest, she talked about bringing it to Market just last week. And the pigeon smelled wrong. Something's happened. Something bad."

As she talked her words came faster and she bustled around my apartment, tidying up as she went. At this rate if we didn't find Mrs. Chu the entire building was going to become dangerously clean. But now I was starting to worry too. Mrs. Chu had her routines and it wasn't like her to deviate. And a shifter's nose was the closest thing we had to forensics here in the Twilight. If Auntie thought the bird smelled wrong, I believed her.

"Is there someone we should tell?" I realized I didn't know if Mrs. Chu had any family nearby.

Auntie shook her head. "She has us, her sisters."

A sinking sense of dread landed in my gut. I was afraid I knew where this was going. When Mrs. Chu talked about her sisters, she was referring to Auntie, Bev, and Grandma.

"Have you heard from Grandma?"

Auntie's lips tightened. "Lydia is out the sloth, training the new patrols. She didn't go to the Ranch this week."

The feeling in my gut worsened. Auntie wasn't leaving my apartment. Which meant she was expecting me to do something. But I wasn't sure what.

"Should we send Bev a pigeon?"

"Already did that, but this isn't right. I can feel it. You need to get out there."

I closed my eyes as if trying to shut out the reality of this shark shifter looming over me in my apartment. I just got my ink, I was supposed to be on duty and I could not be gallivanting around in the Wilds to chase after my landlady.

"Why me? Why not you?"

"I can't go. It's too far inland."

My nightmare seemed prophetic. For so many years, I had been juggling one responsibility after another, getting my mom to her treatments, working extra shifts to pay for it all, while making sure Jasper and Ava got to school. My time here in the Veil had given me an unprecedented level of freedom and I often felt guilty about it. But I'd earned it. And I'd made a lot of silver to send home to ameliorate my guilt.

I just wanted to buckle down, do my job as a Slayer, and get my Midnight Rose to carry out part B of my plan.

"Auntie, I have work. I can't just leave to go to the Ranch."

"Hmmph. Jackie treats you like her own cub. It's only right you should do this."

Ahh, there it was, the guilt and duty card. Her words landed hard because they were true–Mrs. Chu had brought me into her home, given me a sweetheart deal, and looked in on me like family. Which meant I was the one who had to go find her.

I ground my teeth in frustration. "Fine. I'll go."

Her shoulders sagged as the tension drained from her face. "Good."

"I'm going to need a map to Bev's Ranch."

Auntie nodded and I handed her some paper and pen. She drew the map while I hunted for some clean clothes and got my kit together. By the time I came out, Auntie had made a pot of rice, fried me some eggs, and steeped a pot of oolong.

I studied the map while Auntie poured me some tea and set

a heaping plate of food in front of me. She shook some furikake onto the rice and suddenly I was ravenous.

"Thanks for cooking."

"Thank you for going to check on Jackie." Auntie sounded considerably calmer now.

She reached into her giant canvas bag and pulled out a square of folded waxed cloth. "Here's some musubi I picked up at Market."

The bulging state of her canvas bag meant that she had come early, tried Mrs. Chu, gone to Market, looked for Bev and then come back here to pound on my door. No wonder she'd been so agitated.

Auntie rifled through the bag some more. "This is from the Apothecary. Jackie needs this medicine soon."

I didn't understand why Mrs. Chu needed medication. She was a shifter and they were incredibly strong, resistant to any number of mundane illnesses, and they could shift to heal just any condition. If my parents could shift, they probably would have ameliorated the worst symptoms of their illness. My dad might still be here. But they were only human, and Black Wait had hit them.

On the other side of the Veil, the haves and have-nots had different health care. Our family didn't have the health care that could deal with the tumors and blood cancer that was the hallmark of the Black Wait. The money I sent reduced the severity of Mom's symptoms, but didn't cure her.

That's why I was here, so I could get the Midnight Rose to her. Vamp blood would cure her.

But Mrs. Chu didn't need vamp blood, she had shifter healing. So what did she need medication for?

But I didn't pry.

I thanked her and after she finally left, my mind raced with how I was going to carve out time to take a visit to the Wilds where Bev's Ranch was. It wasn't far, but it was definitely an excursion that would eat up a whole day.

I'd already slept away my two days reprieve from patrol duty, unfortunately. If I was going to find my landlady I first needed to skive off of work.

8

MISSING OUT

Cordelia spotted me first as I entered the dorms of the Dojo. Situated in the rear of the massive complex, it was a warren of semi-private rooms available to any and all Slayers. Some, like my friends, lived here permanently, or until they could find their own places. Many were used as temporary housing by Slayers who patrolled beyond Seattle, but came into the city for brief visits.

The Hinterlander fell in beside me as I made my way deeper into the barracks. "Good morning! We missed you yesterday."

"Yeah, I was sleeping off the effects of visiting the Tarim."

Cordelia raised a sculpted eyebrow. "That bad?"

I gave her a brief rundown of what I saw but I left out my experience of touching the crystal tower. Something told me to keep that to myself for now, at least until I had a better understanding of what exactly had happened.

Cordelia was dressed in strictly functional clothing today, foregoing her silvery cloak that marked her as a fae from the distant coastal lands. While the cloak was impressive, she claimed that it didn't offer her any benefits for patrol duty.

Instead she opted for simple leathers that protected her body and forearms. Her milky, translucent sword rode across her back, and her rope whips hung coiled at her hips. Despite her short stature and delicate, porcelain doll looks, it was well known within the Slayers that Cordelia was a fierce warrior. After only a few patrols she was already starting to make a name for herself on the streets as well.

She really was the best of us. Not that I would tell her that out loud. I would never hear the end of it if I did that.

Wen and Ulf shared a room that had a picturesque view of the north end of Denny Park and a clear line of sight to the wreckage of the Space Needle. Their room adjoined a common area with a modest kitchenette that connected to another room shared by two other Slayers, Russ and Joey. Russ had a range magic that was useful in the Wilds. Joey had been a sniper back on the other side of the Veil. They were always staffed on the Caravan route so we rarely saw them. While I would have liked to get to know more Slayers, I did appreciate that we often got the run of the common area.

Ulf had decorated their door with a single protection rune. The door was slightly ajar and I could see Wen on his bed, cross-legged with his eyes closed. His mouth curled up into a small smile when I stepped inside.

"I always know it's you, Roxy."

"Really?"

"Your footsteps are unique."

This again? I sighed. "I know, loud, right?"

Wen opened his eyes and they twinkled with amusement. "No, not loud. Forceful."

Cordelia coughed and brought up her hands to cover her mouth. I shot her a dirty look and she turned away, continuing to cough loudly.

The guys kept a tidy room, no doubt sweeping the bamboo floors daily. Wen's side was especially minimalist, with only a long strand of mala beads on the nightstand. The dark wooden beads shone with a high polish, but one that came from the touch of Wen's hand on the beads rather than any lacquer.

In contrast, all manner of weapons and armor studded the wall on Ulf's side, an homage to his passion–armed warfare.

Ulf sat at the other end of the room with his leathers laid out on his bunk. His broad shoulders hunched as he pored over his armor with a critical eye. On the table next to him was a pile of rags and a bottle of leather cleaner. The fae could be a little full of themselves, but one thing you couldn't fault them for was the way they cared for their weapons and armor.

Ulf had been appalled when I explained to him I could see the various weak spots on armor and weapons. He'd patiently worked through each portion I'd identified on his gear, fortifying his armor and even forging replacement links at the Dojo's forge. He turned to me and held up a sleeve of chain mail.

I rolled my eyes but gave it a once over and shot him a thumbs up. He grunted with satisfaction and went back to cleaning and inspecting the rest of it.

Cordelia admired a helm, the gleaming silver surface carved with elvish runes. I'd never seen Ulf wear it, but it was a beauty. Clearly Cordelia thought so too given the careful way her fingers ran over it.

She gave a low chuckle when she got to the wicked looking mace hanging on the wall. "This reminds me of what Aislinn was carrying the day we went for our Trials."

It figured that Aislinn would wield something with that kind of bashing power. The tall fae warrior was scary enough already. Showing up to mentor your trainee with a mace like that was sheer overkill–a true hallmark move for a Freak of Seattle.

I had gotten Kotori for my mentor and for reasons I didn't understand, my uncle Samuel had taken me to meet her where she liked moonlight at an underground fight club. That had been intense but in case I hadn't been intimidated enough by the way she'd crushed her opponent in the cage fight, Kotori also wielded a naginata.

So I guess when we all got our own trainees, we were going to have to do something suitably intimidating. Which made me a little glum. We were supposed to getting matched up with our trainees today. By strange circumstance, I had already been paired with Finn previously, which I assumed meant I wouldn't have an additional trainee assigned to me today. But everyone else was getting their trainee today, which meant we should be teasing each other about what outlandish thing they would do in order to make a good first impression on their trainee.

But I wasn't going to be there. And even worse, I was going to need my friends to cover for me to boot. It wasn't a great feeling.

Taking advantage of my friends was not something I was comfortable with, which is why I brought food to bribe them. Even Wen leaned in closer when I opened my basket and allowed the steam to emerge.

Ulf lumbered over and peered into the basket. "Hmm."

In addition to the musubi Auntie had given me, I had added some minced greens and tofu steamed buns in there for Wen because he was a vegetarian.

Cordelia eyed the big fae as he pulled one of the musubi out. She grabbed one for herself then handed a veggie tofu bun to Wen who had fully opened his eyes now.

I was pretty sure they didn't have SPAM in the hinterlands where Cordelia was from. I couldn't imagine Ulf had eaten it before either.

I pointed to the musubi. "These have uh...a ham topping. I should warn you that I added chili crisp to these to spice them up."

Ulf smiled. "I am not afraid of a little spice."

Cordelia arched an eyebrow at him and seemed to settle her weight for a fight. She waved the musubi under her nose airily. "Hinterlanders fear nothing."

Ulf said, "In the Reach, our children grow up eating pepper candy."

Cordelia sniffed. "Only unsophisticated palates would consider that spicy."

Wen rolled his eyes at their antics and popped his steamed bun into his mouth and chewed. After a few bites his eyes widened a bit and he looked at me. Were his eyes watering just slightly? He smiled around his mouthful and winked. Maybe I'd been a little heavy-handed with the chili crisp in the filling of the buns too.

We were both familiar with Cordelia and Ulf's routine at this point and there was really nothing to do but to wait for the process to run to completion. The two of them stared at each other for a moment and then at the same moment they both ate their musubi.

They both chewed quietly for a moment, eyes watering, nostrils flaring. Ulf broke first.

"Not spicy at all." He choked back something that sounded like a cross between a gasp and a hiccough.

Cordelia swallowed and covered her mouth delicately. Her eyes were red around the edges. "Bland. I'm sorry, Roxy, but these are nearly tasteless. My baby niece would eat these by the handful."

I sighed and pulled a jug of milk out of my basket and set it on the table between them. Their eyes both locked onto the milk before jumping back to each other.

This time Cordelia broke, swiping up the bottle and chugging so fast that milk ran down her cheeks. Ulf barked a laugh that died quickly as Cordelia drained the bottle dry and set it back down.

I could have made him suffer, but I did have an agenda. I

pulled the second bottle out and offered it to my friend who gratefully drank.

When the milk was gone I said, "Sorry I missed patrol duty with you guys yesterday. How was it?"

Ulf opened his mouth but all that came out was a pained wheeze and his eyes teared up again. Cordelia snickered and then her laugh, too, was constricted down to a thin whistle. Wen cut in and saved them both.

"It's been fine, Roxy, but that's not really why you're asking, is it?"

Leave it to Wen to cut to the chase.

"You got me. I need some cover. I need to leave town. Today."

That sobered up my friends.

We were all aware I had just missed two days of patrols already. I rushed to explain, and sketched out my plan to find Mrs. Chu. Wen's face took on a sympathetic expression when I got to the part about Mrs. Chu's medication. I was hopeful there would be a very reasonable explanation for everything, I just needed them to cover my shift so I could make the trip.

Cordelia pointed out the obvious. "We just got our ink, Roxy. You can't start off by skipping your first day. What would your uncle say?"

Then her golden eyes widened. "What would Kotori say?"

"I know, but who else is going to go find Mrs. Chu? I'm practically the only family she has. Besides, I barely woke up from the whole experience at the Temple. Maybe tell Kotori and Samuel I need another day to recuperate...?"

Cordelia and Ulf both frowned, united for once in their displeasure with me.

Ulf said, "We cannot lie to them, Roxy. "

I sighed. He was right. This wasn't school and I couldn't play sick. It wasn't right to ask them to lie for me.

Cordelia put her hands on my shoulders and brought her

face close to mine. "You should find another way. Today is a big day and we've worked really hard to be here. Not showing up sends a bad message that you don't value your position here."

I sighed and pressed my forehead against hers. "I want to be here but Mrs. Chu needs me."

Cordelia let go of me and stepped back. "You're choosing to miss this first milestone with Slayers, Roxy. You have responsibilities here and now you're bailing on them and we will have to explain why you're not carrying your weight."

Her words stung. I wasn't flaky and I didn't like feeling like everyone would see me that way–like I didn't care about being a Slayer. It was the furthest thing from the truth.

Wen piped up. "Since I am paired with Roxy for patrol duty, I think only I would have to explain about Roxy's whereabouts."

Cordelia put her hands on her hips. "No, Wen. Finn would have to explain too."

I winced.

Cordelia was right, I needed to talk to Finn too.

Wen said, "I can train Finn today."

Ulf grunted assent. "That's true, Wen won't have a charge today."

We all turned to stare at Wen. It hadn't occurred to me that since Wen had declined to get his ink, he wasn't part of the new rotation. I had no idea what was next for Wen but I hadn't wanted to pry. But Cordelia and Ulf were curious too. What was Wen going to do?

Wen held up his hands. "I talked to Tanner. He said I was welcome to stay on and reconsider getting inked with the next class of candidates."

His face gave away nothing but I sensed Wen had made up his mind and wasn't getting the ink. Did that mean he wasn't going to be a Slayer anymore?

"Regardless, since I will not have a new charge, I can

assume Roxy's duties with Finn for a day. More importantly, Mrs. Chu's health may be in danger. One missed day does not compare to doing the right thing for your family."

Wow, I needed to take some notes from Wen. His logic cut to the heart of the issue. Cordelia chewed her lip.

"Kotori will find out. And then what? We just got into the Slayers, Roxy. We have duties now. Isn't this why you got your ink?"

Everything Cordelia said was true, but I couldn't let Mrs. Chu down. In all the time I'd been in Seattle, she'd taken care of me a lot more than the Slayers. I owed her. "It's just one day. Finn will be in great hands with Wen and I'll be out to the Ranch and back soon."

Cordelia clenched her jaw. "Why do you always have to do things the hard way, Roxy?"

She stood and headed for the door. "I have to go. Some of us are taking their duties seriously."

As she headed out Ulf rose too, scratching at his beard. "Thank you, Roxy, for the snack." He looked awkwardly at the door Cordelia had just exited. "She's right, you know."

I nodded and waited, because he seemed like he had more to say.

"But maybe you're also right. Both duties are honorable, who can say which should be more important?"

He sighed and gathered up his gear. "I will speak with Cordelia. I cannot lie for you, Roxy but I can endeavor to... avoid your uncle and Kotori for a while."

It was the best I was going to get, I knew it. I held up a hand and Ulf's big hand swallowed it in a crushing grip. After that, he slipped out the door after Cordelia.

Wen's eyebrows drew down in concentration. "Roxy, you have to tell Samuel why you need this shift change."

I knew that, but I was afraid. "What if he says no?"

Wen nodded. "He may. But I know you have already

weighed the possible consequences and determined that the risk is worth the reward."

Well, I hadn't thought quite that far ahead, but his words sent a rush of gratitude through me. At least someone had faith in me.

"Thank you for understanding."

He held out his arm and we clasped forearms. "Roxy, I don't feel that you should do this on your own. As soon as I wrap up my shift and work it out with Finn, I will come join you."

"I appreciate it, but you don't have to do that."

"I want to. I'd feel better if you had backup."

For the first time since Malia had barged into my apartment, I felt a moment of peace. This was something the Slayers had given me, that feeling of knowing someone was fighting at your side. Wen was offering to do that for me even though I wasn't going to be on Slayer business. If Wen really wanted to get somewhere, he could do it fast. He'd told me that it wasn't exactly flying, but to me it might as well be because he seemed to walk on air in giant leaps.

I leaned over and gave him a quick hug. "Thank you for offering. It's really not necessary."

Wen didn't let me leave until I gave him the location of Bev's farm.

Hang in there, Mrs. Chu. I'm coming.

Finding Samuel when he wasn't on shift wasn't hard. He had his own housing offsite, just like I did, but he was always at the Dojo anyway. I had never thought much about it before but after my conversation with Auntie about how Mrs. Chu didn't have any family in Seattle, I realized the same could be said of my uncle.

Until I had moved to Seattle, Samuel had no other relatives in Seattle. The Slayers were his family.

My dad had left, crossing the Veil again to return to marry my mom. He'd had me, Jasper and Ava and while our lives hadn't been perfect, it had been filled with caring. That had always been what carried me when the struggle threatened to overwhelm me. The knowledge that we loved each other and were there for each other helped me get through those dark days after Dad had passed.

But Samuel had never been part of that. He'd been just a mythic figure in Dad's stories. The strong Slayer uncle who was far away behind the Veil. Now I was here, but we weren't close. Samuel was still larger than life, and while he was my uncle, he was a Slayer first.

Which was why I didn't want to tell him that I was skipping out on my first day as an inked Slayer.

But Wen was right. I had to tell my uncle, who was also my upline boss.

I had wanted to avoid any sort of confrontation with Samuel. I'd been trying hard to live up to the expectations of the spiritual leader of the Slayers, but a small part of me worried that I kept falling short. I had barely made it through the Trials. Aislinn and Kotori had almost convinced Samuel to boot me out during the Trials and I never felt like I was on solid ground with him. But there were glimmers of hope. Like when he gave me my father's spear. Or like when we'd talked before the inking ceremony. Those brief glimpses of approval from Samuel had given me something I'd desperately wanted. Something I'd stopped getting from my dad after he'd gotten sick. Something like acceptance.

I didn't want to damage that.

As I walked through the hallways of the Dojo, I breathed in

the scent of wood and armor that permeated it. I loved walking through this place. Knowing I'd earned my spot here. I hated feeling like I was shirking my responsibility to the Slayers. To Samuel.

I stared at the double doors to the Armory, took a deep breath and pulled the doors open.

Samuel looked up, his Maker magic a low hum of color around him.

"Roxy. I hope you're feeling better now after the Renewal."

I'd almost forgotten about that. "Yeah. I was wiped out for a couple days."

My uncle frowned. "I wished Tanner had told me that he planned to bring you. We probably should have discussed it beforehand."

I shrugged. I was so low in the hierarchy that I wasn't sure the discussion would have been much use for me. But I liked to think that my uncle would have at least warned me about that last part.

I wondered if I should tell him about it, about how I'd felt my magic soar there. But then, maybe he already knew. "Uh, you've gone before, right?"

Samuel shook his head. "No. Only Tanner, his father, and grandfather before him went for the Slayers."

Oh.

It hadn't occurred to me that the other senior members of Slayers hadn't gone before. That meant none of the Seven Freaks had gone. Aislinn's fury made a little more sense now. Maybe she'd felt slighted by Tanner?

And maybe I had to ask myself why Tanner had singled me out instead of bringing one of the more senior members of the guild. But I didn't have the slightest explanation. I wasn't the star of my class–that was Cordelia.

I wasn't sure what to say now. Given that I was here about

something else, maybe I was better off keeping my magic surge at the Tarim Temple to myself.

"It's about my shift today," I started.

"I'm sure you're looking forward to it."

When my uncle smiled at me, I felt a lump catch in my throat.

I swallowed hard. "I am, but something's come up."

He raised his eyebrows.

I clasped my hands together, trying to still the restless sensation in them. "It's Mrs. Chu, something's wrong and she needs help."

Samuel leaned forward, "What's going on?"

In a rush of words, I blurted out the visit with Auntie and that I had to get out to Bev's ranch.

Samuel frowned. "If it's about the meds, we could just send a courier, Roxy."

I'd thought about that. It hadn't solved my problem.

"That won't make sure she gets them. We don't actually know where she is. I have to go."

Samuel shook his head. "No, Roxy, you don't have to go. You are choosing to go at the expense of your other duties here."

I wrung my hands a little. Then I made myself stop. "It's just for a day. Once I track her down, I can come back."

Even as I said the words, I knew they were hopelessly optimistic.

Samuel stood up. "Roxy, this is about more than your shift. This is about your commitment to the Slayers."

My heart sank. This was exactly what I was afraid of–that Samuel would have a lower opinion of me.

"I'm not going to tell you not to go. You're a grown up and you can make your own decisions."

That sounded like a test–one I was failing. When Samuel's face went stiff, it reminded me of how my dad looked when I dropped a weapon or took a hit. Like he expected better of me. I tried to shrug it off but it hurt just the same.

"Well okay. I just wanted to let you know."

I dashed out before I changed my mind, and before I let Mrs. Chu down too.

9

FIELD TRIP

I packed lightly, almost superstitious about how much provisioning I would need. As if the notion of packing more would mean that I would be gone longer. That I would be truly letting the Slayers down the way Samuel had accused. That made me feel a little nauseous.

Samuel had given me his karambit, one of the few times I'd felt like he'd given me a vote of confidence when I was undergoing the trials. The karambit had a six-inch blade chased with silver, and etched with intricate whorls and runes. I loved the wicked curve, the perfect balance of it that I could spin around a finger. Its most notable feature was the delicate crystal reservoir. This blade could drink from the undead and I'd used it on my first exsanguination of a vamp. I'd found a good leatherworker and procured a custom case for the blade that I could strap around my calf.

Not for the first time, I mourned the loss of my father's spear, which was buried in some dark corner of the Box. I vowed that someday I would brave the Box again and recover my legacy.

I stuffed two apple cider donuts into a waxed paper pouch

and some river demon jerky. Hopefully I wouldn't need much more than that for this excursion.

I caught a ride with some merchants who were headed north. Thankfully this part of the plan was easy. I flashed my patrol bandana and they were more than grateful to let me join. They were a small party, not big enough to warrant or afford Slayers protection out in the Wilds. So a little barter for the trip was more than worth it. I just kept a vigilant watch while I rode north in the back of the lead wagon. More than fair.

After the tense exchange with my uncle, I was grateful for the ride to the Wilds. Anything to give me space and time ease the sting of his disappointment. To stop imagining the way my dad would look at me if he'd been there.

As we passed the Sentinel stones that marked the northern border of Seattle I was again struck by the feral nature of the Wilds. Just beyond the small border of our pocket civilization, nature ran riot. The greater Seattle area had stretched for miles in all directions, the epitome of urban sprawl. After a hundred years of forced reclamation it was hardly recognizable.

The temperate rainforest of the Pacific Northwest covered nearly all traces of humanity's past intrusion. Here and there some decaying bit of concrete poked through the greenery, but for the most part, from here to the limits of the Veil, Mother Nature again ruled with an ivy-laced fist.

Deep in these jungles hid the true dangers behind the Twilight Veil. Seattle was the glamorized version of it, the version that still fit into humanity's vision of itself as being if not the top of the pyramid, then at least somewhere in the upper third.

But in the Wilds, vanilla humans were reduced to soft-bellied, toothless, fangless creatures who were blind in the dark and couldn't smell their food or predators to save their own skins. Perils of rogues roamed the darkness, hunting anything with blood. Packs of feral shifters had been spotted as well, sometimes clashing with the rogues as they fought for the choicest hunting grounds.

And if that wasn't enough, according to my father's stories, neither of those two threats compared to the demons that lurked in the depths of the Wilds.

I stood and stretched, working the kinks out of my lower back, and made my way to the front of the wagon. There the driver had the relaxed stance and sway of someone who spent more time on a moving vehicle than actually walking. His face was obscured by a wide-brimmed gray hat and all I really could see was a hawk nose and salt and pepper beard. He held the reins to a pair of robust chestnut color horses that pulled us along at a good clip. To be honest it seemed like the horses were doing everything by memory, and the driver was simply holding the reins out of habit.

As I sat down next to him, the driver eyed me warily, his eyes lingering on the silver mesh collar around my neck before nodding in greeting. "How can I help you, Slayer?"

It was odd, frankly, getting this measure of respect from a man easily my senior by a few decades, but the title of Slayer held a lot of weight in Seattle.

I tilted my head towards the proud stepping horses. "Nice horses."

He twitched the reins. "Can't beat Morgan horses. They're smart, friendly and run like hell when I tell them to. Never know what you'll come across out here in the Wilds."

"And you usually do the route without a Slayer running guard?"

He chuckled grimly. "I ain't got the silver for Slayers. Even if I wasn't just running carrots and potatoes. But rogues and shifters don't care much for vegetables, so they pretty much leave me alone."

The driver grinned and pulled up his shirtsleeve, exposing

a deeply tanned and almost skeletally thin arm. "Besides, who would want to eat something as tasteless and stringy as me?"

He twitched the reins and the horse whickered amiably. I'd been watching him as he spoke, and while his tone was light, I noticed that his eyes darted left and right, searching the dark corners of the forest around us. And for someone who seemed so cavalier about his travels, he had jumped at the opportunity to bring me along.

"Something's changed, hasn't it?"

The driver's mood darkened considerably and he stared into the distance for a long moment before he spoke again.

"Yeah, something's different."

His fingers tightened on the reins convulsively. "The Wilds are...too quiet. I've been up and down this path for years now. I know these trees like the back of my hand. I can't see much, but my ears are sharp, always have been. Sometimes I'd hear a pack of shifters creeping alongside me as I came south with a load of potatoes. They'd follow for a while, decide they didn't like how I smelled, and move on."

"And now?"

His gaze searched the darkness again. "Now, I don't hear anything. It's like the Wilds are empty. Like everyone went on a trip and left the lights on. It's damned unnerving."

That was definitely odd. "You mentioned shifters. What about the rogues? Did they ever give you trouble?"

"Yeah, that's the really scary part, isn't it? The way the shifters and rogues fought, you'd think if the shifters were gone, then you'd see more rogues, right?"

My stomach did a little swirly motion as I guessed where he was going with this.

"No rogues. No extra vampires. Just...quiet. It's not right."

~

THE LITTLE CARAVAN dropped me off at a fork in the road. According to Auntie's directions, the Ranch was just a mile from this branch and the forest was already thinning out into arable farmland. The merchants were comfortable making the rest of the trip without a Slayer watching over them. I wished them an equally uneventful trip on the way back.

I pulled out the donuts and decided now was a good time for a snack.

I tightened my pack over my shoulders and began hiking while I chewed the ushi oni jerky and swigged some water to choke it down. No matter how many times I ate it, I could never quite appreciate the taste–only the energetic effect.

The rough roads out here made my skateboard useless. This would have been a lot easier on my deck but I was counting on the demon jerky to give me a little boost. The sugar from the apple cider donut wouldn't hurt either.

The Wilds thinned out here, the trees giving more space between them. Further north of here were the farms that kept Seattle fed, built upon the remains of Washington's best wine country. The Slayer's farm wasn't far from here either, we had passed it on the way here.

To outsiders, the turnoff to the Farm wasn't obvious, obscured by thick clusters of bushes and trees. But now that I had my ink, a tingle of awareness had shot through the nape of my neck when we'd passed and I could swear I almost heard a whisper in my head. This had to be the Tarim crystal at work, the same way it sparked when we bumped fists with other Slayers.

I'd thought wistfully of stopping in to see Akhil and Altan. They didn't come up to the city much but they'd come for the Inking, which had been nice. At the Farm, there were other Slayers I'd never met but heard much about. Like Ben and Brianna, the boomer twins. Their powers were so disruptive that they preferred the Wilds. Also Frank, the shrieker. Talents like Frank's were not as useful for taking vamps in close quarters.

Instead, Slayers from the Farm patrolled the vast swathes of the Shadow Ridgeline and the Twilight Forest. Those places had been twisted with magic and dense with shadowy creatures. Unsurprisingly, rogues came through the Veil there and many of Seattle's power players paid Slayers handsomely to be the first line of defense.

As eager as I was to meet more Slayers, I hadn't wanted to slow down the caravan, and if this just turned into a pharmacy delivery, there was no need to involve anyone else. I'd be back to Seattle by the end of the day and excursion to the Wilds would be brief.

The funny thing about the Ranch was that it wasn't a ranch at all. It was a farm, officially named the River Rock Farm. But only herbivore shifters lived there and the moniker of "the Ranch" had stuck.

According to Auntie, Beverly had set up the Ranch as an alternative to living in Seattle. She said Bev had put it as, "Not everyone is dumb enough to want to live under the thumb of some macho alpha."

Bev built the Ranch into a kind of pastoral halfway house for shifters who didn't want to roam the Wilds, but also chafed at the idea of the rigid structures within Seattle. Auntie said there were usually anywhere from thirty to fifty residents living at the Ranch.

"They're all free spirits," Auntie said. "Bev wouldn't have it any other way. In her mind it's all about the freedom to choose. They come and go when they want, and as long as everyone plays nice, everyone can stay as long as they like."

Auntie had speared me with a sharp look. "Mind yourself around Bev, Roxy. She puts up with you because you're one of Jackie's, but she's got no love for the Slayers."

Well, that explained all the hard looks I'd gotten from her in Mrs. Chu's apartment.

The Wilds thinned out further and the land opened up to the north. A waist-high wall of rough stone appeared, marching into the distance in a straight line. Inside the wall the fertile land of the Wilds had been somewhat tamed, brought to heel under the ministrations of several large plows. Neat furrows of earth drew parallel lines across the Ranch. I spotted the plows in the far corner of the field, massive triangular blades of beaten metal that looked about as tall as I was. A thick leather harness hung limply from the crest of the plow.

Wow. Who did they have pulling that? A rhino?

I hunkered down behind the wall and waited, listening for any signs of activity. Auntie had made it sound like the Ranch was a constant bustle of activity, with each resident expected to put in some effort to ensure the survival of the enterprise. So far, the Ranch seemed to be like the Wilds on our way here—unnaturally quiet.

The wind played through the trees behind me and brought me insect calls and small birds. As I examined the field, I noted that several rows of plants had been obviously trampled, a detail that stood out amongst the rest of the neat and tidy rows. Flies buzzed around a massive orange and green gourd that had been smashed open, the sticky seeds splattered across the ground exactly like blood from a knife wound. A faint fuzz of black mold had taken hold on the exposed inner flesh of the gourd.

So someone, someone big by the look of the smashed gourd, had left the field in a hurry. And no one had been back since. The rest of the plants were still in good shape, and I didn't see any weeds taking root, so it stood to figure that it had only been a few days. Enough for the mold to get started.

I settled back on my haunches, letting my eyes roam into the distance, looking for details of the expansive stone and wood ranch house that dominated the center of the Ranch. More well-tended fields stretched across the northern border of the Wilds, all of them quiet. If there was any place to find out what was happening, it would be in the house.

None of this seemed right, not by Auntie's estimation of the Ranch.

I thought about the pigeon. Auntie had said there was no note.

Maybe it was nothing. I really wanted it to be nothing.

Maybe everyone was just on a break. For a few days.

But I knew that wasn't likely. I didn't know Bev very well, but well enough to know that was thin. So much for my hopes that this would be just a quick excursion.

Auntie had been right. Something bad had happened. My heart squeezed at the thought of Mrs. Chu not being okay.

I stood and vaulted the rock wall and began picking my way across the field, making my way to the main house. Bev liked me only marginally, and openly disliked the Slayers. If I were lucky, she'd open the door to tell me that to my face. Somehow, I didn't think I would be that fortunate.

10

THE RANCH

I made it halfway across the field. Then, as I stood completely exposed between neat rows of plump pumpkins, the front door to the ranch house clicked, the sound carrying clearly to me through the still air. I had no cover.

I went flat, squashing myself into the nearest furrow between the rows of plants. Dark, wet soil squelched between my fingers as I tried to grab the dirt and pull myself down. I held my breath and peered through the vines toward the house.

The door swung open on well-oiled hinges and a broad-shouldered figure stepped onto the porch that spanned the width of the house. He filled the door frame and his dirty blonde hair was shaved down to bare stubble. Naked to the waist, he wore only a rough set of trousers and tall work boots that looked well-worn and of high quality. His arms and chest were covered in ropy muscle, and his skin was lightly tanned and crisscrossed with old scars, the hallmarks of a life of hard labor and hard times. His eyes were strangely light, almost colorless and so dilated his pupils looked outlined in white light.

A vampire. A vampire at the Ranch. My heart hitched in my

chest. Despite Bev's history of taking in strays from the Wilds, I seriously doubted that she was boarding any vampires here. Whatever was going on here, I wasn't simply going to give Mrs. Chu her medication and go back on my merry way. What had I gotten myself into?

Yes, I had done countless shifts with Slayers and dealt with any number of rogues–but now I was alone. Slayers always fought in pairs or trios. That was our strength. Alone and on the ground, I was at a huge disadvantage.

My heart thumped so hard I was worried the vamp could hear it.

The vampire carried a heavy axe, the kind used for splitting wood. The axe rested negligently across his broad shoulders, his right hand lightly gripping the handle. His hands were huge. From across half the field it was obvious they were outsized, even for a man his stature. I had a momentary flash, a vision of this man crushing my face with one hand like palming a basketball, his thick fingers worming their way into my ears...

I must have made a noise because the vampire turned, his eerie bright eyes scanning right over me. Thank the goddess for all my training because it took everything in my forebrain to override my hindbrain's instinct to pop up and run back to Seattle as fast as possible. I forced my hands to relax, willed my back to unclench. There was no way I was beating a vampire at a dead run, especially true since I was starting from the ground. I had to hope he missed me.

I hunkered down and tried to imagine myself blending into the dirt. The porch was just slightly higher than ground level. Did he have enough elevation to see me beyond the pumpkin plants? I exhaled slowly, stretching it out across four heart-beats, careful not to disturb even the smallest leaf.

Watching this axe-wielding vampire flashed me back to my harrowing detour in the Fangs when I had been surrounded by three hungry vamps from the Shadow Den. That seemed a lifetime ago. I had staked and drained a few vamps since then but had zero illusions that I was a match of this one.

But my other skills had grown. I let my eyes go to that other vision, where the lines of the building and objects around the vampire came into focus. Maybe I could distract him.

The ranch house had classic lines, and was well made, but Seattle had humidity which meant no building could withstand it or termites for long. I narrowed in on the eaves above the vampire and the knothole in the wood beams above.

Bit by bit, I broke the particles and let the wood dust and termite sand trickle down. This was a tiny working of my magic, and the recoil was weak enough for me to ignore it. I was ready for a mild wave of nausea and nearly jumped when my ink pulsed with heat. The ink over my heart chakra tingled and my skin went hot and cold down my neck.

Aanya's words echoed in my head. Was this what she'd been talking about? Sweat beaded on my hairline and started to tickle. Seconds felt like hours as I watched the wood particles fall and then dust the vamp's head.

"Feck!" He startled and his head snapped up to glare at the offending wood beam.

The vamp reached up and punched the beam. More wood dust fell out.

"This feckin' place."

"Felix, what are you doing?" a gravelly voice yelled from inside.

"This damn place is falling apart!" Felix complained.

"Get yer arse back in here."

"Understood, boss."

Felix hefted his axe, and returned inside. The heavy door closed with a slam and I sagged with relief. After a few moments where it didn't appear that Felix was going to come back, I inched slowly backwards on all fours.

I aimed for the herb garden on the east side of the building.

After what felt like a century later, I made it to the tall planter boxes. I scuttled behind them and sat down, my breaths coming hard like I'd run a marathon. My hand went to the back of my neck, but my skin felt normal again. What had happened to the recoil?

And what were vampires doing here on Bev's ranch? An axe wielding vampire named Felix had nearly caught me and even worse, he had a friend inside. His boss.

My mind raced, struggling to process what this meant for Mrs. Chu and Bev.

How many vamps were inside? At least two.

I needed to get a closer look to see what I was dealing with. I got into a low crouch and bent at the waist as I raced to the east wall. I moved slowly beneath the window line, praying that Felix and friend did not suddenly decide to check on the back gardens. Since the vampires hadn't left sentries outside, it stood to reason that they didn't want to be seen. Which meant hopefully they wouldn't see me as I snuck around.

The ranch house was large, which was good and bad. Bad because I was presently trying to sneak in, good because maybe it was too much territory for just a few vamps to secure. This improved my odds of getting in, and hopefully out. Ideally, with Bev and Mrs. Chu in tow.

As I approached the cellar door, I was painfully aware that I had no real plan.

My assets right now included me, my hammers, a couple of blades and my little bit of Breaker magic. My magic was not especially useful here if I wasn't trying to bring down the roof of Bev's ranch. I didn't have an army but maybe I didn't need an army. I hoped.

I didn't know what I would be facing inside, or what condition Mrs. Chu was in. I ground my teeth. She was fine. I was going to be stealthy, and sneak in and sneak her out. The vamps would never even know I'd been there.

As I skulked along the exterior, I let my magic assess the structure. There had to be a back way in a place this size. I was so busy looking at the building I almost tripped over a door in the ground. The cellar door.

I stared hard at it, the polished handle beckoning.

The root cellar probably didn't connect to the ranch house. Also I didn't know what I would find down there. It probably wasn't smart to go down blind. What if there was a peril of rogues hanging out down there in the darkness along with the potatoes?

I scanned the exterior of the house again. Probably it was safer to find an open window and focus my efforts on the main house.

I froze as Bev's rough voice floated up through the cellar door. "For goodness sake, you make enough noise to wake the damned, Roxy. Get down here already."

11

THE BEST LAID PLANS

I dashed over to the cellar door and pulled it up. The interior was pitch black and smelled of cool, damp dirt. "Bev? Is Mrs. Chu with you?"

"Yes, yes. Jackie recognized your footfall. Says you walk like a small buffalo but I'm not sure about that. My buffalos are a lot quieter than you."

I looked around the vegetable garden quickly then eased myself under the door and let it close gently over my head. It was like stepping into a chill bath and my skin broke out in gooseflesh. My magic sparked and the interior of the cellar lit up in glowing lines of pale green light. The cellar was large, maybe half the footprint of the main Ranch house and laid out in a long rectangle. At the far end, a set of stairs led up to what I assumed was the house.

Sturdy shelves had been built off the support beams that supported the Ranch and I made out shadowy piles of potatoes and carrots, as well as the gleam of neat rows of jars. After a moment in the darkness I also caught the sharp aroma of fruity alcohol coming from a stack of wooden kegs at the far end.

"Stop lollygagging, girl, and get over here. Jackie needs your help."

Bev's voice came from behind the shelf with all the jars. I rounded the corner and found the two of them shackled with thick chains at the wrist and ankles. The chains wrapped around one of the support pillars, giving the two of them maybe a few feet of slack. The chains were thick links of steel that stood out in my magic sight like looping whorls of green light.

But that wasn't what caught my attention. Mrs. Chu lay on the dirt floor. Even in the darkness I could tell she was wearing her favorite satin windbreaker, something she would never let get dirty. I crouched. Her breaths came fast and shallow, like she was winded from a long run.

Bev squatted next to me, her chains clinking. "She needs her meds."

I fumbled through my pockets and found the package Auntie had given me. Relief softened the harsh plains of her face and Bev plucked it from my hand. "Good girl."

Bev ripped open the package, and pulled out a small metal cylinder with a nozzle at one end, and a trigger along the body. She put the device in Mrs. Chu's hand. "Here you go, Jackie. Roxy brought it."

Mrs. Chu put the nozzle in her mouth and squeezed the trigger, inhaling sharply as she did. The cylinder hissed and the tension drained out of Mrs. Chu's body, her breaths coming slower. She sank against the wall and clutched her meds to her chest.

Bev pulled off her coat and made it into a makeshift pillow. She pulled Mrs. Chu down to the floor. "Get some rest, Jackie."

Mrs. Chu pawed around until she found and grabbed my wrist with surprising strength. She gave a wan smile. "Thank you, Roxy. I knew you would come."

Her words sent a splinter of guilt into me. I hadn't wanted to come. I had wanted this to be someone else's problem.

Her head sank into the pillow and in moments the only sound in the cellar was her deep, even breathing.

Bev put her hand on my shoulder. "You did good."

I wondered again what kind of ailment Mrs. Chu had that hadn't been cured by her lycanthropy. Her illness was so unnerving I barely registered Bev's complement.

"How did you know I was coming?"

She shrugged, a subtle movement that hinted at the strength in her big frame. "I knew what Malia would do when she got my pigeon. Jackie said she knew what you would do."

I hoped the cellar was dark enough that Bev wouldn't see the flush on my cheeks or sense the heat on my neck as I recalled trying to bargain my way out of coming out here. My only relief was that I'd lived up to Mrs. Chu's expectations, and gotten her meds here in time.

This was still only half the job, though. I put my hands on the thick links of the chain and felt my magic worm its way into the crystalline structure of the metal. I'd been practicing at this. Anything with a regular molecular structure was getting a lot easier to Break. Bone. Ice. Metal.

"I'll break the chains. Can you carry her out?"

Bev grabbed my wrist and pulled my hand off the chain. "No! We can't leave."

"What?"

Bev shook her head. I wanted to shake her, but I wasn't a match for the hefty wereshifter. Why was she refusing to leave?

I tried sweet reason. "Mrs. Chu can't stay like this. We need to get her out."

Bev frowned.

I gestured broadly to the root cellar. "Auntie told me to make sure you were okay. Being locked up in your own cellar is not okay. I'm pretty sure the vampires upstairs are not okay. We need to go."

Bev folded her arms. "We're not the only ones here, Roxy. I have over a dozen hands here at the Ranch and I don't know what's happened to any of them. Those vampires came down on us hard two nights ago. I know I lost at least one in the fight and I'll be damned if I'm losing any more. This is my home. I'm not leaving until everyone is safe."

Frustration had me grinding my teeth. It was already a miracle that I'd found Bev and Mrs. Chu and they were unguarded. Wait, why *were* they unguarded?

"We have to leave before your jailers come back, Bev!"

She shrugged. "They rotate in and out, drug us and then leave thinking their tranqs do the job."

"They don't do the job?"

Bev's lips twisted. "They work on Jackie. I'm an alpha though. They don't know as much as they think they do about shifters."

Shifters were impervious to just about everything except silver. The fact that these vamps had a tranquilizer that worked on the shifters was terrifying. And also suggested a chilling level of either scientific expertise or straight up enchantment. But drugs didn't seem magical. More clinical.

Mrs. Chu stirred. "Can't leave."

I knelt down. "Please Mrs. Chu. We have to get you home."

She opened her eyes. "I'll be fine."

They had lost their minds. "You are not fine. You are in a cage. I can break you out."

"No, no. Bev is right. We have to stay or the vamps will know."

I ground my teeth in frustration. "We'll come back for them, just let me get you out of here first."

Mrs. Chu said, "No. You have to get help to spring all of us."

What she was asking me to do was impossible. "They may all be dead. But you're alive and I'd like to keep you that way."

She raised her nose and sniffed delicately. "No one else has died."

"Yet," I said.

Bev growled.

"How did this even happen?" I asked helplessly.

"They drugged our water supply."

Frustration made my voice sharp. "I don't know how we can get all of your people out here."

She bopped my head. "Think, Roxy. You go get some help and come back as quick as you can. Show me that your Slayers are worth half a damn. These vampires have to be violating some part of the Pact, right? Get your boss out here to do his damn job."

I bristled at her characterization of the Slayers but I held it in. Bev didn't deserve my frustration. In truth, I wondered why the Slayers didn't patrol out here in the Wilds, why the Ranch was so obviously unguarded.

Bev seemed to notice my discomfort and her tone softened. "We're not fighters here. Everyone who comes to my Ranch... they're here because they're sick of the politics, the constant fight just to live in Seattle. We can't do this without help."

This mess was just getting deeper and deeper, and I had a sinking feeling that the bottom was nowhere close.

"Fine. What can you tell me about the vampires, then? How many are we dealing with up there?

"At least seven."

Despair threatened to overwhelm me. I had me, an ailing werewolf, and a peace loving vegetarian shifter on my side. That wouldn't be enough to deal with two vamps let alone a peril of seven.

But that explained why they hadn't left anyone to guard

Mrs. Chu and Bev here in the root cellar. The Ranch was enormous, with a sprawling layout that included multiple barns.

I drew in a calming breath. *Just gather intel first, Roxy. Panic after.* "Who are we dealing with? Are they Shadow's Den?"

Seattle's vampires were controlled by two primary courts, the Shadow's Den and the Court of Mist and Mind, and I had a working understanding of how they both operated. I didn't have any real reason to suspect the Den, other than a bias against them since some of their low level hitters had tried to snatch me off the street a while back. And this didn't feel like the kind of thing that the Mist and Mind would do.

At least, it didn't feel like the kind of thing that Tyee Wilder would do. I wouldn't say I knew the vampire princeling well, but we'd scraped against each other enough times for me to know that his playboy persona was just a front. Whatever his role in his mother's court, it wasn't just to be a pretty face. And as infuriating as he was, whatever was happening here at the Ranch didn't seem...refined enough to be his work.

Bev shook her head. "They don't smell like the Den. I'm not sure--"

Mrs. Chu huffed. "I told you I caught a whiff of Mist and Mind."

"Once. You smelled it once."

I cut in before the ladies could start arguing. "Mrs. Chu, you're sure?"

She nodded. "It's faint, but it's there."

I wasn't going to say it, not here in the root cellar with my aunties chained up, but my instincts rebelled against the idea that the Mist and Mind were behind this.

Mrs. Chu's eyes narrowed as she noticed my moment of hesitation. "What did I tell you, Roxy? They're not like us. No matter how pretty he is, that vampire is a predator."

I trusted Mrs. Chu and I agreed with her to a point. Tyee was dangerous. But I didn't think he would do something like this. *Would he?* For whatever reason, mention of Tyee Wilder, the son of the Night Queen, seemed to skew my critical thinking skills. I had to get my head in the game.

"Where did you--"

Shouting voices broke in from above us along with the pounding of feet and slamming doors.

Bev grabbed my arm and thrust me towards the door. "Go, Roxy! They can't find out about you! Get out of here!"

Heart hammering in my throat I ran to the cellar door and pushed it up a fraction of an inch, even as my back crawled with tension with the thought of a peril of vampires barreling down the stairway from the house.

The back of the house looked clear. With another glance back to my aunties I pushed up the door and clambered out of the cellar. I was just lowering the door back into place when a pair of vamps rounded the corner of the house and let out a screech as they spotted me.

My magic flared hot and bright behind my eyes and I focused on the vampires. Vampires were preternaturally fast, but still slower than my sensei. Plus I knew these guys were going to run straight for me. My magic shot out and found the crystalline calcium structures of both pairs of pumping legs.

I juiced my power and four femurs snapped with a staccato sound like firecrackers going off at New Year's. The vamps screamed and went down in a tangle of flailing limbs. It would take them at least a minute to come back from two broken legs, giving me a sizable head start on them.

Then the recoil rushed back to me like an invisible tsunami of power. Like a fool, I ducked. Thank goodness Kotori wasn't here to see it. The recoil hit me like a pro-league fastball, a gut-wrenching wave of wrongness that spun my vision and threatened to empty my guts from both ends. I fell to my hands and knees and dry heaved, the sting of bile filling my mouth. My abs clenched so hard that the pain curled me into the fetal position.

No. I had to get up. I hadn't just left Mrs. Chu and Bev locked in the cellar so I could get caught by some vampires. I pushed myself back to my knees, fighting past the hot, sick feeling in my gut. When I blinked the tears out of my eyes I got a great view of the two vampires army-crawling towards me.

Sometimes the key to doing something is just having the right motivation. I got to my feet, still swaying, and began stumble running towards the woods. From the back of the Ranch the field was maybe two hundred feet deep before the Wilds reclaimed the land in its shroud of pines and ferns.

More shrieks sounded as another half dozen vampires rounded the Ranch from both sides and they all made a beeline for me. A shock of adrenaline snapped the world into focus and I bolted for the forest. If I made it into the Wilds I stood a chance.

If I made it.

I ran faster.

12

CHASE

It was a close race, and I only made it into the Wilds first on some dumb luck, but after how my day had been going, I was deeply appreciative of any luck that fell my way. The field we ran across looked like Bev's crew had just harvested all of this season's potatoes, and the ground was filthy with dark pits that were perfect for grabbing your feet and wrenching an ankle.

My magic sight mapped out a path in glowing green where the ground was solid. I kept mostly to the raised humps of earth between the rows and hop-skipped my way to the forest. Behind me, a sudden snap and yell let me know that one of my pursuers had landed in a potato hole and had hopefully broken something really painful.

As I neared the edge of the forest I took a chance and threw my magic out in front of me. Trees aren't nice neat crystal structures like metal or bone, and living trees were about the hardest thing for me to Break. But my luck held out and I found a tree with a rotten core, a hundred foot pine with a shining beam of pale white light running through its center.

Aanya had mentioned that I would be getting training for this, but experimenting on my own probably wouldn't hurt.

Probably.

If I could do all of this on the run from a peril of vampires and live to tell the tale, I would have to tell Kotori the story. It might even impress her.

I eyeballed the distance and shattered its rotten core when I was maybe fifty feet from the edge of the forest. The pine tree exploded like a bomb had gone off inside it, showering the field with whizzing chunks of wood. Out of the corner of my eye I watched the closest vampire to me take a chunk of wood the size of a football to the face. It would have been so satisfying if any of the shards had nailed one in the heart but I wasn't that lucky. I put on a burst of speed and ducked under the tree as it crashed onto the edge of the field.

The tree landed with a deafening boom and rush of air. The blast of air pushed me in the back and nearly sent me to the ground. I thought I heard some distinct squishing noise, which I hoped was at least one more of the vampires, but I didn't dare look back now.

The recoil coalesced around me like a darkening on the edge of my vision. I reached out with my mind and clutched at it, like trying to catch a flying knife. On the back of my neck, my Slayer Ink flashed, an instant of heat then gone. The rest of the recoil slammed into my gut like a size twelve combat boot and I fell to my knees, my stomach clenching.

The vampires howled, their hunting cries bouncing off the trees as they closed in behind me like a pack of hungry dogs.

Okay, a less than optimal first try. I scrambled to my feet and fought past the dizzying nausea. Escape the bloodthirsty peril first, refine the recoil process later.

∾

GETTING up the tree had been the easy part, surprisingly. Staying up here was another issue altogether. I was no stranger to stakeouts, but doing so while clinging to the damp and sticky side of a tree was considerably harder. I shifted my grip, trying to ignore the sap that threatened to glue my fingers together. At least I knew the slender branch I was standing on was more than enough to support my weight.

The vampires had quieted. One of them had finally gotten smart, and they were hunting silently now. Still, if I stretched my magic sight as far as I could, I could sometimes detect when one of them broke a branch in passing. By my best estimate there were at least four sets of fangs in the Wilds with me, still long odds for my survival. My best bet was to hide out until they gave up the chase. I hoped my hands were up to the task.

I tried to picture what Wen would do in my situation and hugged the tree, conserving my energy, and kept my breathing slow and even, trying to blend into the tree. A partial curtain of needles hid me from below, but it wasn't perfect.

Just as my mind was starting to drift, the lead vampire stepped into view about fifty feet from my tree, headed in my direction. I pressed myself into the tree and tried to think of pine cones and needles. Two more vampires appeared twenty feet to the left and right of the first. Great, now they were being methodical, sweeping through the forest. I definitely preferred the chaotic hunt.

Thankfully they were all intently focused on the ground, looking for signs of my passage. I congratulated myself on circling the immediate area around this tree to confuse my trail. The three vamps spread out and made their way towards my hiding place. When the lead vampire was nearly below me he stopped and began sniffing around the trunk of my tree.

I held my breath and froze. My fingers burned from strain and pain shot through my wrists as the muscles in my hand cramped.

The vampire sidled up to the tree, pressing his face close to the bark, sniffing intently. Slowly, carefully, I peeled my hand away from the tree, trying to uncramp my muscles. As I adjusted my grip my eyes fell on a series of shallow scratches across the base of my thumb. Red blood smeared across my palm, mixed with sticky brown sap.

The vampire's head tilted up.

I let go of the tree and stepped off the branch. My duster flared around me as I fell and I had a brief moment of satisfaction as the vampire's eyes widened in surprise. I drew Thor from my belt, my fingers wrapped tight around my hammer's stainless steel head.

The vampire opened his mouth.

I hit him like a load of bricks, my thick soled hiking boots slamming into his chest. The sharpened point of Thor's handle entered the vampire's chest just above the clavicle, in the soft area between the collar bone and the neck. My momentum drove the stake deep, piercing through skin and viscera. The vampire gave a pained gasp as we hit the dirt and I felt Thor pierce his heart like popping a water balloon. By the time I was getting to my feet the vampire had dissolved into ash.

Roxy 1, vampires 0.

I still had two more vampires to deal with. I thought longingly of my spear, lost within the depths of the Box last month, as I drew Loki with my off hand and prepared to meet the other two vampires.

I FLIPPED Thor right side up in my right hand, and reversed Loki in my left. Every other Slayer I'd met had commented that my hammers lacked reach, but I still couldn't bring myself to fight with anything else. It felt like dad was with me whenever I brought them out.

The vampire on my right looked like he'd been an accountant in his previous life. The one on my left had been turned as an older woman, looked like a librarian who moonlighted as a wrestler, and she beat out the accountant in height and reach. Waiting for them to come at me was a recipe for disaster, so I took the fight to them. I figured to take the easy--easier--one first and went for the accountant.

Vampires are apex hunters, with increased strength, senses, and reflexes. They're built to kill almost anything that crosses their path, something they learn very quickly to use to their advantage. What they don't see very often is their prey charging towards them.

I had to get out of here. Mrs. Chu was counting on me. I had to get back to show my uncle Samuel that I wasn't the train wreck Aislinn claimed I was. I screamed, letting out all my pent up frustrations, and charged at the accountant, my hammers held high as I ran.

The vampire hesitated a beat, clearly taken aback by my reckless abandon. I used that split second to shatter the tree next to him. Shrapnel peppered his body and knocked him back. He backpedaled to dodge the falling tree and I caught the recoil on my chin just as I was about to pounce on him. The ink on my neck flashed like sunburn.

The recoil buckled my legs again but this time I went with it, turning it into a messy forward roll. My shoulders took out the accountant at the knees and he toppled over me. I came up with my hammers and brought Thor down on his head. Thor's steel head smashed his eye in and the vampire screamed, numbing spittle spraying across my face. The accountant spun from the impact, going down to the ground. I raised Loki, following him down and aiming to stake him through his back.

Then two hundred pounds of vampire librarian hit me in the back like a runaway freight truck. My breath exploded as we hit the ground and rolled, sky and earth spinning wildly around me. The librarian's hands clutched at my throat, long dirty fingernails raking hot lines of pain along my shoulders. We rolled to a stop with her on top of me and she reared back, her mouth opening wide, yellowed fangs dropping down.

I swung, wild, with both arms. The point of Loki's stake caught her in the mouth and tore out her cheek, flinging gray bits of flesh. Enraged, she grabbed me by the shoulders and slammed me into the dirt.

"Stupid cattle," she growled.

Brilliant light flashed across my vision and a deafening ringing tone blotted out my hearing as my head struck the ground. I kept swinging and bucking, desperate to keep the vampire at arm's length.

Another voice said, "Idiot. Hold her down!"

Hands grabbed my arms, more than two. Panic rose hot and prickly in my chest. More vampires had caught up to us, at least one more, assuming the accountant had gotten back into the fight.

My vision was still bonked but my magic sight had nothing to do with my eyes. I found the arms holding down my right arm and snapped both the elbows, causing that vampire to collapse to the dirt. I wrenched my arm free and swung up to knock the librarian off my hips.

Someone struck me across the face. If you've never been hit by a vampire, I strongly recommend against it. I had a feeling whoever hit me was holding back, but this didn't prevent it from feeling like I'd just run full speed into a brick wall. And if getting knocked nearly senseless wasn't enough, then my recoil landed.

Breaking the vampire's arm hadn't been a big working. Maybe it was because I'd used my magic twice before in rapid succession, but this recoil socked me in the gut like a prize fighter's sucker punch. I would have doubled over in pain if it hadn't been for the vampire holding me down with her legs. As it was my body spasmed, and then my back arched like crazy, lifting my hips and the hefty librarian into the air. We both fell over sideways and the next thing I knew, my arms were free, the pain had passed, and my vision was nearly clear.

Clear enough to see four very irritated vampires coming for me. The librarian was clearly the leader of this little peril, with the other three vamps arrayed out on her flanks. The tear in her cheek was already healed and she eyed me with disgust.

I have that effect on people.

I'd fetched up with my back to a big pine tree. This was a plus. I only had to deal with vampires coming at me from three to four directions, instead of all of them. I flipped Loki around, thankful that I hadn't dropped either hammer, and prepared to punch a hole in their line and put more distance between us. No time for fancy staking maneuvers here.

The librarian fished around in her mouth with a dirty finger and came out with a tooth. She flicked it away. Her voice was husky with rage. "You Slayers think you can go where you want, do what you please, all because of some stupid Pact."

More talking meant less fighting, and I appreciated the breather. I shrugged. "Hey lady, I don't make the rules, I just follow them."

Somewhere in Seattle, the irony of my statement was causing Cordelia an intense headache of unknown origin.

The librarian grinned, showing me a mouth full of bloody teeth. "Well, you're in the Wilds now, Slayer. We make the rules out here."

That sounded odd. "Who's we?"

She didn't bother to answer my question, just waved her hand at me and the other three vampires jumped at me. I dodged the fastest one and let him slam into the tree, but that pushed me away from my cover and then I was out in the open, with three vampires circling me. This was exactly why we were trained to fight with our partners.

The librarian sounded bored now. "Just finish her off. We have work to do."

I couldn't help it. "What, is it, canning season again? Need to put up all the rutabagas before they go bad?"

Her eyes flashed with anger. I saw another flash in the distance, a ripple of gray monk's robes and resolved to keep her talking. "Wait, wait. Not rutabagas. You look like more of a parsnip woman to me, right?"

"You Slayers are all the same, strutting around like kings."

She raised her arms expansively and shrieked with rage. "This was never for you! The Twilight was never meant for you simple humans."

I swung Loki, pushing back one of the vamps who sidled too close. "So, what, this was supposed to be a vampire theme park? Bet you'd have a great Halloween theme night."

Her eyes narrowed at me. "Slayers are so cocky. You all think you're protecting Seattle. Protecting the Pact. Did you ever consider that maybe it's the Pact that protects you? When the Pact is gone you'll--"

I never got to hear the end of her rambling because that was when Wen finally caught up to me and wrapped one of his chain whips around the neck of the vampire closest to me. All the vamps looked up at the same moment.

Wen dropped down from the trees, his robes fluttering in the wind, and stomped on the vampire's back. He jerked his chain back and took the vampire's head off in one stroke. I used the distraction to lunge forward and stake the next vampire in the chest. He had half a moment to stare at me stupidly as he dissolved to ash.

The librarian bellowed, a sound like a hunting horn that shook the trees. From the distance came answering cries and howls of more vampires. In seconds the trees around us broke and dozens of vamps appeared on the run.

Wen said, "Down!"

We'd practiced this before. I fell to my knees and covered my ears.

Wen brought both his whip chains up and went into a tight spin. His chains lashed out around us, stirring up a mini cyclone of dirt and torn foliage. The wall of the cyclone picked up speed and spread out, flinging rocks as it went, some of them knocking down vampires. The librarian stood stoically in the face of the wind, not even raising her hand to protect against the flying rubble.

The cyclone increased to howling intensity as Wen's speed built. Then he leapt up and slammed back to the ground. The pressure wave behind his cyclone burst outward, knocking down every vampire within a hundred feet. Except the librarian.

Wen offered me a hand. I grabbed his wrist and stood. All around us the vampires struggled to their feet.

As usual, Wen minced no words. "We should go."

"Let's boogie, then."

I threw my arm over Wen's shoulder. His magic sparked around us like a bubble of crisp, cold air and then we were bounding straight up into the trees. Wen landed on a thin branch as lightly as a bird. Below us, the librarian stared at us with hard eyes as her vampires swarmed angrily around her.

Wen flexed and we bounded off the tree, cold air whipping at my eyes.

"Where to?"

"The Farm. We need help."

13

BACK TO THE FARM

Bev had told me to bring back help which as far as I knew was the Farm. The only problem was that I didn't know if I would have any better luck with Akhil than I had with Samuel. But I had to try.

Wen's powerful bounding had evaded any further vamps and gotten us to the Farm in record time. I hadn't been back here since the Trials and it looked so quiet and unassuming now. Never mind that the river was crawling with river demons and there was a werejaguar in the house.

This was the place where I'd first proved that I had what it took to be a Slayer. Back then Ulf and I had been on opposite sides. I'd slammed his twin into the bread cutting board and threatened to cut off his fat red braid. Ulf and I had come a long way since then, our trust forged in the battles we'd fought back to back in the Box.

Now I was a Slayer and staking vamps like a pro. Well, two vamps tonight anyway.

Wen had done all the work, but I was the one breathing like I'd run a marathon.

"Nice work back there."

"Thank you for saving me some."

I grinned at him and for a second it was just like we were back on our beat, doing our patrols in Seattle proper. But we weren't in Seattle, and the grin slid off my face as I thought about Bev's instructions to me.

I was to fetch the Slayers, bring back an army and rescue the shifters at the Ranch.

Wen looked at the stables. "You going to look for Akhil?"

I nodded. The stablemaster was likely to be with the horses.

"I don't even know where to start," I admitted.

Wen gestured to the blood on my hands. "Start there."

That was a good idea. An easy way to get a Slayer's attention was to talk about vampires.

I straightened my shoulders and made for the stables. Like everything else at the Farm, the stables were meticulously maintained with rakes hung up and stools neatly stacked. A horse nickered and I looked over to see my nemesis, Crabby Agnes. She stood fifteen hands, her chestnut mane looking sleek like it had just been brushed. Maybe it had. Akhil and Altan prized these horses and it showed in the way they took care of them and these stables.

"Hey girl. No sugar cubes today."

She snorted and tossed her mane.

I didn't have Cordelia's magic touch with the horses, but Agnes and I had reached a truce, sealed with sugar cubes.

I peeked in at the stall next to Agnes. Cordelia had grown fond of Smoke, or maybe it was more fair to say that the big black Friesian had been totally eating out of Cordelia's hand the last time we were at the Farm. She loved horses and they loved her right back.

Me, I had a healthy respect for the beasts and kept a wary eye on Agnes's deadly hooves and her penchant for biting.

The rear door of the stable opened and Akhil stepped in.

"Roxy, I wasn't expecting to see you here."

I hadn't seen him since the night of my inking. In truth that had only been a few days ago but so much had happened since then. I wanted to tell him what happened at the Tarim Temple but this visit wasn't about me. It was about Bev and the Ranch. The lightbringer always had a way of putting me at ease. His simple clothing of faded jeans and cream cable knit wool sweater was a disguise. This man dressed like a fisherman but moved like a warrior. The absolute assurance in his bearing, his calmness and gentle voice worked on me the same way it worked on the animals–I trusted him.

So I explained what was going on at the Ranch.

Akhil's face registered concern, so I made my pitch, "and that's why they need us to go over there to get rid of those vamps."

He steepled his hands together and set them under his chin. The silence stretched out between us and the tension was getting to me. I tried to tell myself it would be okay. He hadn't said yes, but he hadn't said no either.

"Mrs. Chu said she smelled Mists and Mind?" he asked.

I frowned. "Once. She caught a scent, once."

"I don't like it. This is a matter that Samuel should take up with the Queen."

Desperation made my voice sharp. "We don't have time for that."

"Roxy, this is not something that we should rush into. There is something larger at play."

I didn't care about the big picture. "I was there Akhil. Bev and Mrs. Chu are in a cage. *A cage.*"

Akhil put a hand on my shoulder and gave me a gentle squeeze. "It's a terrible thing. Why don't we go to the ranch house and talk things out. I can send a pigeon to Samuel."

I closed my eyes in despair. I tried to remind myself he hadn't said no yet. "Sure."

THE KITCHEN here at the farm could feed an army, and often did. Long scarred communal tables stretched out across stone floors of the dining hall. The swinging doors there gave way to the surprisingly industrial kitchen.

Wen tossed a handful of peanuts into his mouth when I pushed through the swinging doors. A steaming pot of tea rested on the counter in front of him. Altan was leaning against one of the stainless steel counters, his flask in hand. He always looked like he'd just come off a bender, but it wasn't clear to me that shifters could even get drunk with their metabolisms. Altan wiped on a hand on his green flannel shirt and then took a swig. The scent of gin permeated the air.

The last time I'd been here, we'd been put to work cooking and washing. It was supposed to teach teamwork, and it sort of had, at least in the sense that many hands made light work. But it had also drawn dividing lines between us as old enemies had squared off and new enemies were made. It had been the first time I had seen Marnie in that light and now it left a bad taste in my mouth.

I was grateful tonight that the kitchen was mostly empty. I gathered the rest of the Slayers were either getting some rack time upstairs or were out on patrols.

"Roxy! Sounds like you got a little exercise tonight," Altan called out.

"You could call it that."

"Don't you get enough fun up in the city proper?"

I shook my head. I knew Altan was teasing me, the were-jaguar's mood boisterous as usual but I wasn't in the mood for kidding around. Mrs. Chu was waiting for me and I needed to deliver.

"I'm sure Wen told you that there is a peril of vampires holed up at the Ranch."

Altan took a big swig and his face turned serious. "Sounds like trouble."

"They need our help."

Altan's face screwed up in thought. "Bev is real private, keeps to herself."

"I know. But she told me to get help and that's what I'm trying to do."

Altan looked down at his flask, the dented bottle showing the wear of many years. He looked over at Akhil who had followed me in but had kept his own counsel while I had spoken with Altan.

Altan scratched the stubble on his neck and his words rolled out slowly. "Bev has told us more than once to steer clear of the Ranch. Doesn't seem right to get involved now."

Frustration made my face hot. I must have looked like it too because Wen quickly offered me a mug of tea. The scent of pu'er, earthy and rich, tickled my nostrils. I took a sip and immediately burned my tongue, which saved me from saying something sharp to my senior Slayers.

"She needs us. The vamps have Bev and Mrs. Chu in a cage. A cage, Altan." My voice rose at the end, an edge of panic ringing out.

Altan's face grew stormy and I knew I'd got him. He put his flask into the pocket of his flannel shirt.

"Lightbringer, I don't like the sound of that," he growled.

Akhil nodded. "I've sent a pigeon to Samuel."

I blew out a breath, frustration tightening my shoulders and every muscle in my neck.

"We fight as one, Roxy."

Those were the words Akhil had led with at our inking.

Saying them now reminded me that I needed help to liberate Bev's people, that I couldn't do it alone. I ground my teeth and my cheeks grew sore.

Altan said, "She makes a good point, Akhil. We can't allow a peril to take root on our doorstep."

Akhil shook his head. "We can't go rushing in. Everyone is out on patrols right now and Roxy mentioned that Mist and Minds may be involved. This may be bigger than what we can see."

The werejaguar slammed his palm on the counter and I almost jumped. "We have a lot of shifters who are part of our family, Akhil. There's some with relations at the Ranch."

Akhil's response was smooth, and even. "And those who choose to live at the Ranch do so freely, choosing to live outside our bounds, outside the bounds of the Pact. They are well aware of the consequences of their choices."

I cut in, even though I knew this conversation was well above my paygrade. "Master Akhil, if the Court of Mist and Mind is involved, then we should be involved. What if they're planning something that will affect the power balance in Seattle?"

Akhil smiled wryly. "Perhaps you inherited Samuel's knack for politics? Yes, if the Court is involved, we need to know, but we will not--" His eyes focused on Altan, holding the werejaguar's gaze meaningfully "--involve ourselves before we know the full scope of the situation. That is why I have sent a pigeon to your uncle, Roxy. I'm sure he would be thrilled to learn you uncovered a plot by the Mist and Mind?"

"Ah, actually, if you didn't mention me in that pigeon, that would be even better."

Akhil said, "Too late."

The Lightbringer pointed to me and Wen. "You two will return to Seattle before I send another pigeon heading to

Seattle and resume your duties as dictated by Kotori and Samuel. That is an order, given to you by one of the Seven."

His words echoed with the weight of our inking ceremony.

Wen and I nodded.

I didn't really know what I expected of coming to the Farm, but it certainly hadn't been this. This seemed so clear cut to me, a situation where the Slayers could make a difference, especially with someone who already had a poor opinion of us. If we knocked down the vampires while we did it, that was just win-win, wasn't it?

He turned to Altan. "You will take the last wagon and make sure our newest recruits return to Seattle in time for their next duty shift. Until we hear from Samuel or Tanner, the Slayers will make no moves on the Ranch. Is that clear?"

The werejaguar seemed to deflate under Akhil's stare. "I still don't like it."

"It's not our job to like or dislike it. We follow our orders."

Akhil's gaze turned to linger on me.

"Shouldn't you two get going?"

I TRIED to tell myself that at least I'd gotten Mrs. Chu her medication. She'd be fine until my uncle made his decision. I had to believe that he would choose to help Bev and the other shifters. If he decided that it wasn't the Slayer's problem, then what were we doing it all for?

Wen seemed to notice my black mood and quietly allowed me to stew. At the front of the wagon, Altan seemed to only be interested in making his flask last the entire trip to the city. About fifteen minutes into our ride, something that had been nagging at me finally hit me and I turned to Wen.

"Did you jump all the way from the city to catch up to me?"

His mouth curled into a small smile. "Well, I took a few breaks."

I leaned back against the wooden bench and let that sink in. The ramifications of that were enough to perk up my spirits, even as we were dragged back to town. I'd used my magic maybe three or four times against the vampires today. Even if I'd managed the recoil properly, the experience would have still wiped me out. I wondered what Kotori would say of my performance today. Undoubtedly she would tell me to do better.

"How do you do it?" I asked.

"Do what?"

I waved my hands in the air. "All of it. Every time I use my magic, I have to deal with the recoil or else I'm puking up my guts. The more I use it, it seems like the recoil gets worse. How did you get out here so quick without losing your lunch?"

"Ah. Well, this is part of why I didn't get my ink with the rest of you."

Altan turned a little in his seat, seemingly intrigued.

Wen raised a hand and gestured to Altan. "When you look at Master Altan, what do you see?"

"An exemplar specimen of the jaguar shifter."

Altan barked a laugh. "A for effort, but flattery gets you nothing."

My quip got a smile out of Wen but he pressed on. "Have you ever wondered if shifters deal with recoil the same way you do?"

The idea was so obvious I was stunned into silence. Altan chuckled, a sound like rocks being crushed. He tipped his flask at Wen. "Not bad, little monk. There's few can say they've managed to shut Roxy's mouth."

I turned to Altan and blurted out the question without thinking, only later realizing the question might be totally rude. "Do you feel the recoil when you shift?"

Altan really belted out a laugh, slamming his fist on the

wagon hard enough to shake us all in our seats. He pulled a long swig off his flask, wiped his mouth, and gave me a pitying stare. "What do you think?"

I looked back and forth between Altan and Wen. Altan seemed to be daring me to say something. Wen just looked like his usual, placid self, although maybe he looked a little expectant. "You...don't?"

This time Altan tipped his flask to me. "See? You can learn."

My mind raced with implications I'd never considered before. "But you're partially magic. Or all magic. Mostly. How can--?" Ideas pinged around in my head like bouncing balls, refusing to be caught.

Wen took my hand and I settled down a little. He cupped my hand in both of his and a little thrill of power passed over my hand like a wave of cold air. The feeling circled and in moments a tiny vortex of clouds had formed in the palm of my hand.

I felt the same sense of awe and wonder as when my dad had first told me about his adventures in Seattle. The same dizzying expansion of my perceptions as the first time I'd used my own magic.

The little vortex played over my fingertips and faded away. Wen's magic dissipated smoothly until nothing was left except the cool, clean feeling in my palm. Instead of a recoil, there was simply a light breeze that brushed through my hair.

Wow.

I bowed my head to Wen, aware that he had shared something very personal with me.

"Thank you."

Even Altan was impressed. "That was nicely done. Takes humans a lot of years do to anything that clean."

Wen looked at me with an apologetic look. "Roxy, when I see you use your magic..."

His lips turned down in a grimace. "You're forcing it."

From anyone else that would have stung, but after Wen's display I was in too much awe to take offense. "Well, yeah, I know I'm still learning."

Wen waved his hand. "No, it's not a matter of your level of skill. It's how you actually use your magic."

We hit a rut in the road, jolting the wagon sideways. I wobbled in my seat, which was par for the course so far in speaking with Wen. "Sorry, how do I use my magic?"

Wen looked around for a minute and then asked Altan to take us off the wagon path. Altan looked in the direction Wen indicated and grinned. He twitched the reins and we headed through the trees.

The wagon immediately began to struggle over tree roots and ground cover. I grabbed onto the bench with both hands to keep myself from pitching out of the wagon. "What are we--?"

I lost track of what I was going to say because Wen stood in the middle of the wagon, as steady as one of the sentinel stones, his hands light on his hips. The wagon bounced and yawed under his feet but he stayed in place. Even Altan had trouble staying on his bench.

Wen pointed at my hands, white-knuckled on the edge of my seat. "That is how you use your magic."

He pointed to his own legs. Through the light fabric of his linen trousers his knees and ankles were in constant fluid motion. He wasn't even facing forward but somehow he knew how to compensate for the rocking of the wagon to keep himself still.

Wen said, "You use your magic to resist what the world around you wants to do. I see where the world wants to go and I use my magic to join the flow."

I was hoping for some kind of epiphany, but Wen's statement bounced off me like I was about to bounce out of this wagon. Before I could ask him anything, something under the wagon cracked with a sound like a gunshot and Altan pulled back on the reins. The wagon mercifully stopped and my guts sloshed to a halt.

Altan leapt off the wagon and did a quick check on the horses before ducking under the wagon. He muttered a stream of curses and crawled back out.

"Well, the axle's come off. Wagon's stuck."

He popped his flask open and took a swig.

"I'll need to head back to the Farm, Frank has some tools I can use to fix it."

I said, "We'll come along to help."

Altan's nose twitched. "Nah. It'll be faster if I go alone. You two stay put."

He pointed in the direction we've been heading. "Bev's Ranch is just through there, so remember what Akhil said about staying out of their business, hear? I'll be back soon."

I blinked, parsing what he was saying and not saying. He'd told us where the Ranch was and that he was leaving.

The spotted pattern on the back of Altan's neck darkened, the hair thickening as his shoulders broadened, bulging muscles adding to his already wide frame. His face shortened and his ears turned up as his body lengthened. He fell forward onto his forelegs, in full jaguar mode. He winked at me with one lazy golden eye.

I got the feeling he was showing off a little, after Wen's little talk, and then he was gone, disappearing into the forest like a dark, silent shadow.

Okay, Altan had just given us our out. Wen and I were free to go and Altan could claim innocence with Akhil and Samuel. Assuming Wen and I got back here in time.

That left Wen and I standing alone in the dim purple light of the Wilds, with only the sounds of birdsong and animals to keep us company.

Wen said, "He's very subtle."

I almost laughed at Wen's dry tone.

I didn't understand Wen's impromptu magic lecture, but I wasn't an idiot. Mrs. Chu was counting on me. I had to make sure she and the rest of my aunties were safe and sound for mahjong next week. I tilted my head in the direction of the Ranch.

"This is our chance. We have to go to the Ranch."

14

VANTAGE

Wen was always better at geography than I was. Trust him to find some high ground. River Rock Farm spread out below us as we perched on the gentle hill Wen had found. We hid in a small copse of trees and hoped that no vampire patrols were headed up this way. The night air smelled of crushed grass and juniper and if it weren't for the fact that we were now directly disobeying Akhil and on the run from vampire patrols, it would have been a nice moment.

By now, the vamps at the Ranch had to be looking hard for us. Maybe they thought we'd run off, or maybe they thought we were getting reinforcements. We'd bested that patrol because we'd had the element of surprise which was how Slayers typically worked.

Slayers 3, Vamps 0.

By now they'd had time to regroup and beef up their defenses. More worrisome, we didn't know how many there were. Bev had counted at least seven. I wasn't so naive as to think all of them had come out after me and Wen tonight.

I tried to bring Wen up to speed.

"That east side is where the herb garden and cellar are. Bev and Mrs. Chu are locked in there, unguarded."

"Does it connect to the main house?"

"Yes."

Wen rubbed absently at the bald dome of his head. I noticed that despite all our exertion, he wasn't sweating. I really needed some more pointers from him. Or maybe more cardio.

Wen pointed at the north barn. "What's in there, do you think?"

I wasn't familiar with the layout of the Ranch. I knew they processed a huge amount of herbs and essential oils. The north barn was larger and newer looking. I wonder if it had more equipment in there for distilling.

As we stood there debating the merits of which way to approach the Ranch, the air began to chill around us, growing heavier and wetter. A low fog crept in and I could imagine that in an hour the entire valley would be shrouded in fog.

That was good. Really good. It would give us the natural cover we needed to approach the Ranch.

"The north barn is largest and probably gives the best place to stay undetected while we try to determine how many of them there are."

Also, if Bev was correct and the other ranch hands were being held hostage somewhere, maybe some were in the barn?

So far my half assed plan was to try to locate as many of the ranch hands as possible, then go tell Bev, bust her out and add to our merry band of misfit soldiers to liberate the hostages. It wasn't a great plan, but it would effectively double our numbers.

"North barn, then cut over to the greenhouse, right?"

"Actually, I would consider the greenhouse first, *ma bichette.*"

I whirled in surprise, my hammers out in a practiced flick.

Behind us stood the Prince of Mists and Mind, a shadowy

figure partially obscured by the rising fog. I couldn't help the quickening of my breath. Tyee had snuck up on us somehow. Mrs. Chu's warning echoed in my head.

He's dangerous.

He did look dangerous. And compelling. Tyee stood with the assurance that said he was in charge and knew it. He took a step closer and I could see the intensity in his face, the shadows making his jawline look like it was chiseled from granite. I was used to seeing warmth in his rich brown eyes, but now they looked as dark as newly turned earth.

He was the heir to the Night Queen and though he usually adopted an air of idle amusement, today he'd abandoned it. As the breeze kicked up, his dark hair danced lightly on his suit and only the Prince could manage to not look ridiculous in a tailored blazer while out in the Wilds.

His lips quirked at the sight of my hammers, a subtle challenge that made me bristle.

I'd got the better of him once but that was when he'd been drugged and I'd put Bashir's spelled silver chain around him. I had my own chain now but I doubted Tyee would give me the opportunity to loop the silver over him. Not that I was planning to attack him. None of this felt like Tyee's mode of operation. Despite what Mrs. Chu had smelled, even Bev had been less than convinced. But a few questions were in order.

"What are you doing here?"

"The same thing you are, Slayer."

I blinked. That was the first time he'd acknowledged I was a Slayer. Though my ink wasn't visible, he knew somehow. Either he sensed it, or goddess forbid, scented it on me the way Mrs. Chu had. More likely he was keeping tabs on the Slayers. I didn't flatter myself with the idea that he was keeping tabs on me. What would my uncle do if he thought Tyee had informants inside the Slayers?

He inclined his head in a brief nod to Wen, who returned the gesture with equanimity.

Wen pointed at the greenhouse. "Why do you suggest the greenhouse?"

"Because I believe they are in the barn presently and approaching from the greenhouse would reduce the likelihood they'll spot you."

Or it was a trap.

I didn't like that thought. Tyee's power base was in the city proper. There was no good reason for him to be out here. Which left plenty of bad reasons.

Frustration made me clench my hammers a little tight. Deliberately, I relaxed my fingers and slid them back into their holsters. If Tyee had wanted to get the drop on us, he could have easily taken both me and Wen out. He made himself known to us for a reason.

I repeated my question. "Why are you here, Tyee?"

He took a step closer and I made myself stand my ground.

Up close, his eyes pinned me. He wasn't ancient like many vampires of the Mists and Mind court but his gaze held the same ageless power. Like he'd seen more than I could ever dream of.

From the hard set of his jaw and the lines bracketing his mouth, I saw a tension and fury in him that was barely reined.

"One of my entourage is missing. We tracked him to the Wilds."

"You had to come personally? Don't you have people for that?"

"They have Eloise too."

Oh.

For Eloise, the Prince would attend to it personally. They shared a blood bond and while I didn't fully understand it, there was an intimacy there that spoke of longstanding closeness. Of secrets shared. One that I had rejected when he'd offered to heal me in the Box. He'd wanted me to drink and it would have healed me but it would have also created a tie between us. A tie that would jeopardize my duties to the Slayers.

I knew my rejection was no small thing. Vampires had plenty of blood servants, but had very few to whom they shared their own blood.

Questions piled up in my mind, a jumble of thoughts. Who was missing from Tyee's entourage? Why had Eloise accompanied Tyee to the Wilds? How long had she been missing? Did he know I was trying to liberate Mrs. Chu and Bev? Why were they all at the Ranch?

In the end I simply asked, "Is she in the barn too?"

He shook his head.

My plans didn't involve Eloise and Tyee. I had to stick with getting Mrs. Chu and Bev out. Tyee was alone, but he was a powerful force that was now a wild card in my plans. I liked Eloise and had rescued her myself once, but if it came down to Eloise or Mrs. Chu, Mrs. Chu was my family.

I narrowed my eyes. "Look, we have to–

A howl of pain ripped out across the valley, followed by a barrage of yelling and the thundering crack of wood splintering.

Wen held out his hand and I took it. We bounded down the valley to the greenhouse.

15

BRICKS AND MURDER

Based on the level of noise I had assumed we would find a fight, some situation where we could tip the scales, maybe off a few vamps.

I was wrong.

The yells and screams echoed through the Ranch as we crept around the perimeter of the greenhouse. Wen led the way, carefully picking a path that kept us in the shadows. I followed close behind, with Tyee near enough behind me that I could feel his presence at my back.

A pair of tall double doors dominated the rear of the barn, with dirty windows set at eye level. We hugged the building and looked in on a scene of horror.

While the outside barn was weathered wood and dirty windows, the interior was pristine. Gleaming stainless steel tables ran down two sides of the barn. Tall racks of chrome shelving rose high against the back wall. A bank of refrigeration units hummed next to the shelves. This was Bev's herbal distillery and it had been turned into a torture chamber.

A man with sandy hair, dark with sweat, stood in the middle of the barn. He'd been stripped naked and his arms were shackled to thick eye bolts set in the ground. Sweat dripped from his pale and freckled skin and bloody cuts gaped like open mouths across this chest, back, and thighs.

But whoever he was, he bore the abuse quietly.

The noise came from the over a dozen vampires cavorting around him. Several hung from the rafters, screaming insults and spitting. The closest circled their prisoner with long spears and struck at him whenever he turned away. With each strike the prisoner gave a little grunt, staggered, and then got back to his feet. Blood sheeted from his wounds, then slowed to a trickle as the cuts slowly closed.

"Goddess. What are they doing to him?" I whispered.

Wen made a disgusted noise. "We have to get him out of there."

An iron hand landed on my shoulder and I looked up to find Tyee staring hard into the barn, his hands on me and Wen. "Go in there and you will die."

I slapped his hand off. "Is that a threat?"

"No, it is a fact. You cannot save that man from over two dozen vampires, Roxy. Even I would be hard pressed to subdue them, and they could kill their prisoner at any time while you were entertaining the rest of them."

His eyes took on a hard sheen. "No, the best thing we can do right now is watch, and learn what we can."

My arms trembled with impotent rage. I knew Tyee was a vampire whose view of life was different than mine, but to see him act so callously, to watch blithely as someone was tortured was too much. It made me even angrier that he was right. Maybe as right as Masters Akhil and Altan. This was so far beyond my abilities. What did I think I was accomplishing here?

Tyee pointed. "Here. This is what they are here for."

I turned back to the window. From the far side of the barn two vampires carried a package between them.

No. My heart dropped into my stomach.

Not a package. A child, bundled in ropes. He was round cheeked and tow-headed. Wearing a green sweater and faded jeans with a hole in the knee. Not even ten years old if I had to guess.

The prisoner went wild, cursing and screaming at the vampires. The child wailed, bucking and twisting but the vampires held firm. The spears advanced again, prodding their prisoner. This time he reacted.

As the first spear landed the prisoner's arm shot out and grabbed the haft of the spear just behind the head. His arm flexed and changed color, the skin rippling from underneath, pale flesh transforming into gray leathery skin. With a shout he pulled and yanked the vampire off its feet. Off balance, the vampire fell forward and the shifter's body melted, neck and shoulders thickened, his chest widened, and a massive horn sprouted from the center of his face.

The vampire screamed briefly before it impaled itself on the were-rhino's horn.

Mother in the moon, there were were-rhinos at the Ranch?

Before the shifter could free his hands all the vampires in the barn sprang into motion, dogpiling him with abandon. Bodies flew and blood sprayed. It seemed to make no difference, the vampires kept coming, piling their weight on the shifter until he was buried under a mass of writhing bodies. Arms rose and fell and bright daggers flashed. The shifter screamed, the sound muffled by the press of bodies.

Beside me, Tyee had gone deathly still.

I nudged him. "What?"

It took him a moment to come back and look at me. "Those aren't blades. They're tranquilizer darts."

His nostrils flared and anger burned behind his eyes. "I can smell it. They're dosing that shifter with the blood of my people. A Mist and Mind vampire."

I turned back to the horrific scene where the imprisoned shifter was slowly succumbing to the effects of vampire blood. More vampires appeared with what looked like medical equipment--empty IV bags and surgical tubing. They went to work, efficiently starting two lines and drawing off the rhino's blood. "Why? What are they doing?"

Tyee's voice was tight with emotion. "A better question is where are they getting the blood?"

Wen put us both in our places. "No. The best question is what are they going to do with that shifter's blood, and why did they need to force him to shift before they took it?"

The question gave me pause. I was caught up in the vampires torturing an innocent. Tyee was focused on finding his friend. But Wen cut to the heart of it. What were the vampires hoping to accomplish?

Wen leaned in close to the window. "Look."

Tyee and I pressed in close. From the far end of the barn, the vampires parted and a tall, muscular vampire walked in. All those in the room ducked their heads in deference. Tyee made an irritated noise.

"O'Malley. Damn his teeth."

O'Malley was tall and lean, covered in the kind of ropy muscle I associated with street fighters who had learned their skills the hard way. His red hair was trimmed short and his pale skin was freckled under its neat mustache and beard. He wore a pale gray vest over a crisp white dress shirt, with the sleeves rolled up under a pale gray vest. His forearms were crisscrossed with scars all the way to his knuckles. Whatever his life had been before he'd turned, it hadn't been an easy one.

"Who is he?"

"The Pact Breaker."

The words dripped with disdain and set my skin prickling in high alert. The Oceanic Pact was what kept humans alive in the Veil. Whatever I might think of my visit to the Tarim

Temple, the Tarim wield magic and control on such an astronomical scale that it served to keep the vampires, fae, and other supernaturals in Seattle in line. Tyee's mother was the Queen of Mists and Mind and vamps who swore fealty to her also were bound by the Pact.

If O'Malley wanted to break the Pact, that was dangerous indeed.

A few months ago, I'd rescued Tyee and Eloise from a cave. They'd both been drugged and Tyee had fingered O'Malley for the drugging and kidnapping. My rescue had kicked off an adventure that had me venturing deep into the Pleasure District to the Jasmine Bower where the Night Queen held court. Back then, I'd never heard of O'Malley but he'd certainly caused quite a disturbance which had rippled out into my life.

Now here we were, and it was eerily similar. I was here to rescue my people and Tyee was here for his.

O'Malley was doing some mad scientist thing and for the life of me, I couldn't understand what. He moved to the center of the barn where his crew continued to drain the rhino. He brushed aside his minions and squatted next to the unconscious shifter. For a big man with scarred knuckles his hands were surprisingly gentle as he examined the rhino and made small adjustments to the IV lines. He brought the half-filled bag to his face and inhaled deeply. A frown flickered across his eyes and he waved one of his men over, a skinny vampire dressed in dirty overalls.

"Take the child back to the back office."

The two vampires holding the child marched him to the back of the barn where a single oak door stood. I watched his small frame get swallowed up by the vamp guards and despaired. The oak door squeaked as it closed and the sound felt like an echo of how small I felt. How could I help him? How many more guards were back there?

My throat tightened as suppressed fear and rage coursed

through me. Bev was right. I would move heaven and earth to free everyone on the Ranch, no matter what it took.

When O'Malley spoke again I finally recognized his voice as the deep baritone I'd heard inside the main building. The more he spoke, the easier it was to hear the lilt of Ireland in his voice. Had he come through the Gibraltar portal like Finn had?

"Smithy, your men almost overdosed this one."

Smithy wrung his hands and bowed his head. "Yes, sir. Sorry, sir. It won't happen again."

O'Malley's voice was a quiet, reasonable rumble. "This process requires precision. The balance is critical. The instructions I give you are to be followed exactly, and correct results are worth any cost. Do you understand me?"

He was about to speak again when O'Malley stood and, in one fluid motion, grabbed Smithy by the neck and lifted him off the ground. The barn went deathly still as he struggled in O'Malley's grasp.

O'Malley deftly removed the bag from the IV line with his other hand. "Let's see how much you buggered all this up, eh?"

The vampires rushed to rearrange themselves, making a clear path to the right hand side of the barn. There, previously hidden behind the crowding vampires, was another vampire, held inside a cage of dirty iron bars, just large enough to let the creature stand, but not much else. I had a sudden flashback to a miserable night in the Box.

I squinted. "Is that...?"

"That is a rogue," Tyee replied.

Wen asked, "What is he doing with the blood?"

Another vampire approached O'Malley with a stone bowl and a white brick. At O'Malley's instruction, part of the white brick was crumbled into the bowl and O'Malley added a few careful drops of the rhino's blood. As the blood splattered into the bowl the rogue snapped to attention. Smithy clawed at O'Malley's grip, trying to swing away as the rogue reached through the bars. Dozens of hungry eyes tracked the unfolding drama. O'Malley produced an old fashioned syringe from a pocket and filled the barrel with the mixture in the bowl.

Smithy whined. "Please, sir. It won't happen again."

Despite his casual tone, O'Malley's voice was heavy with malice. "You see, that's the thing. It probably will happen again. That's just life. Best we can do is try to learn from it, and refine our processes."

O'Malley thrust his arm forward and the rogue reached out as well, meeting Smithy in the middle. Smithy screamed as the rogue grabbed him and slammed him into the bars. Through the bars, the rogue clawed at Smithy and plunged his fangs into Smithy's face. The entire barn seemed to hold its breath.

While the rogue made a quick meal of Smithy, O'Malley calmly reached through the bars with the syringe and spiked it into the rogue's neck. With one quick motion he depressed the plunger and shot the whole barrel of blood and whatever else it was into the rogue. Then he stepped back.

The rogue pulled back, dragging Smithy's writhing form through the cage bars. The barn was silent except for the sound of splintering bone and rending flesh. He continued to feed with loud, wet, crunching sounds. O'Malley pulled a pocket watch from his other pocket and stayed where he was, glancing back and forth from the rogue to his timepiece.

When Smithy had ceased his pathetic cries and gone still, the rogue stood, his eyes strangely bright. He looked down at his gore-soaked hands and arms, and then around the barn, as if seeing it for the first time. O'Malley put his watch away and approached the rogue.

Tyee tensed.

O'Malley unlocked the cage door and swung it open, sweeping the mess of Smithy's body out of the way. Every other vampire in the barn took a step back, but O'Malley stepped forward and put his hands on the rogue's shoulders. "Welcome, my friend. We've been waiting for you."

The rogue grinned, his mouth a horror of blood and mangled flesh.

The rogue's face lost its manic expression and its fangs shrunk. The glint of bloodlust faded from his eyes. "Thanks, boss. I needed that."

O'Malley smiled and his delight transformed his face from predatory to roguish charm. It was disturbing.

"Bosco. It's good to see you back."

O'Malley opened the cage and Bosco stepped out and embraced him. Blood dripped off his face onto O'Malley's vest and down the white shirtsleeves. My stomach roiled.

O'Malley released Bosco and knelt, getting close to Smithy's mangled remains. "Turns out you did okay, Smithy. Sorry how it all turned out."

He stood and turned to the barn full of vampires. The entire building was silent as a grave. "Well? What are you waiting for? There's work to do!"

That broke the spell and the barn was a hive of activity again. Some bent to draining the rhino's blood. More moved to the darkened corners of the barn and dragged out more cages, each one holding a thrashing, feral rogue vampire.

Tyee's veneer of calm had soured into a miasma of anger and barely contained violence. I took a half step back, reminding myself that I was standing next to an apex predator. An angry one.

My voice was a bare whisper. "He's raising an army."

Tyee nodded, the cords in his neck tight. "It would seem my intelligence on O'Malley is sadly out of date."

"He's building an army and he's doing it out in the Wilds. The Slayers don't come out here. No one would know until it was too late."

This was why Mrs. Chu and Bev hadn't been harmed. They

were being kept, caged, for this. To be tortured and drained of their blood. Hot, roiling rage bubbled up in my gut and tingled along my arms, driving me to swing my hammers and smash something, anything.

"It's not an army. They're abominations. He's desecrating the blood of my people to turn rogues into those...Renfields."

I got the feeling I was finally seeing some real anger from Tyee. We'd brushed against each other before, but our conflict had always had a playful edge, which was irritating as much as it was thrilling. Now when our eyes met I saw some of the same white-hot anger I felt in myself. I think he saw it in me, too, and more than a little electricity seemed to jump between us. The very air between us felt like it was charged with energy.

Wen cut into our little discussion. "We need to leave. There are too many of them."

Tyee's jaw clenched and I got the feeling he wanted to burst into the barn and claw his way through dozens of vampires just to get a shot at O'Malley. Worse, I had the feeling I would follow him in if he did it. It would be glorious, but it wouldn't do Mrs. Chu and Beverly any good at all if I got myself killed. And Kotori would never let me hear the end of it. She would use her kitsune magic to haunt me in the afterlife, I was sure of it. No, we had to live to slay another day.

I risked grabbing Tyee's arm. He was so tense his arm felt like stone. It said something about how much this had shaken him that he barely reacted when I touched him.

"Eloise. Focus on Eloise."

Only after a long moment did his eyes return to a semblance of normal. The rumble of emotions in my own gut subsided as well, the fires banking down to glowing hot coals I knew I could ignite again with barely a thought.

Tyee's eyes drilled into mine and I felt the coals stir. "Yes, we'll find Eloise first. And your friends."

I already knew where my friends were. I needed to figure out how to release the rest of the ranch hands.

"We have to free everyone."

Tyee's gaze turned to the barn windows. "We will burn this to the ground."

I could understand the desire, but I didn't think Bev would be on board with it.

"Let's focus on getting our people out."

He squeezed my hand once, giving me the barest slide of our skin, and then vanished in a swirl of mist.

16

PLANS WITHIN PLANS

Wen and I waited it out, watching the grisly activities in the barn and counting how many went back into the house. I hoped in the meantime that Tyee didn't yank out Eloise and raze the ranch house while I was stuck out here.

Tyee was a patient predator normally, but these weren't normal circumstances. I also didn't know how much time we had. Bev and Mrs. Chu were shifters, and most of the ranch hands as well. Now that we had seen what O'Malley had in store with them, it was clear he wasn't going to kill them. At least not immediately. Oh no, what he had planned for them was much, much worse. But his plans took time.

But it wasn't clear O'Malley needed Eloise. That meant she was food to him and his rogues. Tyee knew this.

I counted twenty-three vampires in the barn. Add O'Malley, plus that axe-wielding Felix guy who had nearly seen me from the porch. That was at least twenty-five vamps. Slayers never cleaned out perils that large.

But O'Malley was doing something to stabilize the rogues, shortening their blood madness. They were obedient to him, like servants. Renfields, Tyee had called them. O'Malley was building an army and he was doing it right here out of Bev's barn. Even after tonight, if that concoction worked, they would have six more vamps to add to the current peril.

When the vamps in the barn looked like they were going to be busy for a while, Wen and I snuck back around to the herb garden. All the windows had their curtains down and lights out so we couldn't tell where the ranch members and Eloise were being held. Eloise wasn't a shifter so it was also possible she wasn't with them. The rear ranch doors had windows above them and that was our best option to get a look inside.

Wen gave me the signal to watch as he bounded to the rear doors and climbed up to lie flat across the rafters above the door. The wait felt endless as I held still and watched the barn while Wen perched precariously across the rafters and pressed his face against the glass panels.

I breathed in the scent of herbs and chicken manure for what felt like a century until my nose was finally numb to the smell. Wen moved like a feather on the breeze and joined me behind the large planter.

"They have a large number of vampires clustered around the dining hall. Maybe the hostages are there."

I nodded.

A hush came around us like a cool embrace and then the scent of pine hit me. Tyee formed from the mist to join us.

"Eloise is not in the dining hall. I sense her elsewhere."

When he said sensed, I wondered if it was the blood bond. That made me uncomfortable but I just asked, "Where?"

He tipped his head to the west wing of the house. "There, in the bedrooms."

I really didn't like that, but maybe they would have fewer guards on her because she was a human. Like me. Like Wen. It might be easier to go after Eloise first.

"What about your other guy? Is he there too?"

Tyee shook his head. "My sense of him is fainter."

"Let's make a deal. We help you free Eloise. You concentrate on finding your man. Then you help us free the shifters."

Tyee seemed to consider my words. "Eloise and Conti are my priority. I don't have any alliance with the shifters."

Vamps and fae were sometimes so similar in their political outlook. You were either enemies or allies. Family was the only exception to that. They didn't weigh doing the "right" thing.

But I didn't have that luxury. I had my loyalties, but I also had to sleep at night and be able to look at myself in the mirror in the morning. I had come for Mrs. Chu and her only. Bev barely tolerated me, even with Mrs. Chu in the room. But after what I had seen tonight, there was no way I could live with myself if I didn't get Bev and her people out of this mess.

And I couldn't do it alone.

Tyee would be a huge asset with his fighting strength and his insight into O'Malley. My theory was that it took a vamp to know a vamp.

"And I only came for Mrs. Chu, but we have to deal with this situation."

Tyee's lips twisted bitterly. "I'll burn the Ranch down and everyone inside it. That solves the problem rather neatly."

That had quickly gone downhill from having no alliance to suddenly burning it all down the ground, including the shifters.

"I'm not going to let you do that."

"How do you propose to stop me?"

I scowled at him. "You need me and Wen. The Ranch is crawling with O'Malley's vamps. You won't be able to get both your people out at the same time."

Wen tilted his head as if weighing my words, but didn't chime in.

Tyee's nostrils flared and I saw the mental machinations he was going through. We didn't know what condition Conti or

Eloise were in. Furthermore, if Conti's trail was "faint" as he'd said, that likely meant Conti would need blood. There was no way that Wen and I were helping with that.

I pushed my hard sell. "Eloise knows me. Wen and I can bring her out, freeing you up to search for your man. You don't have time to do both."

I had him and he knew it. What he didn't know was that I would have helped Eloise anyway.

Tyee came to the only conclusion I left him. "I would appreciate your assistance with liberating Eloise. In return, I can endeavor to create a distraction that should enable you to release the hostages."

"Solid plan."

"However, I make no promises about the barn. I cannot permit O'Malley's abominations to leave."

I looked at the iron set of his jaw. "Maybe we could table that for after we get our people out?"

"Agreed."

"Then the Slayers would appreciate your assistance in liberating the shifters."

Tyee smiled, the tips of his fangs just peeking out past his lips. "You're here officially, then?"

I tried not to puff out my chest to sell the bluff. "I'm here aren't I?"

Tyee made a show of looking past me and Wen. "Oh, I just assumed that if the Slayers were interested in the welfare of the Ranch that they would have sent a few more hands than just... you two."

I couldn't resist throwing his words back at him. "Well, it seems your intelligence on me is sadly out of date."

"Hm. Touché."

After a moment he said, "Very well. An alliance, then."

Wen opened his mouth but before he could say anything I

grabbed Tyee's hand. Tyee's fingers gripped down on my palm like an iron vise.

"Swear it. Swear it on your power. This alliance gives the Court of Mist and Mind standing of favor with the Slayers."

Goddess. I hadn't expected him to call my bluff quite like this but I had nowhere else to go now. I ignored Wen's worried expression. "You know I don't control your standing with the Slayers."

Tyee's gaze hardened. "Ah, but you can still swear it on your power."

I could. But should I? "What I am swearing to exactly?"

"That you will rescue Eloise first and get her to safety."

I nodded. I could do that. It didn't feel right to put Eloise before Mrs. Chu but I knew Mrs. Chu wouldn't leave without Bev and Bev wouldn't leave without assurance that all the hostages were sprung–which I needed Tyee for. So Eloise was the first piece of the puzzle.

"There doesn't seem to be much safety around here at the moment. What if I take her to the Farm?"

Tyee shook his head. "No good. I'm not trading one hostage situation for another."

Well, that hadn't been my intent, but clearly Tyee had a different opinion of the Slayers than I did. "Well, I'm out of ideas then. Do you want me to just drop her in the Wilds somewhere?"

"Beyond the southern border of the Farm, past the river, there's a large pine, split by lightning. Do you know it?"

I narrowed my eyes at him. I did know of that particular tree and wondered how Tyee had become so familiar with the terrain around the Farm. "Yes…"

"I will agree to that location. It is close enough to the Slayers domain to deter third parties, far enough away for my security. Neutral ground, yes?"

For my peace of mind I would have rather left Eloise with

Akhil, but Tyee had a point. And Eloise was ultimately his responsibility, not mine. "That works. And after I get her to safety you help me free Bev's crew."

"I swear it."

He held out his hand and I put my karambit in it. He pricked his palm and handed me back the knife so I could do the same.

A hot, tingling sensation wrapped around our joined hands. Tyee's eyes widened just the barest bit at the sensation. The small wound sealed instantly. I thought about that time when he'd shared his magic with me so that I could take a message to the Night Queen. This felt different. More personal. I let go when the feeling faded and pulled out Loki to hide the trembling in my fingers.

"All right. Let's go get your girl."

17

ELOISE

Wen carried me over the roof of the Ranch to the west end. Things were definitely quieter here, as I had hoped. We stopped above the last room and dangled over the eaves. The walls of the Ranch were thick bands of green light, but my magic found its way into the crude mortar that sealed a window of thick glass. I signaled to Wen and counted down with my fingers.

When I reached one I pushed in the window and the pane fell in with a thump. Wen flew off the roof in a gust of cool air and shot through the window. I grabbed the eaves and flipped over, throwing my legs through the window. As I landed the recoil from my small magic hit me, warming the ink on my neck again. This time I traced the feeling as it worked its way through the ink until it dissipated through my skin. I held on to the feeling as long as I could. I had a feeling I would need it later.

The first impression as I landed in the darkened room was a thick scent of sweat and fear. A shiver ran up the back of my neck and without a thought my hammers were in my hands and my magic sight drew the room in glowing lines. The room was a simple box with a bed along the opposite wall, built out of rough cut timber. Even in the dim light I made out the crumpled form of a body on the bed.

Other than the three of us, the room was empty. Wen moved to guard the door and waved me to the bed. I stepped lightly across the floor, acutely aware of how much noise my feet made. I'd really have to get Wen to teach me a few tricks. Later.

I knelt at the side of the bed. A heavy braid of blonde hair spilled over the top of a thin sheet that was thick with the smell of unwashed bodies. I stowed Thor and pulled the sheet down slowly, dreading what I would find.

"Elo--"

I jerked back as the figure in the bed moved. I mean, she really moved. There was a blur of movement and a flash of metal. Years of training saved my bacon as my back arched away even before my brain registered the knife heading for my eyes. As I pulled back I caught the wrist and stopped the blade inches from my face.

The blade trembled and the arm strained against me. Wow, she was strong.

I pulled the sheet the rest of the way and Eloise lunged up with her other hand. I pushed up with my legs and bore her back onto the bed.

"Eloise! Stop! It's me, Roxy!"

Wen leapt over to the window and twitched back the curtain, brightening the room marginally. Eloise's eyes widened as she focused on me.

"Roxy? What are you doing here?"

I eased off and let her sit up. And I definitely noticed how deftly she put away her little knife, tucking it casually into her braid as she made like she was straightening her hair.

"We're here to get you out. Tyee is here too, looking for someone else."

Wen went back to the door and put his ear to it. "We can't stay here. Can she move?"

Eloise swept away the sheet, exposing a heavy manacle around her ankle. I sent my magic into the manacle and found a convenient mesh of rust damage that allowed me to crumble the hinge of the manacle with minimal effort and noise. Eloise whispered her thanks as she opened the manacle and rubbed at the raw skin around her ankle. Splotchy purple and red bruises covered her lower leg and she hissed with pain when she tried to bend her knees.

"How bad?"

Eloise grimaced. "Nothing permanent, thankfully. O'Malley was careful enough to assign one of his more skilled thugs to my care and questioning."

That struck me as odd, considering that Eloise was a pastry chef who seemed to be far out of her element here. I had assumed that as a human Eloise was simply being kept around as food. "Questioning? What was he hoping to get out of you?"

"It would seem that Mr. O'Malley has better intelligence than we expected."

I'm sure I must have looked even more confused.

Eloise's eyes narrowed, as if considering her next words carefully. "He knows who I am."

I had a feeling our conversation was heading out over very thin ice. "And just who are you?"

Eloise held my gaze and spoke very slowly. "I am a trusted associate of Tyee Wilder's vast bakery operations." She gave me a little wink.

"Right...And in your, professional, baker's assessment, what do you think we're dealing with here?"

Eloise levered herself to sitting on the edge of the bed with a groan. She looked like she'd been put through the wringer. "Something terrible. I have to get to Tyee."

She fell over almost as soon as she was upright. I caught her around the waist and got my shoulder under her arm. As strong as she was I could feel how unsteady she was, her muscles trembling just from trying to stay upright. Wherever we were going, she was going to need a lot of help. I hugged her close to my chest. For all she looked like a baker who enjoyed overindulging in her own treats, she was surprisingly solid under my arm.

"Okay, let's get you out of here. You can fill me in on the way."

We did the three-legged race to the door and waited as Wen listened through the door.

"So...do you find yourself...baking...for Tyee often?"

Eloise smiled tiredly. "You've saved my life twice now, Roxy. I trust you enough to speak a little more plainly."

She might be ready to get chummy, but I knew who she reported to. "Are you sure? You won't get in trouble with your – ah–employer?"?"

Now she actually laughed. "Firstly, I'm not going to tell you anything you haven't earned. And secondly, Tyee Wilder might be my prince but he's not my owner. He doesn't get to say who I can be friends with."

Oh.

Of all the things I had expected to come out of a temporary alliance with Tyee, this had been nowhere near my radar. Back in Boston, I hadn't had a lot of friends, since I'd spent most of my time taking care of my folks, and then my siblings. Jasper, Ava, and I were tight. There had been no real need for friends.

Here in the Twilight, I'd figured to operate much the same way, until it became clear that my uncle Samuel was going to do his level best to keep me at arm's length. Falling into a kind of unorthodox family with Ulf, Cordelia, and Wen had been just the thing I didn't know I needed, and now I couldn't imagine life in Seattle without them.

Were Eloise and I actually friend material? I guess some

things were organic and I didn't need to overthink it. Although things might get awkward if I ended up spending more time with Eloise because what if one day Tyee was on the other side of my hammers? Wouldn't that put Eloise and I on opposite sides?

Eloise laughed again at what must have been clear anxiety on my face. "Relax, Roxy. I won't be asking you over to my house for a girl's night any time. We're both professionals. We can keep it professional. Tyee is wonderful, but I need another woman I can speak with. As a peer."

I would be lying to myself if I said I didn't feel a little zing of discomfort at her mention of Tyee. But she was right, I couldn't let some vampire prince dictate my relationships so however this played out with Eloise, this was just between me and her. Hopefully. Also, it couldn't hurt to have a connection to the Court of Mist and Mind outside of Tyee, and clearly Eloise was more than a mere baker.

And it was appealing. As much as I adored Cordelia, her fae nature would always be between us. Eloise was human, subject to the same kind of power imbalance that forced us to struggle to survive every night in the Twilight.

"So, as a peer, what are we dealing with here? What is O'Malley doing to those rogues?"

Wen said, "Whatever they are, they are not vampires."

Eloise raised an eyebrow. "Yes. O'Malley is creating Renfields. A creature who passes through their Hunger but does not learn to strengthen their mind and control their hunger."

I considered that. "But they're still strong? Still drink blood?"

"Yes, but--"

"So in a fight, still functionally a vampire."

Eloise grumbled but stopped when Wen held up a hand. I reached out with my magic and got ready.

I leaned into Eloise and whispered, "So how do I tell a Renfield from a vampire?"

Wen dropped his hand and I popped the lock. This time the ink on my neck barely got warm. The subtle touch was definitely a winner.

I froze as the door cracked inwards, revealing a dark shadow just on the other side, about the size and shape of a side of beef. The vampire had to be over six feet tall, his dirty head poorly shaved, with patches of stubble behind his ears and cracked scabs at the nape of his neck. A greasy red nylon tracksuit stretched over thick shoulders and a broad back. Legs like tree trunks threatened to burst the seams on his pants. I'd seen him in the barn, but from afar. I wasn't too excited about getting close and personal with him.

Eloise went deathly still under my arm. "They look like that. Just like that."

As WEN and I moved to push the door closed the vampire turned and looked at me, his dull brown eyes staring right through me and into the room. His mouth hung open and a runner of dark-colored drool wobbled from his bottom lip. The vampire's hand came up, like a massive ham moving just short of the speed of sound, and smacked the door open. The door cracked me in the wrist and numbed my arm to the shoulder. Wen was kicked back by the impact.

Tracksuit lumbered into the room, brushing Wen aside like an errant bit of litter, knocking the monk onto his butt. The vampire raised a meaty finger pointed accusingly at Eloise.

"Master says you stay in your room!" His voice was deep and raspy, like he hadn't spoken in a long time, the words slurred together into an almost unintelligible mush. A gut-heaving stench wafted past the rotten remains of his teeth.

The Renfield turned his head slowly until his eyes locked on me. It was like staring down a massive animal. Something sparked in his eyes and past his dirty lips I caught a glimpse of his crooked fangs dropping down.

I didn't wait. I shoved Eloise back towards the bed and went in low. The bigger they are…

Tracksuit's arms swung clumsily through the air where I'd just been a second ago. I drove my shoulder into his hip joint, putting all the strength of my legs behind it. Wen was already in place and his whip chain wrapped around the vampire's legs just as I made contact.

Physics did the rest and the Renfield crashed to the floor with a roar. I rolled off before he could grab me and came up with both hammers out, stakes ready for business. Tracksuit thrashed, trying to free his legs, squirming around like a landed fish and generally making enough noise to wake the dead. I stabbed and missed, sinking Thor into his right shoulder and drawing an even louder shout from the vampire.

Goddess, what a mess.

Wen shouted as the vampire's struggles dragged him across the floor. "Roxy!"

I finally got smart. I yanked Thor free and kicked the Renfield across the face, my lug soled boot tearing away a chunk of his cheek. That gave me a moment to stow my hammer and pull my spelled silver off my waist. With a flick of my wrist I flipped the silver chain over the Renfield's torso and drew it tight.

Tracksuit's cries went up another notch as the silver made contact.

Normally spelled silver induced pain in vampires as well as paralysis. The more the vampire fought, the more the magic reacted, ratcheting down on the captive vampire to subdue them. It was powerful, elegant magic that was vital to our profession and a crucial edge that allowed someone like me to stand toe to toe with vampires with supernatural speed, strength, and reflexes.

Tracksuit knew none of these things, and he acted like it. He thrashed, nearly pulling me off my feet while jerking Wen further across the floor. He twisted and nearly pulled my arm out at the shoulder. He screamed in pain, guttural cries like an animal being slaughtered. The silver chain grew hot in my hands as the spell cranked up its response to the deranged vampire.

I wrapped another hand around the chain, desperate now to keep the Renfield from breaking free. Wen had his feet braced against the foot of the bed, his back arched to keep his whip chain taut, both hands white-knuckled. We were both out of hands to do anything else. In moments someone would hear all this racket and come to investigate.

Eloise's warm breath tickled my ear. "Let me give you a hand with that."

Her arm snaked around my waist and plucked Thor from its holster. I loved my hammers. They were my dad's hammers, and literally no one other than me had touched them since he'd died. But I had a rabid Renfield on the end of my silver chain, defying all reason and still fighting the spell work, and I didn't see how Wen and I were going to get out of this situation.

Eloise stepped gingerly around me, still limping heavily on her right side. She hefted Thor in her right hand and spun the hammer to face the stake side down. Huh. The lady clearly knew her way around weapons. Her baking skills truly were wide and varied.

Her eyes narrowed and I watched her assess the Renfield, waiting for the right moment, timing her move just right. I'd done the same plenty of times before. Tracksuit arched again and I slammed my boot into his shoulder, straining back on the silver chain, my forearms burning with exertion. At the top of his arch Eloise brought the stake down with ruthless efficiency, her aim straight and true.

Thor's sharpened end slid into the Renfield's chest like a hot knife through butter. Eloise slammed her other hand onto the head of the hammer and plowed the stake home. Tracksuit froze, a roar dying in his throat. Wen and I fell to the floor as the vampire dissolved into ash and our restraints went limp.

1 down. 24 more to go.

My arms fell to the floor and I had to force my senseless fingers open. Slick sweat covered my neck and face and my heart pounded in my ears. Wen rolled up to his feet and began coiling his whip chain. Eloise stopped above me and held out Thor to me, handle first. I grabbed the hammer and Eloise leaned back, pulling me to my feet. Eloise grunted with pain as she bore my weight. When I was up she let go of Thor.

I may have snatched it back and stowed it with a little more speed than strictly necessary. "I need to get you out of here."

Eloise frowned. "I need to rejoin my prince."

Technically her prince needed to rejoin us after he'd secured Conti. That was what our bargain was. I hoped he would hold up his end of the deal because we were desperately outmatched here.

I got my shoulder under her arm again and marched us to the door. "Your prince sends his regards and asked me to remove you from harm. Let's go."

Wen checked the door again and we eased ourselves out of the room and crept down the hallway. This end of the Ranch must have been used as a dorm, as doorways opened off the long hallway at regular intervals. All the rooms were open and the entire wing was quiet.

Eloise peered into the first room we passed. "All empty, as I guessed. They've got everyone stashed somewhere else."

I shuffled us forward, keeping us apace with Wen. "How did you know?"

She tapped one delicate ear. "They blindfolded me, but no one ever covers their prisoner's ears. I could tell who was coming and going, and the nature of the sound outside the room indicated that the space was empty."

That was seriously impressive. Kotori-level impressive, actually. I resolved to watch what I said around Eloise from now on. In fact, if I was within shouting distance of her, I'd have to be careful.

At the intersection I pointed to the right. "Let's head out the front. It's away from the barn where everything is happening. We might have a chance to get across the field and make it back into the Wilds."

We made it just outside the main building when the howls of a peril on the hunt echoed from around the far corner of the house. I dragged Eloise over to Wen. "Get her to where we agreed. Then go to the Farm and get help."

She struggled in my grip. "No! I need to get to Tyee!"

The vampires rounded the corner. It looked like four, maybe five, led by the axe wielding vampire I'd seen on the porch earlier.

Wen loosed a whip chain from his sleeve. "We should stay together. Fight as we've trained."

I shook my head. Eloise was fighting me but she didn't have the strength to break free. She wouldn't last twenty feet if we had to run for it. "Not with her we can't. Our priority is to get her to safety. I'll buy you some time."

"This is a bad idea."

"Do you have a better one?"

The vampires closed to within a hundred feet.

18

BAD BARGAINS

"Go!" I yelled and shoved Eloise at Wen.

Wen grabbed her around the rib cage and was gone in two bounds, leaving me to deal with O'Malley's goons.

I whirled to confront our pursuers and I didn't like what I saw. It was Felix, axe wielding vamp, in the lead. With a field separating us, he'd been a terrifying figure. Up close, he did not improve. Those eerie pale eyes glowed with an otherworldly light, high contrast to his scarred pitted skin. When he flashed his fangs at me, my heartrate kicked up in fear.

Felix was flanked by three other vamps, thankfully all smaller than him. But that didn't make them less of a problem for me. On his right, a vamp with fair skin and hair black as sin on one side, and bleached white on the other. Her harlequin hair was tied up in two high pigtails. She cracked her neck, her deliberate movements chosen to intimidate her prey. She wore so much leather that she creaked when she moved, the leather rippling with menace. To my dismay, I hadn't seen her in the barn. That upped my count of vampires on the Ranch to 26.

Next to the Harlequin vamp were two dark haired males I

did recognize from the barn. They worried me even more than Felix. They had deep brown skin and sharp cheekbones. Maybe brothers. They wore tracksuits, one in red and one in white. I would have found it amusing if I wasn't so outnumbered. They had that tight rounded musculature of gymnasts, but they moved like street fighters. Like me.

You fall to the level of your training, and fortunately, I'd trained a lot. So though my primal hind brain was telling me I was toast, my magic had already been lasering in the best targets for breaking.

I saw the alignment and ligaments and with the advantage of the rooftop height, I kicked downward, aiming for Felix's neck. Thor on the left hand, karambit on my right. One boot to his neck, a hammer strike into Harlequin's skull and my magic splintering out the femurs of the tracksuit brothers.

It almost worked.

I flinched at the last moment. Again. The tracksuit brothers stumbled and fell to the ground with groans. Two down, twenty-three to go once I finished these two off. A rush of satisfaction surged in my gut, quickly replaced by the recoil and a sickening sensation like a punch in the gut. Harlequin dodged my hammer as Felix went down.

She hissed and lunged at me. I got the karambit up but she smashed my hand so hard the blade clattered down the ground. The pain of the hit radiated up my arm and combined with the after effects of the recoil, I vomited.

I ducked to buy myself a second but Felix got up and then it was over for me.

The big man grabbed my shoulder, his thick fingers digging in until my whole arm went numb. He squeezed harder, crushing the joint of my shoulder until I cried out in pain and his pale eyes lit with pleasure. "We caught dinner, Jem."

Jem gave a harsh laugh, her black and white pigtails

bobbing. "More like an appetizer." Her eyes went to the streak of vomit down my chest. "Well, maybe clean her up, first."

Wen was long gone, hopefully to getting Eloise to safety. Tyee would be preoccupied with finding his man Conti. We were out in the Wilds, far from help and I was alone with these two. O'Malley's vamps didn't care about the Pact. They would drain me here, on the spot.

All of my time in Seattle had been wasted. I was going to lose everything here in the middle of nowhere and my family would never know.

Jem came over and punched me in the gut. She hit like a heavyweight boxer and if she'd punched me in the jaw she would have broken my neck. As it was, my teeth cut my lip and I groaned while waves of nausea washed over me in a sick flood. My breaths came in pants now between the pain and the fear.

She laughed and punched me again. "Gotta tenderize the meat."

This time her hit was higher and she nailed a rib. The pain was so intense that blackness narrowed my vision to a pinpoint. When I could see again, I spat at her and I could see blood in my spittle. Her eyes went dark with bloodlust and her fangs extended.

Felix lifted me up higher like he was inspecting a glass of fine wine and then stopped when he saw my spelled silver chain looped at my waist. His lips twisted in disgust. "Slayer. O'Malley will want to see this."

Jem sneered. "Some Slayer."

She reached over and yanked Thor and Loki out of their holsters and flung them into the night. Rage and frustration warred within me as I struggled against Felix's iron grip. My dad's hammers were lost, a dire sign of how my mission was going.

I had been given a momentary reprieve, and the adrenaline

flooding my body left me sagging against Felix's meaty arm. But a part of me suspected whatever O'Malley would have in store for me would be exponentially worse than Felix and Jem's plans.

O'MALLEY PACED IN FRONT ME, his steps echoing on the Spanish tile of the entryway. The entryway was spacious and clean, if a little sparse. It vaulted to a high point past us to the living room, with sturdy beams of oak. A skylight peaked above us. Across from me was a large square mirror over a scarred oak console table. To the right of that stood a lonely coat rack. A spring of dried lavender hung on the back of the door. The decor, or lack thereof, said a lot about its owner's personality and taste. Bev's farmhouse was clean, with solid furniture and the dried herbs were the one spot of color that decorated the space.

I tested the chains Felix has used to loop around my wrists. They were old and a little rusted, probably brought in from the barn. I sent a tendril of my Breaker magic to work on the weakness inherent in the rusted metal.

Aanya had said the recoil needed a path. A way that involved my ink. The tattoo was still fresh enough that if I concentrated I could visualize the lines buried deep in my skin. And it did outline a path of sorts, a winding, twisty path that ended at the center of the pattern, right over my chakra. Now I just needed to convince the recoil to take the path.

Breaking the chains wasn't the problem–the problem was Jem, watching me with her beady eyes.

I took a breath and tried to channel Wen's serenity. Jem had tossed my hammers, the loss of which scraped me raw but I could mourn them later, after I'd saved my own bacon.

At least I still had my spelled silver chain because none of the vamps could touch it.

My karambit was still with me, too, tucked into my boot. I couldn't do much with it now chained up like I was, but that could change.

O'Malley sent Felix out to tend to the tracksuit brothers, who had been writhing in pain outside. I would have been more proud of that bit of breaking if it weren't the fact that I knew it shouldn't have taken those vamps out for so long.

They weren't healing as fast as they should have. Which could have meant a couple of things. One, they weren't getting enough sustenance. Two, they were very young vamps. Given that they had a house full of hostages to feed on, I could assume they were very young vamps. But vamps that fragile should have been deep in the throes of the Hunger. Except the tracksuit brothers hadn't been insane with bloodlust. They'd been following cues from Felix and Jem, which should have been impossible.

After what I had seen in the barn earlier, I could only conclude that the tracksuit brothers were recently rogues who'd received O'Malley's unholy concoction.

And now the monster himself had me in his sights.

"It looks like you've crippled Jun and Kenichi."

I shrugged. "You know what they say. Don't skip leg day."

I was tall, but O'Malley was a hair taller and when he leaned in, we were eye to eye. His pupils were so dilated there was only a slight rim of green cornea visible. Vampires didn't need to breathe and their stillness was yet another eerie reminder they were undead. The contrast between the two of us was stark–me with my escalating heart rate and the rise and fall of my chest, him scrutinizing me with predatory stillness. We were so close I could have counted his freckles.

"It's like you broke their bones from the inside out," he whispered.

I had.

"It's a rare talent that can do that. There's a rumor of a

legendary Breaker who was a Slayer...what was his name again?"

I couldn't help the way my pulse ticked upward, the pressure surging so much my ears throbbed.

"Ah yes. Lim. Gabriel Lim."

My father's legacy should have been a point of pride for me, but too often it had caused me to bump into some rough spots. This had to be the worst of them all, to be at the mercy of this vampire and for him to have assumptions about me because of Dad. I could tolerate it from the other Slayers, but I wanted their goodwill. Hearing about my dad's reputation from vamps made me queasy.

O'Malley tilted his head like a raptor sighting prey.

"You must be Roxanne Lim. What a pleasure to meet you."

His fangs flashed against his red beard and I found myself relieved when he stood straight again and his pale face was not so close to mine.

I let out a breath I hadn't realized I was holding. "I can't say the same."

He laughed, throwing his head back like I'd shared a joke with him and Jem.

"Tell me Ms. Lim, did you cross the Veil?"

I nodded tightly.

"Didn't it feel amazing to survive the Crossing? To know that you carried the blood of the chosen to be here?"

I had never looked at it that way—as being chosen. But it was true that most didn't survive the Crossing. All anyone knew was that it was hereditary. My father and Samuel had crossed the Veil so I knew I could and that my brother and sister could. We didn't know if our mom could, which is why she stayed in Boston.

But O'Malley's question reminded me that I'd had a moment of exhilaration when I'd crossed, followed by horror when I realized how many who'd attempted the Crossing the same time I had, yet hadn't survived.

So yes, I'd felt incredible reaching the Twilight, but I hadn't considered myself chosen. I was my father's daughter and I'd been certain I could cross. Mostly.

My face must have revealed a bit of what I was thinking because O'Malley pointed at me. "You did, didn't you? You felt the power that the Veil could bring you, and the freedom to breathe here without knowing you'd die of Powder Lung, tumors, or blood cancer."

I flinched.

In the end, Dad had died from both tumors and Powder Lung. His last days had been truly terrible. I didn't like to think about my mom, who was presently battling blood cancer. It was the bane of the have-nots. The elites could afford the best treatments, eradicate the cancers, and live a normal life. Nanites could rebuild lungs and most elites had internal filtering that was keeping their lung tissue healthy. The rest of us were on borrowed time, eaten up inside by the harsh environment the world had become, and at the mercy of a medical system that was truly broken. Old resentments flared up and I couldn't help the familiar bitterness that tightened my chest.

Crossing the Veil had gotten me away from all that. But my family was still living it on the other side. Joining the Slayers had been part of my bigger plan to save them. Get the Cure to my mom, get more money to Ava and Jasper. It was early days yet but the silver I'd sent home had helped my mom a lot.

O'Malley spread out his arms wide. "This place reminds us of how we should be living, free of rot. Even better, we see the true gift of what vampires have–perfect health, eternal life, enhanced strength and speed."

Vamps did indeed have all those things, but in my view it wasn't a gift.

Jem smiled, her fangs flashing down. She stared at my silver mesh collar, as if calculating how much effort it would take to get past the enchantments and to my blood.

Metal flakes drifted from my chains. A gossamer thin recoil drifted over me like fog. I tuned out O'Malley and reached out with my magic. Something tickled at the edge of my perception and I held still, letting the sensation come towards me. Instinct made me clench up, fearful of the impending nausea, but I clamped down on the reflex and let the recoil come.

Kotori's voice taunted me in my head. "Are you a Breaker, or not?"

The recoil landed on my neck like a butterfly and my skin warmed like I was standing in the sun. The chains shifted ever so slightly and I clenched my fingers to hold them in place. The heat on my neck faded and it took everything I had to keep the smile off my face. I knew without looking that one tug would pull me free. But how would I get away from Jem and O'Malley?

The front door with its large brass handle was too far. I would never be fast enough to get out that way. I drew in a deep inhale and my gaze wandered up to the skylight. The deep indigo of night loomed above us and I wished I could fly, just launch out of this nightmare like a rocket and bust through the skylight.

O'Malley's voice intruded on my thoughts. "What if I told you that the Veil holds the key to eradicating all those diseases on the other side?"

In spite of myself, I found myself listening.

"That's right. Right here is the fountain of youth. The shifters and vampires hold the key to curing humans everywhere. To alleviating their suffering."

I tilted my head. He was monologuing, but he was saying something interesting.

"And it's free."

My eyes narrowed. Nothing was free.

"With a simple exchange, humans on both sides of the Veil can know the healing effect of vampire blood."

I scoffed. "The vamp blood doesn't survive the crossing."

O'Malley smiled wide. He knew he'd hooked me finally. "It just needs the right vessel, Ms. Lim."

Goddess take him. I knew he wasn't talking about the Midnight Rose. But what was he talking about? Had his mad scientist skills found something that would help my mom? My emotions were all the over the place, the turmoil of his revelations sending me into a spiral of uncertainty.

He steepled his fingers. "But I digress..."

"Tell me, why would a Slayer be out here on the Ranch?" he mused.

My lips flattened as I resolved to say nothing further.

"And alone, no less. But wait, you weren't alone were you?" Now his voice was harsh.

My heart stopped for one impossibly long moment.

"Tell me who you were with and I'll take it as a gesture of good faith." He leaned in close again, and then his voice went low. "We can make a deal, Ms. Lim. A little inside information and I can share a little of the remedy I've created."

Revulsion warred with curiosity inside me. I was not going to reveal any Slayer secrets but I wanted to know about his so called remedy. In that moment, I hated O'Malley and I hated the part of me that was the tiniest bit hungry for something I could use to save my mom. If push came to shove, would I give up Wen to get that remedy for my mom? Maybe this is why the Slayers had to rely on Aislinn putting a geas on us all to keep secrets–because the temptation would always be out there to barter them away. Even for the best reasons.

The wide oak door swung open with a creak and the cool night air filled the entryway. Felix stomped up the porch steps and to my astonishment, he led in a goat on a short length of rope.

I blinked but the goat didn't disappear.

For the life of me, I couldn't understand what was happening but I welcomed the distraction from O'Malley's intense questioning. The odds had just grown worse with Felix's return but now the door was open and maybe I could make enough of a ruckus to get away.

The tracksuit brothers were still on the ground where I'd felled them and one of them scooted closer to the goat. A light-bulb finally went on in my head. Oh no. Vampires could heal almost anything with enough blood. It didn't have to be human blood. While I was relieved I was not immediately on the menu, I didn't want to see this bleating goat get drained.

"Boss, we are running low on livestock." Felix sounded troubled.

Jem giggled. "Guess we'll have to use actual humans for them."

My stomach clenched.

This was the clearest illustration of why the Queen of Mists and Mind and Pierce Yang, King of the Shadow's Den honored the Pact. By agreeing to put down rogues who didn't swear fealty to those two factions, they were essentially protecting their own food supply. Because rogues drained their victims to death and worse, begot more rogues during the process.

Jem pushed past me to join Felix on the porch. She yanked the rope, pulling the goat closer to the tracksuit brothers. My odds were starting to look a little better. Felix and Jem were out there, leaving only one vamp close to me. Unfortunately it also meant I couldn't go out the front door. But I knew another way out.

O'Malley was also looking at the goat.

I amped up my magic, sending it high above me. While everyone was watching the drama unfolding outside, I tried to trace the path the recoil would follow. I concentrated on unfurling the stream of my magic slowly, creating a channel within me to give it room to return slowly. The skin of my tattoos burned with a cool fire. It was now or never.

The glass in the skylight shattered and I dove towards the living room in a forward roll right past O'Malley. With a snap, I pulled apart the brittle chains and ducked as an oak beam crashed down on him. The ceiling in the entryway also came down, sheetrock and framing smashing to the tile. The mountain of debris effectively blocked off Jem and Felix from the rest of the house as I raced to the rear door that led to the herb garden.

Someday, I would be able to break the structure and aim it at the same time. Then the wood could do some real damage to the vamps. Which was yet another reason I had to live to slay another day—so that I could get better at my magic like this.

The recoil snapped back but instead of feeling like a punch in the gut, it felt like a shower of pinpricks up and down my spine. It spread out like an undulating serpent and I was able to ride out the sensation without nausea. If I hadn't been running for my life, I would have crowed with elation.

19

NO ARMY

I yanked open the rear door and hid against the siding for a moment while my heart rate slowed from hummingbird back to human range. A sharp twinge jabbed me in the side, likely the rib Jem had cracked earlier. There was a lot of crashing and yelling back in the house, and I was counting on all the dust and debris to distract them from knowing which way I'd gone out.

The house had four exits. I took this one because I knew it was closest to Bev and Mrs. Chu. The moment of my capture had put me in a dark place. Jem had been beating me to a pulp and she'd tossed aside my dad's hammers. But while O'Malley had been talking, I remembered that even though Wen was gone, I wasn't totally alone.

I had my spelled silver, my karambit, and two angry shifter aunties. It wasn't an army, but it wasn't nothing.

Bev and Mrs. Chu could transform into ferocious beast forms. I had never seen Mrs. Chu do it, but even in her human form she could lift a horse. Hopefully Bev would forgive me for destroying her foyer.

I lifted the door to the cellar. The cool air bathed my face as I leaned in to whisper, "Mrs. Chu? Bev? We have to do it now!"

"Did you bring the Slayers?" Bev asked.

"Sort of. I got one. Anyway, we have to hurry." I reached in with my magic and snapped their chains. I rode the recoil again and my ink warmed. This was something I could get used to.

I heard some clanking and shuffling. Moments later, Bev popped up, her eyes peering around. As she stepped out of the cellar, she held a hand down for Mrs. Chu.

Mrs. Chu looked a sight better than when I'd seen her last and I was relieved her medication was having such an immediate effect. I pulled her in for a quick hug and then pointed to the side of the house where the hostages were.

"I'll go distract them in the front. When they give chase, you guys get them out."

Bev frowned. "That's it? That your plan?"

I admitted it wasn't much of a plan.

But then I asked her, "How many vamps could you all take out in your shifter forms?"

Bev and Mrs. Chu exchanged a look.

Finally Bev said, "Let's hope it doesn't come to that."

We skulked along the perimeter of the ranch house and I explained in low whispers what had happened. That I'd gone to the Farm but the Slayers weren't sure they could or should intervene. That Wen had come to help me.

"Where's he now?" Bev asked.

"Uh...when we were scouting, Tyee Wilder showed up."

Mrs. Chu grunted, her disapproval of the Night Prince clear.

"Two of his people were also captured so Wen and I agreed to get Eloise out and he said he would come back to help with the rest of the hostages after he got his other man out."

At the mention of Eloise, Mrs. Chu's face grew concerned. She liked Eloise and had nursed her back to health once before with her own miraculous soups. The thought of soup made me wistful. Not that I was hungry, but the healing properties would have gone a long way right about now.

My explanation seemed to mollify her as it also explained why Mrs. Chu had caught the scent of the Mists and Mind vampires.

The shouting seemed concentrated at the front door and moving away from us, which was good. Bev and Mrs. Chu had much better hearing than I did so they moved easily around the perimeter of the house toward our target–the dining area.

Bev put a heavy hand on my shoulder. I winced. That was the shoulder Felix had wrecked. "Roxy, I don't like your plan and I don't think we should separate."

"What should we do then?"

"It doesn't look like Wen will be back in time, but it sounds like they think you rabbited to the woods. Our best shot is now and I've got more rifles and shotguns in the shed."

Shotguns might slow down a vampire, but it wouldn't stop them. Maybe if there were more Renfields like the tracksuit brothers, then shotguns would be more helpful. But by the time we got to the shed and back, the vampires might have circled back from the woods.

"No time for shotguns." I replied.

Bev scowled but she didn't disagree. She knew it was a long shot, especially against so many.

We rounded the corner to the dining room windows. Bev got close to the covered windows and listened for a moment before nodding.

I edged her and Mrs. Chu back a step. "Step back from the glass."

My magic wormed in around the glass and with a gentle push the glass fell out towards us. Before it could land Bev was beside me, her arms swelling to enormous size, dark hair sprouting from her wrists. She caught the falling glass, gentle as catching a feather, and set the heavy pane in the dirt, leaning against the house.

She whispered, "Glass isn't cheap, girl."

I decided against reminding her that the coming chaos was likely to make a mess of the dining hall and moved up to the window. Or telling her that I'd blown out her skylight and her entire entryway.

I leaned into the window frame and pulled aside the curtain a little while my eyes adjusted.

The dining hall was a large rectangular room. Opposite this window I saw the open double doors leading to a cavernous kitchen. The long tables of the dining hall had been pushed to the edges of the room and used to block the doors. Bev's ranch hands were bunched in the center of the room, spread out across scattered chairs or lying on the floor. I took a quick head count and ducked back out.

Luck smiled on me for once today when Bev confirmed that most of her crew was in the dining hall. She peeked in with me and pointed out the shortest one, a stocky man in dark overalls. A stubby pair of horns sprouted from his forehead. "That's Chris, my foreman, and he looks the most alert."

But she still looked upset.

"What is it?"

"They all look like they're drugged, And we're still missing two. My nephew and Toby."

"Toby?"

"My nephew's son. Just a child."

My heart sank. *Oh no.* I was afraid Bev's nephew was the victim O'Malley had tortured in the barn, and the child I'd seen was Toby.

"How about this, you and Chris get your people out of here. Mrs. Chu and I will search the barn to look for your nephew and Toby."

Bev frowned but a look at her crew convinced her they needed her to lead the mad dash to freedom.

Mrs. Chu waved impatiently. "Go. Toby knows me. I'll get him out."

I nodded. "That's right. We're getting everyone out, and we'll find Toby."

My voice sounded a lot more confident than I felt.

I squeezed Mrs. Chu's hand. "When the craziness starts I want you to stay next to me, okay? Stay next to me and we'll run like hell."

My landlady gave me a wan smile and patted my hand. I wondered again what was ailing her and why her shifter nature couldn't resolve it for her.

I ducked back into the window. The ranch hands looked like they were in good shape, just dazed or half asleep. A half dozen vampires stood guard around the perimeter, three of them dressed in colorful tracksuits. The other three were dressed more typically, but with the addition of a leather bandolier fitted with a set of throwing knives.

No. I looked closer. Not knives. Tranquilizer darts. The same kind they were using in the barn. No wonder Bev's shifters weren't fighting back.

Taking down six vampires quickly and quietly wasn't exactly my specialty. This was really a job for Kotori. Of my crew I would have delegated this to Wen. But all I had was me, so I'd have to do my best to channel Wen's calm energy.

My magic painted the room in glowing pillars of green light. I focused on the vampires, looking for easy exploits, brittle bones and bad joints that pre-dated their turning. I tried to imagine using my magic in the same way that Wen had stood on the bucking wagon with such ease, the flow of my magic jumping from vampire to vampire like water flowing downhill.

Pale points of light glimmered in legs and arms, and in one vampire, his lower back. I took a calming breath and tried for the kind of zen-like state Wen always seemed to be able to achieve, even when dodging a furious onslaught from Kotori. Something tickled at the edge of my mind and I pulled on it like a string, sending my power after it.

Without looking at her I waved Bev off. "Go around to the other doors. Get ready."

It was almost in reach. I wasn't sure what I was feeling, but my gut told me I was heading in the right direction. If I could keep it up, it felt like my magic would take on a life of its own, like a train slowly rolling down a slope, slowly gaining momentum.

There. I pushed with my magic and the bright point in the closest vampire's ankle exploded with a sound like a gunshot. He grunted and went down on one knee. It happened so abruptly that the other vampires stared stupidly for a few moments as he collapsed, cursing in pain and confusion.

I didn't wait. I let the flow carry me to the next vampire, Mr. Low Back Pain. As easy as pushing a glass off a table his vertebra splintered under my power. He doubled over in pain, his hands flying behind him, which caused him to land unprotected onto his face.

The recoil from the first vampire landed and smoothed itself through the ink on my neck, warming my skin as it faded. The other vamps looked around, scanning the windows and doors. One of them shouted, telling the ranch hands to stay put even as my magic wormed into her shoulder and blew the joint out of place. Her voice went up two octaves as her arm flopped to her side.

The ranch hands weren't stupid. They all struggled to their feet, arms and legs swelling. Things were about to get really crowded in there.

I focused on one of the eaves, the termite eaten board an easy one to splinter. I twisted my magic and a sharp crack ricocheted, sending wood chunks and splinters raining down in a barrage. Chris, Bev's foreman, leapt up in a graceful movement and grabbed a large splinter. He grabbed a second piece of larger wood on top and hammered down on the closest vamp's chest. For his trouble, Chris took a hit of ash to the face.

Four down. Twenty-two to go.

And that's when I missed the second recoil. As smooth as the first three breaks had gone, I wasn't nearly as slick as I thought. The recoil rushed through me in a wave of sickening nausea. I grunted, trying to hold down my rioting gut and focus on the next vampire.

Halfway there and they still didn't know what was happening. I could do this.

My magic found the next vampire's femur, and an old break that had never healed properly. This one was easy, like tearing perforated paper. As I pushed forward the next recoil slammed into my gut like a wave of greasy take out. Pain spiked through my belly and I nearly cried out. Mrs. Chu grabbed my hand and I clutched at her fingers.

"The door," she whispered urgently. "Open the door for Bev."

The double doors leading to the main hall were jammed shut with two long benches. My focus had dissipated and I failed at redirecting any recoil through my ink. I snapped the benches in half and they fell to the floor in pieces. Another dizzying wave of recoil slammed into me and I doubled over and dry heaved.

I got back up just in time to see a massive bison, easily six feet at the shoulders, ram through the opposite doors, tearing them off their hinges. I'd seen bison before on documentaries, quiet animals grazing in herds. Bev was a terrifying proto-bison, a beast from an earlier epoch, with curving horns bracketing her head, and long, shaggy dark hair that covered her hulking frame and trailed on the floor. Hooves the size of dinner plates trampled through the splinters of the doors and benches and ground them to dust. Bev raised her head to the ceiling and bellowed, a ringing, horn-like sound that shook my bones.

The rest of Bev's crew got to their feet and raised their voices in response, a raucous chorus that seemed to shake the whole building. Bev charged into the room and took one of the tracksuits through the center of his chest with one of her horns. The Renfield screamed and flailed, trying to unimpale himself. With a flick of her neck, Bev threw the vampire across the room where he slammed into the wall.

Roused by Bev's call, her crew jumped into action. They tore apart a bench for impromptu stakes and fell on the remaining vampires. By the time I dragged my nauseated self through the window it was almost over, with just a few of the shifters angrily stabbing at drifting piles of ash. I reached through the window and helped Mrs. Chu climb inside.

Bev stomped her forelegs on the floor and the room fell quiet. All the ranch hands dipped their heads in respect to the massive bison. I did another quick check. Everyone looked unhurt and upright. That was good.

Judging the various pile of ashes on the floor, it looked like all six guards were dust.

Nine down, seventeen to go.

Still terrible odds, but now the shifters had a fighting chance to flee the ranch and elude the vamps.

But now that the initial excitement was over, I could see Bev's concern. While they might be strong and able, I only saw fear in the eyes of Bev's crew. These people weren't accustomed to dealing with the darker elements of life beyond the Twilight Veil. Some of them dropped their stakes like they'd been shocked, and many of them clutched at each other, clinging for comfort. They'd simply come here for a simple existence where they could maintain control over their lives. Bev's crew was no army. They'd only won here because the odds had been in their favor. Against the rest of O'Malley's vampires, these ranch hands would crumple like a house of cards.

Bev's head came up, her ears twitching. A moment later all the shifters, too, looked around with worried expressions. My inferior human senses found it last, a low, rumbling sound that I first felt through the soles of my feet, and then as a dull pulse that shook the air in my lungs.

I ran to the window. In the distance, where the Wilds faded into the orderly rows of Bev's vegetable fields, O'Malley stalked out through the trees. Felix emerged just behind him, his axe resting across the top of his shoulders. With his other hand, Felix beat his chest as he hooted, his mouth open, fangs extended.

More vampires and Renfields emerged from the forest, all headed directly for us, walking at a steady pace behind their master. Each of them beat their chests in steady time, like a drum beat for their war cries.

I lost count after twenty of them. Whatever my tally had been before, O'Malley had either made more Renfields, or had more in reserve that he'd been hiding. More than half of his vampires were dressed in old tracksuits, and while they didn't carry weapons, they beat their chests and yelled the loudest.

O'Malley stopped halfway through the potato field and shouted at the house. "I know you're in there, Roxanne Lim. I can hear your rabbiting little heart from here."

My hand crept up to my chest on its own, as if I could shield my heart from O'Malley. I turned and found Bev's crew clustered in a tight group behind her. There was no way they could fight their way through this.

I had my magic, my karambit, my little knives, and my silver. Without the comforting weight of my hammers on my waist, it felt like my dad wasn't with me any more. For the first time, I was truly on my own. I picked up one of the biggest shards of wood leftover from a broken bench. It had the heft of a baseball bat and ended in a sharp point. It would have to do.

I gave Bev a respectful nod. "You've done your part. Get your people out of here. I'll buy you the time you need."

The big bison stared at me for a moment, liquid black eyes that seemed to see through me. She gave a little chuff, then turned around and herded her people out through the ruined doors.

Their impromptu stampede gave O'Malley's onward march some pause and I hoped Bev and her folks would give everyone a run for their money.

It was only after they'd cleared out that I realized Mrs. Chu had stayed behind. She stood ramrod straight and held my gaze as if daring me to say anything. I knew she was at least as stubborn as me, so there really was no point. We still needed to find Toby and I was afraid I knew where he was–in the back office of the barn. If I was lucky, all the vamps and Renfields were here.

But also if I wasn't lucky, all the vamps and Renfields were here. My body ached from the busted ribs Jem had given me and the expenditure of my Breaker magic. I still had something left, but not nearly enough.

I had to think about Toby. That little kid was counting on us.

Mrs. Chu reached out and grabbed my hand, her grip surprisingly strong despite her obvious fatigue, and together we walked out to meet with the Pact Breaker.

20

A TEST

I wished Bev's ranch house had been built on a hill so that I could look down on O'Malley, Felix, and the Renfields but I wasn't so fortunate. Bev had situated her ranch in a shallow valley, which meant the army of undead coming towards us would soon loom over us.

Felix hefted his axe against a beefy shoulder and made a show of baring his fangs at me. My eyes were mesmerized by the axe head. That axe scared me more than a hundred Renfields, reminding me that I was only human. I didn't have super speed or super strength or rapid healing. One hit from that axe and I was losing a limb or my life. My hands trembled. The missing weight of Thor and Loki in my palms was a painful phantom sensation I couldn't scratch.

When O'Malley and his goons were just ten yards away, he stopped and held up a fist for the rest of them. The entire peril came to a halt, obedient as a trained Doberman.

He spread his arms out expansively, theatrical in the extreme. "Ms. Lim, I have a proposition for you."

"Can't wait to hear it." I was proud that my voice didn't

crack. Mrs. Chu's grip on my hand tightened until my fingers tingled.

O'Malley tilted his head towards Bev and her crew, fleeing into the Wilds. He didn't seem in the least concerned. "You've cost me quite a bit today. Shifter blood is hard to come by, and I had a lot invested in this venture."

The vampire smiled. He clearly loved the sound of his own voice. "But the true mark of foresight is to recognize when a setback is actually fortune smiling down upon you. And you, Miss Lim, are my fortune."

I made a show of turning out my empty pockets. "Sorry to disappoint you, but it's another week until payday, and I'm honestly broke until then."

Felix growled at that and took a step forward, bringing the axe off his shoulder. Seriously? As if a six foot vampire wasn't threatening enough, he felt the need to swing an axe around.

O'Malley held out a hand and Felix stopped. "I'm not talking about anything as boring as silver, Roxy."

He said 'silver' like it was a bad word. "Hey! Only my friends call me Roxy."

O'Malley's face darkened, the ease gone from him now. It cheered me a little, to know that I was getting to him. It meant we might get to the fighting and the killing a little sooner than later, though.

He opened the buttons on his leather vest and reached inside. I tensed but when his hand came out he held three glass vials. They looked similar to the tranquilizer darts the others had used on Bev's crew, but these three were all different colors.

"I think we can be very good friends. After all, what kind of friend wouldn't help out a friend's sick mother?"

My heart skipped a beat and Mrs. Chu gave me a little tug, as if to hold me back. I swore I saw O'Malley's smile grow a fraction as he heard it.

"Powder lung? Blood cancers? Neural rot? Which is it,

Roxy? Which one of the modern world's creeping terrors is slowly eating your mother alive?"

He jiggled the vials, which clinked loudly. "Which one of these will save her life?"

The scene around us suddenly went very quiet, and my world narrowed down to the little tubes of colored liquid. O'Malley was clearly an accomplished scientist if he was able to concoct the drugs needed to subdue the shifters and also force the rogues through their Hunger. I'd always known that vamp blood would be mom's cure, but the only way to get it to her would be to ship her a Midnight Rose, one of the most closely guarded artifacts in the Slayers. Even though I'd gotten my ink, I still didn't have my own Rose. Transporting the Rose would be an even more dodgy proposition and I had concocted a rather elaborate plan where my brother Jasper would bring my mom to the Veil border and I would cross over with the Rose to get her the cure. Never mind that my mom wasn't well enough to travel that far but it had been the best plan I'd managed to date.

But what O'Malley was suggesting would shortcut my plan. If I could believe him, he was holding the vials that would heal my mom and I wouldn't need the Midnight Rose. It sounded too good to be true. The bigger question was, what did he want for it?

It was an effort to keep my voice steady. "How do I know those even work?"

And it was the wrong thing to say. O'Malley's grin widened and his fangs dropped. He knew he had me. He spread his arms wide, indicating the small army of Renfields behind him. "I was under the impression you were familiar with my work. I only came here because I needed the shifters for my soldiers. But finding you, that's more than I could have hoped for. Because I don't need the soldiers if I have you, Roxy."

I did not like the sound of that.

O'Malley tilted his head. "Breaker magic is rare. Why waste it on the Slayers? You hold the very power of destruction and chaos in your hands."

He made me sound terrifying, like a megafauna tromping out of the Pacific to terrorize Seattle. But I was just in the fledgling phase of my magic. And I wanted to be a Slayer. I loved being a Slayer. I was scared that everything would end here and now and I'd never get to fulfill my duties as a Slayer.

"Where are your Slayers now? If they truly acted as they do in the stories, they would be here, would they not? Aren't you just a little disappointed that they haven't arrived to save you? To save all these shifters?"

Ouch. That one hit home.

"They hide behind their walls and tend their little garden but outside the city is where the true Twilight is. Out here, only the strongest and the smartest survive, not just those lucky enough to inherit Legacies."

An image of Tanner jumped into my head, resplendent in his shining armor, straight sword at his side. I had the sudden realization that if Tanner had to fight O'Malley, I wouldn't have the greatest confidence in Tanner to emerge the victor.

Mrs. Chu clamped down on my hand hard enough to make my knuckles ache. It was enough to shake me out of my daze and pull my attention away from the glass vials. My landlady pulled me towards her with a sharp whisper.

"Keep it together, Roxy. Look around us."

Goddess, she was right. While O'Malley had been talking his Renfields had slowly inched forward until they stood arrayed around us in a large crescent. A little longer and they would have us surrounded.

O'Malley continued talking, and now I saw that he, too, was making small movements towards us. "The Slayers don't deserve you, Ms. Lim. You can do better than them. You can break the system that holds them up as the arbiters of peace in

Seattle. Join me and I will save your mother and show you how strong you can really be."

I pushed Mrs. Chu until she was behind me and started backing up. "You sound like you want to destroy the Slayers."

Now O'Malley's eyes glinted like there was fire behind them. "And in doing so I will save humanity from its own short-sightedness."

"That's nice. I just want to save the people I care about, from things like you."

O'Malley sighed. "You think too small."

He turned to face Felix. "Perhaps Ms. Lim needs a small demonstration."

My heart stuttered in fear. What did he mean by demonstration? Felix set down his axe and turned to select a slender vamp with gray hair and a floral dress. She wore sensible walking shoes and looked like she should have been someone's grandmother. Her eyes had a vague confusion in them but she obeyed Felix's brusque gesture to move up. Something felt off and then I realized what it was.

You never saw aged vamps. Vamps tended to turn young and attractive humans. Once turned, they ceased aging.

O'Malley patted one of his vest pockets and pulled out a syringe.

Goddess. What was he doing?

Mrs. Chu dropped my hand and growled and then it was my turn to hold her back. Felix grabbed the elderly vampire by the throat. She gave a weak gasp as he dragged her off her feet towards O'Malley.

O'Malley drew a small measure of fluid from one of his vials into the syringe. "I call them Remedies. They're what we've needed for a long time, something to help us crawl out from under the boot of our governments and corporations."

Quick as a cobra strike he jabbed the needle into the elderly vampire's neck. She screamed as the needle drove home and I had to wrap my arms around Mrs. Chu. My landlady growled and cursed at O'Malley as the old vampire twisted in pain, hanging by her neck from Felix's hand.

O'Malley held up a hand. "There is no progress without pain, as you're about to see."

And then I saw it. And I knew Mrs. Chu saw it too, because she went limp and boneless in my arms. The elderly vampire stiffened, her back arching to an impossible angle. Her mouth opened and a thin, keening scream ripped out of her as her skin bulged and rippled up and down her limbs. Where the wave of distortion passed over her, wrinkled, age-spotted skin was replaced with glowing, toned flesh. Her limbs fattened and filled out, covering knobby joints.

Goddess in the moon. I wasn't sure what I had just witnessed but I couldn't help think, if it could rejuvenate an aged vamp, what could it to do for an ill human? For my mom?

Felix dropped her and she landed on the ground softly, cat-like. She brought her head up, a smooth, sinuous movement, and her eyes were bright, clear, and wild. Her face was smooth, her skin radiant, she looked like a vampire who had been turned in the prime of their life. She opened her mouth and her fangs dropped. O'Malley put a hand on her shoulder and the vampire stilled.

He turned to me. "You see? This is the true bounty behind the Twilight Veil, the means to catapult humanity beyond the limits imposed by our leaders. I just need a catalyst. I need you."

The vampire's transformation was astonishing. The idea that my mom could be cured so easily was a siren song that threatened to drown out everything else in my head. But then I looked down at Mrs. Chu and I knew that the Remedy had been created by torturing shifters like Mrs. Chu.

O'Malley caught the look I gave Mrs. Chu and sighed. "Fine. Have it your way."

He gave the reborn vampire at his feet a little shove towards me. She didn't miss a beat, turning the push into a bound and then she was running for me flat out, fangs extended, drool running from her open mouth as she howled. The rest of O'Malley's crew pressed in as they scented an impending kill.

I smelled something else. Something familiar and welcome. Cool, clean air like an arctic wind blowing off a glacier. I pushed Mrs. Chu behind me and drew my karambit from my boot. It was sharp and deadly, but a decidedly close range fighting weapon, and nearly useless as the vampire charged. It didn't matter though, I just wanted her to keep her eyes fixed on me.

When the vampire was within ten feet the chill wind became a freezing downdraft that almost made me shut my eyes. As it was, through my watering eyes I just barely caught Wen as he landed in a crouch in front of me. Cold air spilled out from around him in an expanding ring of dust.

His whip chains were already out and spinning. I grabbed Mrs. Chu and got us both nice and low. The first whip caught the vampire across the cheek, tearing her face open down to her jawbone. It glistened stark white against her bloody cheek. The second whip caught her on the shoulder and knocked her off her feet. She slammed to the ground in a cloud of dust and a tangle of limbs.

And then I heard it. A high pitched cackle that ripped across the valley.

A slow smile stretched across my face. I knew what was coming next. Smokin' Hots incoming.

I yanked Mrs. Chu's hand and backed away. Wen stood and followed us back, his whips whistling through the air and keeping our proximity clear.

Arcs of blue light whipped across the sky, landing with a sizzle amidst the encroaching Renfields. Dark blue smoke poured out obscuring the field, the scent of saltpeter stinging my nose. Heat and smoke rippled around us, masking our heat signatures. Between the smoke and the heat effect, vampire senses lost their edge in finding humans. Smokin' Hots provided a powerful defense but we rarely used them in close quarters because the smoke wasn't great for us to breathe for too long. But here in the Wilds, it provided just the cover we needed to bail.

Wen appeared out of the smoke like a wraith. I pushed Mrs. Chu into his arms.

"Take her and go. I'll follow."

Wen nodded and wrapped an arm around Mrs. Chu's waist. An icy wind swept up and they launched into the air. I pivoted and ran around the perimeter towards the source of the laughter. The sound could only be Altan and he had arrived just in time. I hoped he brought the cavalry.

21

CAVALRY

The skin under my ink tingled as I drew closer to Altan. I let out a two note whistle and he responded in kind. I followed the sound and found Altan next to a massive redwood. He was dressed as he always was, in loose brown pants and a fitted gray t-shirt, but today he had the addition of a large pack that was unrolled on the ground next to the tree. Wen knelt next to the pack, unloading weapons into his pockets. Mrs. Chu stood behind the tree, worry lines creasing the corners of her eyes.

Relief poured through my veins at the sight of the were-jaguar. "Is Akhil coming too?"

He nodded. "Right behind me, on Agnes."

That ornery horse. I hope she stomped a bunch of vampires into a pulp. I would give her sugar cubes for the rest of her life. Altan pulled a pair of bandoliers out of the pack, one belt loaded with hardened wooden stakes and the other with silver blades. He pulled the pair of them over his head and secured them across his broad chest. From the bottommost pocket he pulled out a travel flask that was comically small in his massive hand. He deftly unscrewed the top, took a swig, and licked his lips.

"Been a while since we've had a proper fight. This'll be fun!"

He held out a big hand and in his palm were two Smokin' Hots. "I come bearing gifts."

I nabbed the two tubes and shoved them in my pockets. "Much appreciated."

Wen handed me a grip of short throwing knives with silver etching. I thanked him as I stowed them in my vest. It wasn't a replacement for my hammers, but it was something. These movements were familiar. How many times had I stocked up just like this before going on a run? So many that I'd lost count. The weight of the knives soothed me and in these brief seconds before we were overrun by a literal horde of undead, I just savored this small thing I knew how to do.

Now the list of my assets had multiplied. I had my magic, some weapons, two Smokin' Hots, Wen, Altan, and Mrs. Chu. Soon, I'd have Akhil and his crazy warhorse. It irritated me that I also kept expecting the Night Prince to show up. He'd said he would and though I hadn't expected him to come back solely for me, our bargain had been struck. Here in the Veil, the bargain was worth more than any feelings.

Mrs. Chu coughed, her chest wracking with a deep shudder. She sounded horrible. When I put my hand on Mrs. Chu's shoulder, I could feel her trembling.

"It's going to be ok. The cavalry's here and we're going to get Toby back."

Her mouth firmed into a straight line and she gave me a quick nod.

Altan raised a bushy eyebrow. "Who's Toby?"

When I explained the were-jaguar's face darkened. "This isn't a full-scale rescue mission, Roxy. It's just me and Akhil. We're here to get you out and clear out any pursuers. That's it. We're not going back in there."

The anger I'd felt before rose up again and I fought it back so I wouldn't yell at my superior. "Those vampires were torturing them! We got all of them out except for one last kid! Do you really want to run now, and leave a kid behind?"

"Woah, woah, who said anything about running?"

"If we leave Toby behind we've as good as killed him! Bev's crew can't fight these vampires! That's our job. Or else why do we call ourselves Slayers?"

Altan scrubbed a hand over his face. "Roxy, it's not that simple--"

Mrs. Chu reached up and slapped Altan across the cheek. It startled all of us. She was strong but she might as well have tried to slap down a brick wall. Altan raised his hand to his cheek and stared, wide-eyed, down at Mrs. Chu's angry expression like he'd been cut with a blade.

My landlady trembled with fury. "Saving lives is simple."

Altan's expression changed, his eyes going into the distance. To a threat behind us. We'd just run out of time. I signaled to Mrs. Chu and she stepped in close to me.

"Duck!" Altan roared and I dropped flat, hugging Mrs. Chu tight to me as he sailed over us, claws extended.

I'd never seen Altan fight before because I'd never been assigned to a shift with him. He usually stayed in the Wilds. But now I could see how different his fighting style was compared to say, Kotori.

In the city we fought underground, or in caves, and enclosed spaces. We learned to tuck in for close quarters combat. But here on a sprawling battleground, none of those formations I'd learned were any good. Even worse, the spelled silver chains that we relied on inside the city did very little against these Renfields.

Altan clearly had no qualms about fighting vampires on his own. As he landed his arms and legs swelled, the spotted pattern of hair that ran down the back of his neck extending to cap his shoulders and arms. His face elongated and fangs grew from his muzzle. As his chest broadened the bandoliers tightened but stayed in place. Altan landed on his legs in a powerful half-form as a small peril burst through the trees, about half dressed in tracksuits.

The vampires paused for a moment, taking in the towering half-jaguar. Altan roared, a bone-shaking sound like a book being torn in half. He pulled a stake with one hand and a blade with the other. The vampires howled in response and Altan crashed into them like a surfer diving into a wave.

I'd seen Kotori take on multiple vamps before, and marveled at her economy of movement, the way she made combat look like fine art. If Kotori was one end of the spectrum then Altan was the other. He waded into the vampires like a wrecking ball, arms swinging like sledgehammers. He was like the drunkest barroom brawler ever, armed with stakes and silver.

A Renfield screamed, limbs flailing, as Altan grabbed her by the ankle and swung her around like a rally towel. With a grunt he threw her across the clearing, slamming her into two more vamps who popped up through the trees.

But as jaw-dropping as Altan was, he was only one man, and Slayers always fought in pairs for good reason. More of O'Malley's vampires poured in and soon Altan was fighting just to stay upright. I hesitated, unwilling to leave Mrs. Chu alone, and also understanding that the fight Altan was in was far beyond my abilities.

Thundering hooves sounded behind me and I turned to find Agnes bearing down on us. The massive Friesian swerved at the last second, slamming one shod hoof into the head of an oncoming vamp, smashing it like a ripe melon. I was going to have to bring her a bucket of sugar cubes on my next visit to the Farm.

Akhil jumped lightly from Agnes' saddle and landed on the

forest floor next to Altan. His cream cable knit sweater stretched taut, exposing his brown forearms. Akhil's hands glowed white hot and he blasted an expanding ring of cleansing light around himself and Altan. The vampires screamed as the light caught and burned them.

The two Masters formed up and began picking off the vampires at a distance. It wasn't like how we fought inside the city, but they clearly had their own rhythm worked out. Altan threw stakes and blades, turning vampires into drifting mounds of ash. Akhil shot bolts of fiery light, spearing vampires through chests and foreheads, cooking them where they stood. If any got through their perimeter, Altan pounced, dispatching the vamp with brute strength. They didn't move like Kotori, but it was still an elegant dance of violence.

Akhil's dark eyes found me where I stood protectively over Mrs. Chu. His look became exasperated. "What are you two still doing here? Take her and get going!"

I knew he meant for us to go to the Farm, but we couldn't leave Toby. Mrs. Chu would never forgive me. I would never forgive me. And Bev would probably kill me. Altan would explain to him, and I could use the vagueness of his order in my favor later. It was a cheat, but I would take whatever I could get right now.

Wen said, "I'll stay and help the Masters. You two find Toby and get back as fast as you can."

I hugged him quickly and thanked him. Mrs. Chu grabbed my hand and we ran off back to the Barn.

22

TOBY

I squeezed Mrs. Chu's hand as we raced down to the barn. The farther we ran, my lungs thanked me because we were leaving the hot smoke behind. Pulling up short of the perimeter we peeked in. Most of the cages were empty and I didn't see any guards. Of course, the Renfields that had been injected tonight were up with O'Malley now, battling it out with my Slayer colleagues. I sent up a quick prayer to the moon to keep Akhil and Altan safe. Then I tacked on a request for Toby and Bev's nephew.

Once inside, I ducked low and gestured to the rear door where I'd seen them take the boy. As we crept through the barn, the earthy scent of many herbs hit me. Lavender, rosemary, bay, and mugwort. Despite all of that, it still held the tang of fear and pain to me and I would never forget the horror of watching Bev's nephew be tortured.

Mrs. Chu made a choked sound and I looked over.

"Oh, Wilson. What have they done to you?"

She'd found Bev's nephew.

My heart sank at the sight of the big man, dangling in chains. When I'd last seen him, a dozen vamps had been torturing him, trying to get him to shift. And then they'd brought out Toby and he'd gone berserk with rage, his shift so massive that he'd nearly broken the chains. Those chains had to be spelled silver. Now he was hanging limp and it didn't look good.

Mrs. Chu turned me, her eyes fierce. "Roxy, you have to break those chains."

I nodded and let my magic zero in on the metal. Spelled silver, good condition. But nothing was perfect. My ribs were still aching and I didn't need more recoil pain so I was careful to visualize the pathway for my magic. The chains snapped and Wilson tumbled down. Mrs. Chu and I reached up to catch him and the weight of the shifter sent me down on one knee. We gently set Wilson down and turned him over.

Mrs. Chu placed a gentle hand on his neck and when her head slumped forward in despair, I knew Wilson was never opening his eyes again. Would never see his boy Toby again. Mrs. Chu let out a soft sob and her shoulders shuddered.

I patted her shoulder. "I'm so sorry."

She mopped at her face and when she looked at me, her face was streaked with tears. "We have to get Toby out."

I nodded.

I stood and barely had gotten to my feet when Mrs. Chu jumped and nearly twisted my hand off at the wrist as a dirty, naked Renfield jumped at us and slammed into the bars of its cage. The rusty iron screeched as the cage tipped crazily on one edge. The vampire growled, its arms clutching through the bars, straining so hard the iron tore the skin on its shoulder.

Around the barn the rest of the Renfields picked up the cries and in moments the interior was filled with the howls of bloodthirsty Renfields and scraping, clanging metal.

Mrs. Chu's eyes grew wide as saucers. Goddess I hoped those cages were strong.

"Toby. We're here to get Toby and then run like hell."

She nodded, tearing her eyes away from the vampire. "Right. Toby."

Mrs. Chu lifted her face and took a deep breath through her nose. Her face pinched as I'm sure she got a nose full of blood and guts and unwashed rogues. Her eyes watered but she pointed with a steady hand to the back door. "He's in there. There are guards, too."

Of course there were. O'Malley has been using the kid to keep the other shifters in line. We were going to put a stop to all that. I would break open the door and Mrs. Chu could rush to secure Toby while I took out the guards. Simple.

This was a terrible plan. In fact, it was no plan at all. I was down to a handful of weapons and my landlady. Normally Mrs. Chu was very formidable but today the combination of O'Malley's drugs and her own medical issues had her in such a state that I worried about how much more she could handle. Seeing Bev's nephew Wilson had hardened her resolve though and I hoped it would carry Mrs. Chu through this last bit to get Toby out.

I stacked the throwing knives in my right hand and readied the karambit in my left.

I sent my magic ahead into the backroom and quickly familiarized myself with the layout. It wasn't x-ray vision exactly, but more like a grid where my brain filled in the negative spaces. The more I used my magic under Kotori's brutal tutelage, the more I was able to sense with it. A long, rectangular, split level room. The back half of the room was half buried, accessed by a wide set of stairs cut into the floor. Long tables dominated the space, but I couldn't tell what they were used for, or if anything was on them. Sturdy cages stood at the far end, in the lower section of the room. I'd even bet a fae that Toby was in one of those cages, behind who knew how many vampire guards.

The door was thick, heavy oak but the hinges were metal

and fatigued. The latch, while functional, was also spotted with rust. The question was, creep in quietly, or blow the door off and go for the element of surprise? And where was Tyee? The Night Prince was shaping up to be a severe disappointment.

I had barely sent my magic into the rusting metal hinges when the latch clicked and the door swung open towards us. Before I could get us out of sight a tall female edged through the door, an irritated expression on her face. A dirty green tracksuit covered her lanky limbs.

"Why so noisy!?"

She froze, staring at me dumbly.

I flung my right arm out and threw one of my knives.

This was one of the first things my dad taught me, practicing with an old set of his knives into straw dummies at the far end of our little yard. The back fence was soon pockmarked with damage from my errant throws. I spent that entire summer out back, my shoulders burning, blisters popping on my fingertips as I practiced. One day I finally found the flow, the rhythm, that elation when the blade left my hand and I knew that it would fly straight and true and sink into the target with a satisfying thunk.

It was like dad was behind me, beer in hand, as my fingers released the silver-chased blade. *Bullseye.* In my head, he gave an almost imperceptible grunt of approval as the blade flew, flipping over once in flight before sinking to the hilt into the vampire's neck.

The Renfield's head snapped back, her voice cutting off into bubbling gurgles that morphed into strangled screams as the silver burned through her flesh. Goddess, I guess I was doing this the hard way.

I launched forward. The Renfield was tall, so I jumped up into her, the karambit in my left hand, taking her with a sweeping uppercut into the soft spot under her jaw. My weight slammed into her and drove her into the back room. My karambit bit into her neck. I grabbed the protruding handle of my throwing knife and jerked my arms apart, turning the front half of her neck into a grisly ruin.

The back room was bone chillingly cold, and my breath misted out as the Renfield, and I crashed to the floor. I pushed forward with my blades and finished the bloody task of decapping the Renfield. The vampire twitched once and went still, her bony fingers trailing down my shoulders as her arms went limp. My breath heaved and my heart pounded in my chest like a chained beast trying to get out.

I nearly screamed when Mrs. Chu grabbed my arm and pulled me down behind the nearest trestle table. She clapped a hand over my mouth and pointed mutely into the rear of the room, her eyes wide with fright.

The long trestle tables marched along the long walls, many of them stacked with neat piles of grayish-white bricks the size of both my fists. The smell of herbs and plants was stronger here, despite the cold, and there were bags stuffed full of dried plants on the tables, each labeled neatly.

Between the tables and the walls, things had been stacked and stowed in haphazard fashion, as if they'd been pushed out of the way. Fragrant oak barrels leaned against the walls, still dripping pungent alcohol. I recognized the copper tubs and tubing used in distillation.

Down the stairs, the room darkened, the air thick with pale white mist. In the back left corner, Toby huddled against the dirt wall, his arms shackled with thick iron bands. His face and clothes were dirty, but his eyes blazed with unshed tears and anger.

His ire was directed at two Renfields in filthy tracksuits huddled around a bloody carcass on the floor, maybe an elk. Drool ran thick from their open mouths, their fangs extended. With long-fingered hands they tore at the carcass, tearing off bloody hunks of meat. They sank their fangs into the meat and drank deeply, blood running and congealing down their pale necks. The Renfields seemed to be engrossed with feeding, seemingly oblivious to the fact that I'd just decapped their comrade at the door.

Mrs. Chu whispered in my ear, "This is Bev's cold cellar. What is all this?"

Her eyes were fixed on the long rows of stacked bricks and beyond to the tables in the deeper part of the cellar. There, one of the tables was stacked with compact trays a dozen high. Trays of sleek, manufactured plastics. Within the trays lay tidy rows of glass vials, more than half of them filled with blood. The other half varied in color, some of them even glowing with their own light.

The tables were different, too, expansive slabs of pristine stainless steel. Just the tables alone were worth a queen's ransom here in the Twilight, without even counting the fortune in plastics and crystal-clear glass atop them.

My eyes widened as I looked closer. Even after my short time here, seeing these things set off a strange dissonance in my mind. Centrifuges. Tabletop ovens. Burner plates. Stacks and stacks of heavy-duty hydrogen batteries with coils of heavy cable connecting to the equipment. And more pristine glass than I'd seen in a long time. It was like I'd dropped back into a pharmacy in Boston. A pharmacy making things work during a power outage, maybe.

None of this was found or manufactured here. O'Malley had a line to the other side of the Veil. A supplier smuggling a piece of the modern world to the Twilight Veil, giving O'Malley a technological leg up on his competition.

I stopped counting after I hit twenty stacks. Endless night, there were so many vials.

Tyee had said he'd smelled the blood of a Mist and Mind vampire used to subdue Wilson. O'Malley had combined Wilson's blood with the powdered white bricks to cure the rogue's Hunger. Watching the way these Renfields ate though made it all so ironic. These Renfields still hungered for blood–but the difference from the rogues was that O'Malley was able to control them.

My eyes traveled over the seemingly endless stacked gray-white bricks. With enough shifter blood O'Malley could convert every rogue in the Wilds and have plenty left over for the rogues hiding in the city. It was a neat solution to Seattle's rogue problem. No more rogues, only Renfields and only loyal to O'Malley.

And it would completely upend the Oceanic Pact.

Mrs. Chu had come to the same conclusion. "That monster will drain every shifter he finds to make this."

My spine went cold. I had argued with Auntie Malia about coming out to the Ranch. If I hadn't come, how many more shifters would have been drained and killed, hung up in chains like Wilson? Would I have found Mrs. Chu like that? And what were all the other vials? What else was O'Malley concocting here?

My fingers were clenched so hard on the edge of the table that my fingers were numb. I forced my hand to relax and open, and sensation tingled back into my fingertips. "We're getting Toby out of here."

My nice little landlady's eyes were hard as river stones. "Damn right."

I had the beginnings of a plan. "Okay, what I want--"

Toby screamed, the sound thick with frustration and fear. From his position on the floor, the chains gave him enough slack to allow him to take his arm through a complete throwing motion. A rock he'd found somewhere sailed through the air and connected with one of the Renfields, square in the back of the head.

Kid was a good shot.

The rock impacted with a crack that made me wince and

made the Renfield nearly bite off his own hand as he was feeding. The vampire roared, stalked over to Toby, and backhanded him across the face.

The sound was like a board cracking in half. Toby let out a gasp as his head snapped back and his eyes rolled up into his head. I was moving out from behind the table when I noticed that Mrs. Chu was already halfway to the back of the room, running flat out on silent feet.

Goddess, she really was quiet on her feet. I got moving, aiming for the other Renfield. So much for my plans.

Toby gave it away, looking up at the last second, his eyes going wide at the sight of Mrs. Chu bearing down on the vampire as he hauled back to smack Toby again. The vampire turned just in time to catch Mrs. Chu's right fist. My landlady jumped at the last moment, driving her fist up at what looked like the neighborhood of the speed of sound, right into the vampire's neck. The impact made a combination cracking, gagging sound that generated a brief moment's pity for the vampire.

And then the pity was gone, because I had caught up and waded into the fight with the other Renfield, who deigned to drop the elk carcass and come after me, both of his hands sticky with congealed blood. I threw another blade at point blank range and took out one of his eyes, which only got me an enraged scream. Just when it seemed like I was going to crash into his thick arms, I dropped low and barreled into his knees.

He toppled over me like a bowling pin, and I came up with knives in both hands. I had the karambit in my left, but I had no illusions of exsanguination here, just survival. To my right, Mrs. Chu was in a frenzy, going after the other vamp like a wild animal. My vampire lunged at me, and I used his momentum to drive both my blades into his chest. I pushed back with my legs and slammed him onto the nearest table. He writhed like a worm on a hook, the silver in my knife burning a smoking hole in his chest.

I risked a look at Toby, who stared wide-eyed at Mrs. Chu. My magic whipped out and his chains snapped open. "Get clear!" I yelled.

That snapped him out of it. The boy shook off the broken manacles and ran to the other side of the room. He hid behind one of the heavy tables, his eyes peeking over the edge.

My vampire managed to swing his leg around and buckle my knee. I went down and got an up-close look at the vampire's ugly face, riddled with scars, his nose squashed and crooked. My recoil landed and the world tilted. The vamp struggled off the table and all I could do was fall away from him and not land on my own knives.

The vampire's big, stompy feet came down and I rolled under the table. Too slow, because his stupid boot slammed into my hip as I turned away, lighting up my leg in new and fascinating shades of pain. I kept rolling until I ended up against the wall, under the other edge of the table.

Renfields were strong and fast, but they seemed to be pretty stupid. Instead of coming under the table to get me, this one kept coming forward until he pushed the table to the wall, covering my head. He then proceeded to beat down on the table, as if trying to pound through it to get to me. Thankfully O'Malley had sprung for the really sturdy tables, but the vamp managed to put a number of serious dents in the table, caving in the center.

I risked another shot of my magic, homing in on the corner of the table, where the leg attached, and the current beating had cracked one of the welds. I scrambled out and snapped off the table leg as I went. The table tipped, sending all of the glass vials crashing to the floor. The table leg was a square tube of steel that ended in a suitably jagged edge of torn metal.

The Renfield was still staring stupidly at the collapsed table when I took him through the neck with my improvised stake. He arched back, hands clutching at the end of the table leg. I twisted and wrenched, using the leverage of the steel to rip the vampire's head clean off his shoulders.

Mrs. Chu had her vampire on his knees. Her cardigan was covered with blood and the vampire's face was crisscrossed with scratches. His face looked ready to fall off.

"Jackie!" I threw the table leg.

Without even looking at me Mrs. Chu snatched it out of the air and wound up like a pro ball player. She connected with the vampire's head like it was the bottom of the ninth inning. The vampire's head exploded in a shower of gore that covered the back wall in blood and brain matter. Both vampires keeled over like dead trees.

Wow. "You sure you don't want to join the Slayers, Mrs. Chu?"

She dropped the table leg and pointed a finger at me. "Since when did you decide, you could start calling your elders by their first names?"

Ouch. I hung my head in contrition. "Sorry. Heat of the moment."

Luckily for me, Mrs. Chu had other things to concern her. "Toby!"

The boy ran out from behind his table and slammed into Mrs. Chu, wrapping his arms around her, heedless of the blood on her clothes. Mrs. Chu sniffled and stroked his hair, murmuring softly to him.

I turned away to give them a moment. Not everyone lived like a Slayer. Most people didn't fight for their lives on a regular basis. And Mrs. Chu hadn't shifted. I was sure her wolf form could have taken down a Renfield with greater ease, but now wasn't the time to ask her about it. I filed that away for later.

O'Malley's set up was truly spectacular, top-notch equipment that would impress even on the other side of the Veil. I picked up one of the batteries and hefted it. For its small size it was deceptively dense. These were common on the other side, but I hadn't seen one since I'd come over. There just wasn't a need for them.

But maybe, today, I could use them. We still had to get back out, where Akhil and Altan were assuredly still fighting a massive peril of vampires and Renfields. Wen was here too, but three Slayers still weren't enough. I had to get back out there and help in some way other than just throwing knives.

The battery was built around a central tank of pressurized hydrogen. Sudden, violent releases of hydrogen have been historically proven to be dangerous, so the reservoir tank was a solid mass of green in the center of the battery. But the hydrogen had to be released in order for the fuel cell to work, so that gave my magic a toehold.

It took some finding, but Kotori's lessons paid off handsomely as I wormed my power down to the miniscule level of the fuel release membrane. Amidst the unbroken expanse of green, my magic found a microscopic pinpoint of pale white light. Normally the membrane was only permeable when the battery sensed a power draw, but that didn't matter to me. I only needed to punch a hole in that membrane and physics would do the rest.

The timing was going to be tricky. I pulled one of my utility knives from my hip and began unwinding the gaffer's tape that covered the handle. Still holding Toby, Mrs. Chu watched with skepticism as I worked.

She whispered intently, "That seems like a bad idea, Roxy."

I secured the last bit of tape and examined my work. My magic told me everything would hold together until the moment I needed it. "It's a bad idea for them, not for us."

23

CHOICES

I'd been so fixated on getting Toby out that I hadn't stopped to think about how hard it would be once we had him.

We'd gotten clear of the Renfields guarding Toby but just outside the barn was a battle scene of unholy proportions. I couldn't so much see Wen as I could see his whip chains as he leapt from one cluster to another, the chains a blur of motion. Altan had shifted to an awe-inspiring were-jaguar half form and he moved in cat like leaps, tearing through vampires. Unfortunately, his strikes didn't kill them immediately and decapitation was a slow and grisly business.

Agnes reared and I could see the silhouette of Akhil astride the mighty Friesian, his hands glowing with light. His strikes cleared out a couple of Renfields only to see three more in their place. How much longer could he keep this up?

We didn't have endless stores of magic. Even if I could perfectly set the recoil to my ink, every time, eventually I would exhaust all the stores of magic in my body, or the recoil would overpower any constraints and wipe me out. Bashir had warned me that I set to breaking something too big, the recoil could hit me so hard I'd never regain consciousness. After that warning, I'd resolved to do everything Kotori told me and get more precise about breaking small things.

Unbidden, an image of my dad rose in my mind, near the end when he'd started rambling. How he talked about breaking the world. I hadn't understood it then, but now that I had been using my breaker magic, I had a vague idea what he might have been talking about. At some point, Dad must have taken a recoil hit so big that it had knocked him unconscious. I wanted to avoid that at all costs as it seemed a good way to get dead quickly when in an altercation.

I blinked away the memories, and mentally calculated the distance to Akhil, Wen, and Altan. Mrs. Chu was wiped out, her adrenaline-fueled offensive on the Renfields clearly taking its toll on her now as she moved tentatively.

I looked down at Toby, he was breathing hard, his thin chest heaving from exertion.

"My friends are over there. I need to go help them."

He blinked, his pale blue eyes wide and confused.

I pointed at Mrs. Chu. "Do you think you could lead Mrs. Chu out to the main road to the wagon pickup?"

He nodded, his face brightening. "Yes. I know where that is."

"Great. I'll go–"

A crack of bright white light pierced the purple haze and then I saw Akhil slump over on Agnes. *Oh no.* He'd exhausted his magic and was surrounded by a rapidly contracting ring of Renfields. Sensing a kill, the vampires stepped over the piles of ash of their brethren and closed in, a writhing swarm of arms and teeth, clutching for the unconscious Slayer.

Wen leapt over them and snagged the Lightbringer off his saddle, bounding away in unbelievable leaps. Altan smacked Crabby Agnes on her rump, and she whinnied loud before rearing and stomping another Renfield skull before she galloped off in the direction of the Farm. Altan seemed to grow even sleeker, his limbs extending from his warrior half form into a massive jaguar and racing off after them.

Watching them escape was at once a relief and terrifying. I was totally alone now and still had to get Mrs. Chu and little Toby out of here safely. I'd never known true terror until this moment. In the Box, I'd feared for my own life. Earlier tonight, I'd feared that Felix would cleave me in two with that big axe. But now, as I was entrusted with the life of this child and Mrs. Chu, I was more terrified than I'd ever been.

The barn door flew off its hinges and an enraged O'Malley flew out. His form had morphed into a grotesque half bat, half humanoid frame with giant leathery wings sweeping outward from his spine.

Toby shrieked and ducked behind me, his screams piercing my eardrums.

O'Malley launched at Mrs. Chu, and I threw all the knives I had in rapid succession as his wings beat down on Mrs. Chu's head. One tore through a leathery wing, the other punched into his shoulder. He lurched, wings folding and morphing back into human limbs, blood running down his pale arms. To my horror he wrapped one arm around Mrs. Chu's neck and she elbowed him in the chest to no avail.

Desperate now, I flung my Breaker magic at the same time I aimed Samuel's karambit at his thigh. I blew out his right knee and my blade carved into his left upper thigh before he kicked me off and my recoil exploded behind my eyes.

I fell backwards into a heap and scrambled to my feet, blinking rapidly to clear my vision. When at last I was upright, O'Malley had backed away, dragging an unconscious Mrs. Chu, one pasty freckled forearm under her chin, blood dripping onto her sweater. After I'd busted his right knee, he'd shifted weight to his other leg where my blade stuck out of it, taunting me.

I hadn't gotten the karambit deep enough for the crystal to meet flesh and drink. I'd been aiming for the femur but missed.

O'Malley reached into his vest and pulled out a syringe, then plunged into his right thigh. The veins in his arm throbbed, dark blue against his flesh and then the skin itself pinkened and he stood tall again, shifting his weight on the knee I'd busted.

I'd given it everything I had and this monster could still stand. My Breaker magic that he thought so highly of wasn't working out so well for me now. My head hurt like a pounding drum and all I could hear was the echo of my failure and Toby's screams.

Mrs. Chu dangled limply, her delicate chin bobbing as O'Malley moved. My heart squeezed in my chest, pain radiating outward at the sight of her. I'd only come out here for her and everything was going terribly wrong. I had a chance to take Toby and run but I couldn't leave her behind.

O'Malley reached down and yanked out the curved blade, lifting it close to his face. His eyes traveled the gleaming silver surface and stopped at the crystal reservoir. His fingers shifted and I could see that he knew exactly what that part was for. Vamp blood was precious, curing a number of injuries and ailments, but it didn't travel well. Basically, the best way to carry vamp blood was to carry an entire vamp. Barring that, you needed a spelled crystal reservoir, which were in limited supply, the enchantment long ago lost. It was rumored it was the Night Queen who had drunk down the entire Midnight Rose coven who had enchanted the reservoirs.

He was careful not to touch the reservoir but his eyes lit with speculation as he waved the karambit about.

"Well, well, well. It seems we are at an impasse."

That seemed an overly generous assessment of my situation. He had all my weapons and the person I cared about most on this side of the Veil as his hostage.

He smiled and it was not a pleasant expression. "You've cost me a tremendous amount tonight, Ms. Lim. But the upside is that you might be more valuable than this entire operation."

I did not like where this was going. But it made my last play seem the most reasonable.

"Let her and the kid go. I'll come with you."

"In due time. But first, a test." He brandished the karambit. "A Breaker can work with any material, organic or inorganic, right?"

I nodded slowly.

"Then you should be able to break the Crystal on this blade."

His words sent a spike of fear into my gut. "I can't break Tarim Crystal."

He waved the knife a bit. "Yes, yes, it's very special. Crystalline structure, but with sentient properties. Fascinating stuff. You break the Crystal, then you have my word I'll let these two go."

I wondered what Tanner would do in this situation, how would he save the hostage and appease the Tarim at the same time? "No, you don't understand. The Crystal is inviolate. It isn't--"

O'Malley growled and shook Mrs. Chu like a ragdoll. "Silence! I expected better of you, Ms. Lim. You grovel at the Tarim's feet? This is how you honor your father's legacy, and everything he fought for? Gabriel would be ashamed of you."

Anger blazed in my chest at the sound of my dad's name. "Shut up! You don't know anything about my father!"

O'Malley's face split into a fierce grin. "Oh, Ms. Lim, I think I knew your father quite a bit better than you did."

He pressed the edge of the karambit into Mrs. Chu's neck until the edge stretched her skin tight. "Break it. Show me who you really are or the last thing you will see is this tired old wolf's blood spraying across your face."

I closed my eyes, the weight of everything anchoring me to the soil. I wanted to sink into it and vanish. Disappear from the demands of this creature and my own obligations. I thought about my visit to the Temple and how things had gone at the end. What would happen if I tried to break the Crystal?

If I couldn't Break it, he'd kill us all.

But if I succeeded and O'Malley kept his word, Mrs. Chu and Toby could go free. I would have fulfilled the very reason I'd come out here–to get her out. But in turn I would have to go with O'Malley. He wouldn't kill me, but after seeing how his men had tortured Wilson in the barn, I knew there were worse things than death. And I would be forsworn in my oath to the Slayers. Tears stung the back of my eyes and I blinked a few times to keep them from falling. *I'm sorry, Dad.*

Toby whimpered, crouching even lower behind me.

I knew what I would have to do.

"Swear it."

He nodded, his smile widening. "I swear on my blood that if you break this crystal, I will let these two go."

"Unharmed."

"Yes, yes. Unharmed. Now, your turn."

I swallowed hard. It felt like a million years ago, but really it had just been a couple of hours earlier that I had sworn an oath with Tyee on my power. Here in the Veil, oaths had power and I was loathe to keep making them. I had fulfilled my oath to Tyee to get Eloise out, which was how I'd gotten captured by O'Malley in the first place–giving Wen time to get Eloise to safety.

"I swear on my power that if I Break the crystal and you let them go, when you walk out of here, I will go with you."

"Now Ms. Lim, show us just how good of a Breaker you are."

His words put me right back in the ring with Kotori, awkwardly dodging her precise strikes and even sharper verbal jabs. "Are you a Breaker or not, Roxy?"

The Crystal scared me. I couldn't imagine what the recoil from it would be like or whether it would turn me into a vegetable after. But I was a Breaker and I couldn't back down now.

I let my sight narrow down the small reservoir on my karambit. My uncle Samuel was a Maker and his craft was unparalleled. There were no weaknesses in the blade or the tang. The only things to exploit were the joins. When I focused on the crystal itself, a faint chime rang out. But O'Malley showed no reaction, which told me that only I had heard it. The crystal was ringing inside my head.

Inside the finely crafted handle of the karambit, the crystal glowed like a solid bar of green light. Like my uncle's crafts-manship, the crystal was pristine. As my magic dug into it, the louder the ringing got in my head. It got loud enough that I felt my teeth vibrating. I pushed my magic harder, searching for the grain in the crystal, the molecular pattern that would become the shear planes for me to break it.

As I sank into the crystal the resonance of the vibration changed the nature of my magic sight, giving the green light an odd texture I'd never seen before. Wen's advice bubbled out of memory and I let the resonance build and direct my power.

If I didn't break the crystal, O'Malley would kill Mrs. Chu, then come for me and Toby. I had no more cards to play. The realization was terrifying, and freeing, like a leap of faith from a tall building. The recoil didn't matter anymore, only the break-ing, so I concentrated on that, and poured myself into my magic, attuning my power to the resonance of the crystal.

"Any time now, Ms. Lim."

I gave him a sheepish look and shrugged my shoulders, an exaggerated movement causing him to look away from the karambit.

The resonance in my head built to a keening pitch and I released my magic in a single, tight burst. I felt the pulse of magic leave me and it felt just as right as a well-thrown blade. Every cell in my body sang in triumph as my magic crossed the distance between me and O'Malley in the blink of an eye.

I Broke the blade apart, the shaped enamel splitting apart from the tang, the silver edging, and the reservoir.

The blade carved into O'Malley's throat and his eyes went wide with surprise. He released Mrs. Chu as he raised his other arm to stem the bloody gash.

The crystal didn't Break the same way. When I sent my magic through it, instead of seeking out a seam or fracture, it soaked into the crystal, almost on a molecular level. My magic bounced around as if it were swimming in a pool and I heard the ringing of a carillon in my head as I pumped more magic into it. The ink on my spine tingled cool and then icy as I cycled more and more magic into the crystal.

"Please," I told it. "Please Break."

And then I showed it exactly where I wanted to go.

The crystal flowed with my magic, a stream of atoms singing as it sprayed outward, showering O'Malley's left cheek and sinking into the open wound on his neck.

On contact the crystal ate through his skin, a fiery orange outline burning the tiniest bits of him into ash. He screeched like the demons from hell were chasing him and I hoped he was afraid. That he experienced even a fraction of the suffering Wilson had gone through.

Satisfaction at his pain ripped through me, bright and hot, and then the recoil hit. The ink on the base of my neck flared and it burned in an icy ring spiraling outward throughout my skin. My head felt too small, a thousand pounds of pressure waiting to burst within. And throughout it all, the chimes sang through my blood and vibrated along my skin.

I sank to my knees and curled over Toby's shivering form.

O'Malley's wings flared out, a vast expanse of blackness and he lifted off, still shrieking. His take off was jerky, the entire left side of his body sagging like a puppet with cut strings. He collapsed to the ground and his eyes grew round and wide with fear.

"To me! To me!" His voice rang out, the sound nearly knocking me back. No lungs could make a sound that loud. All around, vampires and Renfields turned and ran to their master. I grabbed Toby around the waist and ran. More like stumbled, really, as the recoil from my magic continued to squash my brain into new and interesting shapes inside my skull. I managed a mostly straight line to Mrs. Chu, crumpled in a heap a few feet from O'Malley.

O'Malley screamed in agony, clutching at his face, his fingernails raking bloody tracks down his cheeks. The orange glow from the atomized crystal chewed across his cheek, exposing a broad streak of his jawbone.

I grabbed Mrs. Chu and dragged her away from the swirling storm of vampires collapsing in on O'Malley's position. I spun around just in time to watch O'Malley grab the nearest Renfield by the neck. The tendons on his forearm stood out as he dug his fingers into the Renfield's neck. The Renfield screamed, a high-pitched, thready sound.

O'Malley opened his mouth and his fangs dropped. He lowered his half-ruined face into the Renfield's neck and sank his fangs in.

I kept moving, dragging Mrs. Chu and Toby with me, and unable to tear my eyes away. The Renfield's scream faded and his body seemed to cave in on itself as O'Malley fed and fed and fed. His cheek filled out with fresh pink skin, although the orange glow of the crystal remained under his skin. His eyes found mine, as the vampire in his hands crumbled to dust, across a sea of dozens and dozens of Renfields in a protective ring around him.

Like a massive organism, the scrum of vampires began to move away. O'Malley's winged form maintained the center, and his vampires continued to swirl around him while carrying him away. His eyes stayed fixed on mine as he grabbed another Renfield from the crowd and began draining him.

The vampires moved across the field and faded into the Wilds, moving towards the thickest part of the jungle. In moments they were tiny shadows, and I was left standing over Toby and Mrs. Chu in the trampled remains of the potato field.

Dark metal glinted at my feet, the shattered remains of my karambit. The Crystal that had once filled the handle was gone. I hadn't killed O'Malley but as the Crystal continued to eat away at him in a slow burning path, he would soon wish I had.

24

THE PRINCE RETURNS

Dark mist swirled a short distance from me. I groaned. Too little, too late, Tyee Wilder materialized from the mist and I caught the elusive scent that made me think of cool nights in a forest. He'd carried me once through that mist and it had been an intimacy between us that I tried hard to forget.

I picked up the remains of my karambit and carefully kept my eyes averted as Tyee approached.

His leather shoes were incongruous on the churned earth of Bev's ruined field. He stood silently next to me as I carefully found all the fragments of my knife. It had been a gift from my uncle. I wasn't about to leave it here to be buried with the potatoes.

I checked on Mrs. Chu and Toby. My landlady was still unconscious, and Toby had finally succumbed to exhaustion. I stood and tried to summon my anger with Tyee, but I was honestly just too tired to be mad right now.

"What are you doing here, Tyee?"

He had the decency to look abashed. A little. It was hard to tell. "I gave you my word, *ma bichette*."

Tyee looked around, taking in the massive barn doors, ripped off the building and laying askew on the ground. "But perhaps you didn't need my assistance after all."

Maybe I wasn't too tired after all. I took a breath and pictured Wen, standing on the rocking wagon, at ease even as we rocked over the rough forest floor. The budding ember of anger in my chest flared and my hands suddenly itched for my hammers.

My dad's hammers, lost in the dark of the Wilds, thrown who knows where by some whacked out vampire. I knew he would say they were just hammers, just tools, but it still felt like failure, and that extinguished the rage before it could burn hot enough for me to do something stupid.

Aggravating he might be, I was still going to get some value out of him. "You're not getting out of your promise to me, vampire."

Maybe it was something in my voice, but Tyee's attitude changed subtly, and he dipped his head to me in concession. "Of course. It was not my intention to do so. How can I be of assistance?"

Bring Wilson back to life. Fix Bev's Ranch. Erase all the horrifying memories from Toby's young mind. Find my damn hammers.

He couldn't do any of these things for me, but I knew what he could do. I gestured to Toby and Mrs. Chu.

"You can make sure these two get home safely. Mrs. Chu to her apartment. Toby to his people."

Did he look uncomfortable? "I'm not sure I know where the boy's people are at the present mo--"

I glared at him and he stopped short. "Of course, I will find them, and see the boy safely home."

"I'm serious, Tyee. I don't have time for games."

He held up his hand, where we had exchanged a vow, and

blood. "No games, but I have to finish this." He gestured at Bev's Ranch. "All of it."

I'd been through too much; my mind was too fried to keep up with him. "All of what?"

Tyee pointed at the wreckage of the barn. "You saw what was in there, right? The scale of O'Malley's operation? If he gets this going, he'll turn the Wilds into a factory for Renfields. It all needs to go, or the Pact will be worthless."

He was talking about destroying Bev's Ranch. "You can't."

"I will. O'Malley must be contained."

No. Not after everything I'd been through just to free Mrs. Chu. The whole point has been to preserve Bev's Ranch and her crew.

Tyee's face softened. "Would you have them all come back here, just to be slaughtered? O'Malley's process requires shifter blood. If they return, O'Malley will simply come back to brutalize them again."

Bev wasn't exactly my favorite but the idea of her losing her home like this...

"This is her home. We can't take it away from her."

Tyee's eyes hardened. "If she comes back, it will be her death, and the death of all those who trusted her for safety and shelter. And their blood will be used for O'Malley's ends, which will result in even more death."

My eyes stung. It wasn't fair. Bev had just wanted to be left alone, to live her own life, on her terms. How could I face her and my aunties, knowing I'd let Tyee destroy the Ranch?

Tyee's hand on my shoulder startled me. He was close enough that his usual scent of pine distracted me from the stench of the battlefield. It was comforting and I wanted to reach for that comfort, but I also wanted to punch him in the mouth.

Because he was right. But I couldn't let him do it.

"*Ma bichette*, you don't have to stay--"

I wiped the tears from my face, my anger rising again. My voice shook. "No. I'm staying. You're going. Fulfill your vow to me and get them home."

"But--"

"I'll do it." And the words hurt even more when I said them out loud.

"I owe Bev that much. I'll do it."

Tyee pulled his hand away and the spot on my shoulder felt colder without the contact. He picked up Mrs. Chu in a fireman's carry, quite gently, I noted, and then I lifted a sleepy Toby into the crook of his other arm. Tyee stood with obvious ease, despite carrying two people in his arms. A sharp pang of jealousy scraped across my already raw emotions. Of all the people I had helped save today, Mrs. Chu was the one I cared about, and I wasn't strong enough to carry her out of here.

"Be careful with her, Tyee. She's family to me."

"Of course, m--" He seemed to reconsider his words. "Of course, Roxy. She gave me aid in her home. I will not forget that."

I waved him off and turned back to the wrecked barn. "Go. I've got this."

And I would be damned if I would let Tyee Wilder see me cry twice in one day.

"I will see you again, Roxy."

A wave of sandalwood and smoke enveloped me from behind and then I was alone on Bev's potato field. I pulled the heavy weight of the hydrogen battery from my pocket and stared at my improvised bomb.

Had I known all along that this is where things would end? O'Malley had dozens of Renfields. My bomb might have beat them back for a moment, but there was no guarantee it would have killed any of them. It had always been a losing fight.

Altan and Akhil had known that. They hadn't come to win

some glorious battle. They'd only come to rescue a stupid Slayer who'd gotten in deep over her head.

But my bomb could prevent O'Malley from doing this to more shifters. Or at least, keep him from doing it for a time. Just at the cost of Bev's home, a place she'd created as a refuge for other shifters.

It was an awful solution, but the only one I had. O'Malley could come back at any moment. And destroying the tech meant putting a dent in his operations. Surely the Slayers would see some merit in that, even if Bev didn't.

The bomb was ready. The pinprick of white light shone like a tiny star in my magic sight. The barn was built from old timbers. There were plenty of other batteries in there. Once the flames caught, it would go up like a bonfire.

I threw the bomb and let out a scream of frustration and anger that felt like a rubber band snapping inside my heart. Like my throwing knives I knew the throw was on target as the bomb left my fingers. Kotori's training made tracking its movement easy, even if the pinpoint weakness was miniscule. It could not escape my magic.

I burst the hydrogen chamber and the Smokin' Hot just before it hit the ground inside the barn. There was a momentary flash of white, and then an expanding cloud of heat, air, and dust ballooned from the center of the barn. The barn walls bowed out with the force of the explosion and lifted the roof a couple of feet. When the roof crashed back down it caved in, smashing O'Malley's improvised drug lab to splinters. A glowing red and orange light in the center of the barn quickly grew, sending spears of light out through cracks in the walls.

The recoil rose up like a tsunami. I sensed it with my magic, and now the path was clear. I saw how easy it would be to coax the recoil, bring it home, and land it softly on my ink.

I did none of it. I stayed still as the recoil slammed into me. I was destroying Bev's life. It didn't feel right to not experience every horrible consequence of my actions.

The impulse landed like a mule kicking me in the gut. Suddenly I was on my hands and knees, my fingers curling into the dirt, my stomach violently evacuating its contents. My eyes stung, both from the bile coming up my throat, as well as the spreading smoke and ash from the fire.

The recoil passed, leaving me vaguely dissatisfied. I stood and watched, like a sentinel, as the flames greedily consumed the barn and found their way to the main building. The main Ranch was built out of tougher wood, but fire is nothing if not persistent.

I watched until the smoke clogged my eyes and nose, and I couldn't tell if my tears were from the hot ashes or my bitter disappointment.

$\sim$

I DIDN'T REMEMBER MUCH of the walk back to the Farm, other than a blank space in my head, filled with white noise. Lucky for me, when the haze in my mind lifted, I was looking at the wide road leading to the front of the Farm.

Dread filled me as I continued up the path. I could withstand the consequences of my actions, but what had happened to Akhil? A handful of Slayers in dirty work clothes stood scattered through the fields and they slowly stood and watched as I approached the Farm. Even dazed, I'd made it past the outer wards, so they weren't alarmed to see me, but I felt the heavy weight of judgment in their eyes as they followed me to the front door.

It took all my effort to keep my back straight and my eyes on the wide front porch as I mounted the steps. When I opened the door a blast of sound hit me in the face, voices shouting and bodies bustling around. Just as I stepped inside, a large woman built like a bank vault rushed past and clipped my shoulder, almost throwing me to the ground. She turned and looked like she was about to apologize when she clearly recognized me and stopped dead in her tracks.

"You!"

The noise screeched to a halt and in that instant every pair of eyes turned to me. Several Slayers stood, all menacing glares and hunched shoulders. Between them I caught a glimpse of Akhil, laid out on a bench, his chest and arms covered in bandages. His skin was ashy gray. Between all the burly shoulders I also saw Wen, still hunched over, with his hands hovering over Akhil's chakras. In the sudden silence the only sound was Wen's quiet voice.

A big hand grabbed me by the arm and dragged me outside. Wen didn't look up. Then the door closed and he was gone.

Altan dropped me on the porch. The werejaguar's arms and shoulders were covered in a fine network of fresh pink scars, new battle trophies courtesy of his accelerated shifter healing. His t-shirt had been reduced to mere tatters, hanging by a literal thread. The usual gleam in his eye was gone, replaced by a dullness that frankly scared me more than any of his over eager laughter. With measured movements Altan pulled his flask out, took a sip, and grimaced. He was about to put it away when he paused for a moment, then offered it to me.

I took the flask and sniffed carefully. It smelled faintly of plums and sour fruit. I tipped it back carefully and let the liquid brush against my tongue. Fumes climbed up my throat and nostrils and set my eyes watering. Then the sour flavor of the hooch hit my glands and I almost choked. I handed the flask back to him. His eyes were still grim but at least now he had a bit of a smile.

"What are you doing here, Roxy?"

I coughed. My sinuses were miraculously clear. "I saw Akhil go down. I wanted to make sure he was okay."

Altan's smile disappeared and I took an involuntary step back. "Make sure he's okay? If you cared about your fellow Slayers, maybe you'd follow orders when given, eh?"

It felt like I was in school again, trying to justify myself before my teachers. "I didn't... I... You didn't see what they were doing, Altan. I couldn't leave them there."

"That wasn't your job."

I raised my voice, unable to stop myself. "Our job is to help people, isn't it?"

Altan opened his mouth like he was about to yell back at me and then deflated. "It's not the job we're paid for, kid. Like it or not, that's how it is, now."

He put his hand on my back and got me moving off the porch and towards the stables. "There was a time, Roxy, when the Slayers would have been right behind you from the beginning of your whole little adventure."

At my look of disbelief he actually laughed ruefully. "Yeah, and you know who would have been right there with you?"

"You?"

"Ha! No, your dad would have backed you, one hundred percent. I mean, I would have come along, just for the fun of it. And most like half the Slayers, too. But your dad, he would have been there on principle. That's what made Gabe who he was."

I'd never heard any of the Slayers speak about my dad like this. I'd hoped to hear stories like this from my uncle, but he seemed to shy away from talking about his brother.

We stopped just outside the stables. Altan turned to look back at the main house. "Akhil will be okay. Don't worry about him, he's a tougher nut to crack than you'd think. While I was bringing him back he was prepping a bird to fly back to the Dojo."

Uh-oh. Altan read the look on my face. "Yeah, he let everyone know what happened. Look, I'll give you points for guts, Roxy. What you did here takes some nerve, the kind of thing I haven't seen here in the Slayers for a while now. But we've got rules to follow, also."

The ink on the back of my neck seemed to get uncomfortably warm and I fought the urge to rub my hand over it. "So what now?"

"I don't know, kid. But I do know there's no going around it. Take Smoke and go home."

Altan looked like he was maybe going to say something else, and then turned and headed back to the main house. He didn't say goodbye, and he walked back into the house and closed the door without once turning back to look at me.

Inside the stables I paused and let the rich smell of hay and animals permeate my being. Agnes nosed out of her stall and nickered softly. I wandered over to her stall and held out my hand. The big horse nibbled at my palm.

"Sorry girl, no sugar this time."

Given what had happened to Akhil, even the horse seemed to be in a somber mood. I reached my arms up Agnes' neck and hugged her to me, burying my face in her mane. After a moment I let go and she nosed me towards the doors.

"Yeah, I know. Time to face the music."

25

CONSEQUENCES

I rode Smoke back to the Dojo. The bad news was that Smoke was an enormous black Friesian who was even larger than Crabby Agnes. The good news was that he didn't throw me as I hunched over his powerful form and held on for dear life. Between moments of sheer terror and exhaustion, I still had time to dread the conversation I would have with Samuel once I'd made it back to the Dojo.

I tried to tell myself that all things considered, things hadn't gone terribly. Yes, Bev's property had been decimated but we'd gotten Toby out. Most importantly to me, Mrs. Chu was safe. But then I remembered Akhil unconscious, the pallor of his skin unnaturally pale. The way Altan had talked to me, worry writ large on every line of his craggy face.

What should have been a simple trip to deliver Mrs. Chu's medicine had ballooned into a cluster of disastrous proportions. I'd stumbled into a massive operation and even now, all I understood is that O'Malley had connections to get enormous amounts of modern tech into the Veil and that O'Malley's unholy science experiments were creating Renfields.

And...he might have found a cure for my mom. A cure I

might have destroyed in my fight to free Toby. I didn't let myself
dwell on that.

Altan had given me a lot to think about. Akhil had given me
an Order, twice, which I hadn't followed. At the time, I'd had
good reasons. Now as I approached the Dojo, I could see how it
would look to the rest of the Seven Freaks. To Samuel.

It looked bad.

The Dojo was unnaturally quiet as I neared the front gate.
Where there should have been a pair of guards to receive any
visitors was instead a lone, broad-shouldered silhouette.

I recognized my uncle Samuel's profile, and the rigid set of
his arms. He was dressed in the full complement of his armor,
as if prepared for battle.

Or a funeral.

Samuel's head tilted to track me all the way to the front
gates. As I passed through he disappeared and I found him
waiting for me inside the main courtyard. I hadn't spent a lot of
time with my uncle since arriving in Seattle, but in the little
time we had spent together, I knew him to be straightforward,
and nearly honest to a fault. I wondered how he would have
fared, trying to survive as I did in Boston, without the powers
and status he was afforded behind the Veil.

Without the good health that came from being in the Veil.
Would he have aged like my dad? Gotten bitter at the end?

I stopped just in front of my uncle and tried to not let the
grandeur of his arms and armor intimidate me. Adding a
weapon with longer reach to my kit should be a lot higher on
my priority list. Which reminded me of the spear I'd lost in the
Box and made me feel even worse about meeting my uncle like
this.

"Are you going to say, I told you so?"

He grunted a little, like I'd punched him in the gut, and his
eyes clouded a little. Samuel's voice was rough, and a little too

loud. "It never worked on my brother, why would it work on you?"

That put me back on my back foot, alarmed at the sudden emotion from my uncle. I'd always wanted to hear about my father from my uncle, but maybe tonight I was going to get that in a way I wasn't going to want.

"Uncle, I did what I thought was--"

Samuel pointed an accusing finger at me. "Your ink is barely dry and you're already haring off, skipping duty, disobeying a superior. Is this what you thought the Slayers would be? Some kind of summer camp?"

"What? No! Mrs. Chu was in trouble, Samuel! What did you expect me--"

"I expected you to know your place and do your job! You were given an order! By one of the Seven!"

"They needed our help!"

"Then they should have paid for it! Gods damn it, Gabe, you can't keep--"

He cut off, his eyes wide and wet with emotion. I stared at him. What old argument with my father he was reliving? Samuel scrubbed his face with his hands and growled. He spun on his heel and headed for the Dojo.

"Come on. They're all waiting for you."

I hurried after him. "Uncle Samuel--"

"I tried, Roxy, but everything's been decided. All that's left is for you to come take your medicine."

THE INTERIOR of the Dojo was lit with half a dozen fairy lights set around the walls, but today even those lights seemed sinister. A small cushion had been laid on the floor in the center of one of the fighting rings. My uncle Samuel left me to take his place on the perimeter of the ring, and four of the Seven stared down on me.

My uncle stood on the far left. Bashir next, with his pulwar on his hip. The end of the long blade nearly brushed the floor. Bashir raised his eyebrows to me as I took my position in front of the cushion, but that was all.

Opposite Samuel, Aislinn stared down at me, her golden eyes hard and unblinking. A cloak of glittering moonlight cascaded off her thin shoulders like a waterfall, and a pair of ornate machetes hung at her thighs. Aislinn's mouth was set in a thin line. She'd never been shy about criticizing me.

At the far right, a compact figure in blood red whom I knew well. Kotori's crimson cloak was pristine, as usual, with snowy white fox fur trimming the edge. Unlike everyone else in the room, she had her weapon in her hands, a naginata as tall as she was, topped with an elegant single-edged blade. Her fingers rippled over the shaft and she dipped her head towards the cushion. I had learned many hard lessons about staying on my toes around my mentor. Going down to my knees while she was wielding her favorite blade was not something I wanted to do.

Aislinn said, "Kneel, Slayer."

Well, they were still calling me a Slayer, at least. Keeping Kotori in the corner of my vision, I knelt and carefully tucked my feet underneath me, and rested my hands on my thighs. As I looked up at everyone I realized they had left an empty space for a fifth person in the center of their arrangement.

Samuel coughed. "Since Tanner has sent his apologies, I think it's best if we just get started."

Aislinn sniffed. "Yes, let's be done with this. Bashir?"

On my left, Bashir pulled a folded sheet of paper from his pocket and cleared his throat. In quick, almost monotonous fashion, he read what must have been Akhil's note, sent by pigeon ahead of my return. It efficiently detailed my actions starting from when I first arrived at the Farm, and included details I didn't know, probably based on Wen's account of things. The tone of the note shifted at the end, and spelled out the extent of Akhil's injuries, and a rough estimate of O'Malley's numbers of followers and his strategic assets. The last part must have been Altan's contribution.

Bashir's voice returned to his normal, melodic cadence. "The discovery of O'Malley's forces is an unexpected turn of events that we cannot ignore. It is a clear threat to the Pact and-
-"

Aislinn bowled over him. "And absolutely nothing to do with tonight's proceedings."

She turned her cold, golden eyes to me. "Roxanne Lim, you are hereby--"

"Wait, don't I get to say anything?" My stomach had shriveled down to a frozen stone that sat like a lead weight in the bottom of my gut.

Alarmingly, Aislinn's eyes actually chilled further. "No, I think we've seen enough of what happens when you're allowed to speak your mind."

There had to be a way out of this. "What about Tanner? What does he have to say?"

Kotori slammed the butt of her naginata on the floor, and the sound was like a gunshot, echoing off the walls. Her voice was a furious whisper. "We speak with Tanner's voice, a lesson you have failed to learn, despite the nearly catastrophic consequences of your actions."

I'd thought that this was as low as I could get, but Kotori's voice dripped with disappointment, and I found myself wishing that the spider-vamp had simply buried me in the Box. I shut my mouth and put all my effort into holding my head high and keeping my back straight.

"Roxanne Lim, you are hereby stripped of all Slayer privileges, status, and salary."

The cold sensation in my gut spread until it felt like my

arms and legs were going numb. Kotori stared at me, unblinking, her knuckles white around her weapon. My uncle stared at the floor, his face morose. Bashir looked angry, but he let Aislinn continue.

Aislinn went on for a little bit more, but an odd ringing filled my ears, and her words just washed over me. I was out. I'd spent months trying to get in, and I managed to wreck all my plans in record time. I'd have to go back to scrounging jobs for silver to send home. I'd lost my shot at sending my mom a Midnight Rose, and I'd done so by destroying all of O'Malley's Remedies which might have cured her.

The irony was sharp and brutal enough to make me curl around my gut. I gritted my teeth, stifling a keening that was building in my chest. If I let myself make a noise, I didn't know if I could stop.

When the ringing in my ears stopped, I realized that Aislinn had stopped talking, and that my forehead was resting on the floor of the fighting ring. This was the same ring I'd fought Kotori in, eking out the barest of wins to propel myself into the finals of the Trials.

All that effort.

For nothing.

Footsteps moved past me as the others left. When I raised my head only my uncle remained, still staring at the floor. After a long moment he raised his head. Tears streaked down both cheeks and the usual light in his eyes was gone. Broken.

I'd done that.

As my uncle crossed the fighting ring I stood and dug into my pocket. I moved to block him and he stopped and sighed.

"Roxy, there's nothing you can do."

It took me a moment to master my voice, and it still wobbled a little as I spoke. "I know. I'm sorry I screwed up."

I held out my hands and Samuel looked at me, a question in his brows. He opened his hands and I placed the shattered remains of the karambit in his palms. My uncle closed his hands around the pieces and shut his eyes, shaking his head.

Rather than being sad, he looked like he was getting angry again, and that almost felt good. It would be better if he was mad at me, instead of sad for me. But then he deflated, and he simply walked around me, leaving me alone in the Dojo for the last time.

I'd failed my uncle, my dad, and most importantly, my mom. Maybe Aislinn had been right, and all I was good for was breaking things.

26

HOME

I t had been but a day since I'd left my flat but it felt like a century. When I'd packed for the Wilds, I had been an inked Slayer with all the privileges that came with it. I'd seen the glint of respect in the eyes of the wagon driver and it had soothed an insecurity I didn't want to admit I'd had.

Now I didn't know what I was or what I had anymore.

I didn't have my hammers. I didn't have Samuel's karambit. Most of all, I didn't have a place I belonged to now and that hurt more than anything.

Despair threatened to swamp me as I climbed the stairs to my place. I stripped off my clothes and stood under the shower. Everything hurt. I pressed a hand to my ribs and knew that the fractured ribs were the least of my aches and pains. I turned off the water and pressed my face against the cool tile and let myself cry in a way I hadn't at the Dojo. I cried thinking about the way Samuel had looked at me. Shudders wracked my body and when I didn't think there could be any more tears left, I cried even more. I don't know how long I stood like that but my skin had pebbled from the cold and I dragged myself out to towel off.

The pile of my blood-stained clothes taunted me from the floor and I wanted to burn them all. I stepped over them and went to pull on my sweats and flopped down onto my bed.

I was tired to the bone, and cold. I dragged the coverlet over myself but the coldness had nothing to do with temperature.

My eyes closed with fatigue and I thought about sleeping for a week. But I couldn't avoid the mess I'd made for that long. I thought about Noodle and Dumpling and what I would write to my family. What could I say in a single sentence that could possibly explain what had happened today?

Two sharp raps jarred me from my depressing spiral of thoughts. Eager for the distraction, I went to the door.

"Roxy. It's me."

Mrs. Chu. With a snap, I released the defenses on my door. The wards were keyed to her anyway but not the physical locks.

When I yanked open the door, my landlady was standing there, a bowl of soup in her arms.

She looked a little pale, but the sight of her with the pink and white patterned bowl was very welcome and I felt some of the tightness in my chest loosen up. At least I had gotten this much right.

Mrs. Chu shuffled in and sat me down at my little dinette table with a bowl of soup and a ceramic spoon. I wasn't hungry but I knew better than to argue. Gamely, I took a sip. It was chicken and ginseng and goji berries. Savory and sweet. I took another sip.

She watched intently as I ate and drank, making sure that I got every drop.

When the bowl was empty I asked, "Did Tyee bring you back okay?"

She sniffed. "The vampire returned me to my home. He was...polite."

My eyebrows went up. That was high praise. Maybe she was softening on him.

Mrs. Chu pointed a finger at me. "Don't think I've forgotten what happened at the Ranch. You need to stay away from him. He's entirely too involved in your life."

Fatigue crept up on me again, making me a little woozy. I rested my head on the table and spoke without looking up. "I don't think I'll be dealing with him much, seeing as I lost my job."

The pregnant silence that followed that statement was something practiced and perfected by every Asian elder on the planet. They probably held seminars, possibly even competitions, to see how much guilt and disappointment you could convey just with...silence.

Mrs. Chu finally relented. "Aiya, you're too good for them anyway. You'll find something else."

The vote of confidence from Mrs. Chu warmed me almost as much as the soup. She reached across and patted the back of my neck. "Thank you, Roxy, for coming to get me."

A knock sounded at the door and I started. Mrs. Chu was already here, who else would be knocking on my door?

Mrs. Chu's hand pressed me back down to the table. "I'll get it. I think it's my house guest."

House guest? My sleep-deprived brain struggled to keep up. Mrs. Chu crossed the living space and opened the door. My eyes nearly bugged out of my head.

Bev stood outside my door, dressed in in a tattered housecoat, with a towel wrapped around her head. She had fuzzy pink slippers on her feet. Her eyes lit up when she saw my landlord.

"Jackie, here you are. Toby can't find--"

Bev cut off when she saw me at the table and her eyes darkened. Oh, no. Of course, where else would she and Toby go after I had single handedly destroyed their home?

Mrs. Chu tried to intervene. "Bev..."

Bev turned on her heel and retreated into the hallway. Mrs. Chu turned back to me.

"Roxy, I'm sorry, I should have warned you. They're just staying here until she can find more permanent arrangements."

The door popped open and Bev barged into the room, her eyes intent on me. She brushed off Mrs. Chu's hand from her shoulder and stopped at my table. I didn't bother getting up. I'd destroyed Bev's home. I deserved whatever she was about to unload on me.

Bev's shoulders bunched as she reached into a bag in her hands. She had big, thick arms, heavy with muscle from her ranch work. Whatever she was about to bring down on my head would be propelled by arms used to throwing around heavy weight.

Her hand slammed down on my table, the sound ringing through my apartment. In the silence after, my eyes locked on Bev's hand, and my mind tried to make sense of what I saw. Two hafts of carefully turned hardwood, tapering down to sharp points, crisscrossed in her palm. Gleaming stainless steel topped both wooden handles.

Thor. Loki.

My dad's hammers, lost in the Wilds.

The golden light from my faerie lamps glinted off the steel, dazzling my eyes.

My dad's hammers, here, on my dinette table.

Bev growled, dragging my attention back up to her. I didn't know how my dad's hammers had returned to me, but I found I was willing to do anything to have them back. I squared my shoulders and met Bev's deep blue eyes.

She slid the hammers across the table. "Next time you visit someone's home..."

Her voice faltered for a moment and she closed her eyes, taking a breath. "Next time, don't leave your things behind and expect your host to return them to you. It's rude."

Bev took her hand from the hammers and straightened. Her eyes were bright and wet and dared me to say anything. I settled for the only thing I could think of.

"I'm sorry, Aunt Bev. That was thoughtless of me. I'll do better in the future."

"Hmph. Toby says thank you." Bev turned on her heel and left my apartment without a word.

I inched my fingers forward, afraid the hammers would disappear if I approached too quickly, or touched them too suddenly, like mist swept away by wind. The tip of my finger touched the cool, smooth wood, and my hand curled reflexively around the handle. I marveled at the familiar weight of the hammer and my vision blurred with tears.

Mrs. Chu was at my side. I hadn't even noticed her approach. She really was quiet on her feet. Her hand closed around mine, atop the hammer.

"She knows you did the right thing, Roxy. Give her some time and she'll be back to ignoring you on mahjongg night."

I laughed through the tears falling down my cheeks. Fatigue like a heavy blanket fell over me. Soup and gratitude, both unexpected, warmed my stomach and fuzzed my brain. I vaguely recalled shuffling back to my bed and Mrs. Chu clucking over me as she tucked me into bed.

This time, I slept.

27

FAMILY

I got to The Rose and Horn early and claimed my usual
seat in our usual booth, all the way in, next to the
window. It was the best seat to catch a slight breeze from
outside, a welcome respite from Ulf's post-meal burps. The
worn leather on the bench creaked under my weight and I let
my hands trail over the rough wood of the table, worn smooth
by thousands of hands over the years.

Jake, the skinny owner/bartender who I was sure was at
least half fae, came around with my regular order, a pint of his
house ale and a bowl of his house roasted nut mix.

"You're here early, Roxy." His voice was a deep rumble I
would never have expected from his skinny frame. I had no
idea how old he was, but I guessed that his long gray hair tied
in a neat ponytail had absolutely no bearing on his real age. His
skin was smooth, but wrinkled around the eyes from laughter,
and his regal nose had probably been straight at some time in
the past. I liked to imagine he was a knight who'd retired and
shed his fighting weight, trading his full plate armor for a spotless green kitchen apron.

"Just wanted some alone time with your fine ale." The ale

was, truly, the best I'd found in Seattle. A deep, golden color with a sublime balance of caramel malts and biting bitterness. He even served it just barely chilled.

Jake smiled and returned to the bar.

While the pub wasn't specifically a Slayers venue, there were quite a few other groups of Slayers who were regulars. I wasn't sure how comfortable I would be here, now that I was on the outs. I wouldn't miss Ulf's gastronomical expectorations, but I would certainly miss the beer. And with fewer opportunities to nibble the roasted nuts, I'd have to give up on teasing out Jake's specific spice recipe.

It was just as well. If Cordelia, Ulf, and Wen were moving on with the Slayers, it would be better if they didn't associate with me. Wen would be paired with someone else for patrol duty. Someone else would fill my shoes. I thought about Finn and wished I could explain to him what had happened. Probably Kotori would assign him to someone else to continue his training.

Mrs. Chu's restorative soup and a night of deep sleep had improved my outlook. I would find another way to earn silver for my mom. I had gotten good at hustling jobs before my Trials to get onto the Slayers rosters. I was probably better at the hustle now because I knew Seattle better.

O'Malley had figured out a way to cure blood cancers and powder lung. He couldn't be the only one. I'd start looking for someone else who could do the same. Hopefully someone a lot less crazy.

My friends arrived when I was nearly done with the ale, and I had determined that cinnamon, definitely cinnamon, was a part of Jake's recipe. Maybe a hint of turmeric? The bowl of nuts was empty. Ulf entered first, his boisterous greeting to Jake enough to shake the window behind my head. Cordelia came in next in front of Wen, laughing, apparently at something Wen had said.

As they got closer, I heard the faintest whisper and then louder, as if the ink along my spine was awake. And maybe it was. Maybe this ink tied me to the Slayers forever, giving me this awareness when they were near.

Cordelia stopped laughing when she spotted me, her expression going dark and stony. If Ulf noticed, he didn't give any sign. He signaled to Jake for more ale as my old teammates settled into the booth. Cordelia took her seat next to me, sitting stiff as a board, and the boys took the spots at the ends.

Tension as thick as pie filling oozed off of Cordelia's tight shoulders, her mouth set in a grim line. She set her hands on the tabletop and stared straight ahead, avoiding my gaze. Ulf sighed and put a bag on the table and pushed it over to me.

"Your extra knives. I thought you would like to have them."

I took the bag and tucked it away. "Thanks."

The awkwardness was painful, and exactly what I'd hoped to avoid by coming early. But maybe I'd been gearing up for this all along since I'd decided to come to what I thought of as "our" pub. But it was worse than I could deal with now so it would be better if I just left.

I was glad I'd finished my ale, and I was about to rise to scoot out when Jake arrived with four glasses of ale and two more bowls of nuts. Ulf passed the beer around and I stared helplessly at the fresh drink in front of me. I was out of the Slayers. What was I doing here?

Ulf raised his, well, his beer was more accurately described as a tankard, and said, "To friends and family."

A pang of longing hit me. Aside from Samuel and Mrs. Chu, my family was on the other side of the Veil. I was alone here. Or at least, I was now that I was out of Slayers. I had made one friend here, and a small part of me wondered if Laila would think less of me now that I was off the Slayer's roster.

But Wen and Ulf stared expectantly at me. Three mugs met in the center of the table and I belatedly raised mine. We clinked our beers together and with a look, Cordelia hit my mug so hard some of my ale splashed out before she drank.

Cordelia put her beer back down with perhaps a bit too much force and spilled some of her precious ale. "Just what did you think you were doing?"

I put my own beer down carefully. "I was--"

"You just got your ink, Roxy. We were all there, we all worked so hard for this, and you even dragged Wen into this..." She threw her hands up and growled. Actually growled. Ulf must have been rubbing off on her.

Ulf stroked his beard thoughtfully. "We said you were there for your landlady, yes?"

"Mrs. Chu, yes."

"And she is dear to you?"

A little ring of pain tightened around my heart. "Yes. She opened her home to me when I first got here. She treats me like family."

Ulf's gaze drifted around the table. "I cannot say I would not have done the same if I were in your shoes. If my brothers had needed me, I would have done all that I could to have come to their aid."

Cordelia's face screwed up funny and I could tell she was conflicted. She was not a fan of Ulf's brothers. But she understood his point.

I brushed my finger against Cordelia's hand, and when she didn't pull away I curled my fingers around her palm. She curled her fingers around mine as well, but kept her eyes averted.

"Look, 'Delia, I'm sorry. I didn't mean for any of this to happen. I know that this means things will be different. I don't want it to be this way, but I also can't say I would have done anything differently."

I looked at all my friends and my heart squeezed again. "I'll get out of your way now, so--"

"Idiot." Cordelia's voice was a low, hoarse whisper.

"What?"

Cordelia's hand clamped down on mine until I nearly yelped with pain. Fae weren't quite as strong as shifters, but strong nonetheless.

Wen grinned. "I believe she called you an idiot. It is not inaccurate."

Cordelia's voice grew stronger. "Roxanne Lim, you are an idiot."

And now she brought her head up to look at me and her golden eyes shone with unshed tears. "What makes you think you're free to abandon us?"

"Abandon? Wait, no, I'm not--"

Cordelia said, "Aren't we your family, too?"

The tight knot around my chest sprang open, and it was like a dam bursting inside me. I leaned over until my head touched her shoulder. She didn't pull away.

Cordelia continued, "I can't believe how selfish you're being, just assuming that you're going to go off on your own adventures and leave the rest of us behind like some old furniture you can't be bothered to take with you."

My vision was suddenly quite watery as well, but I found myself smiling. "So, the next time I find myself in a dicey situation, you'd like to come along? For the fun of it?"

She sniffed. "Not if you're talking about breaking the rules again. Maybe Ulf can go."

Wen said, "I could go, since I'm unemployed now as well."

That got everyone's attention and my good mood crashed and burned. "Oh no, Wen, I'm so sorry."

He raised an eyebrow to me. "Sorry for what? Sorry that I made my own decisions, and chose to come help you? You should be more careful of what you apologize for."

Of course, he was right. I raised my ale to him, and he returned the gesture.

"I do, however, find I am in need of a place to stay, now that I have been removed from the Dojo…"

This cue I didn't miss. "My couch is yours, my friend, for as long as you need."

Ulf roared, loud enough to shake the windows, again. "Jake! Four pies!! And four more ales! It's going to be a thirsty night."

We raised our glasses again and I drank deeply of beer, friendship, and family.

28

EPILOGUE: TYEE

The witch's workshop smelled of dried herbs and woodsmoke, and underneath those scents, the feel of the rich earth of a jungle. If serpents coiled around the columns, he was grateful he was immune to their venom. Lush green plants hung from every available surface, a tangle of vines creeping across the brick. Roxy hunched over next to the cauldron, her face dangerously close to orange flames that licked up the sides of the vessel.

Roxy called out, "Yes! That's it! It's holding steady."

Tyee watched one the most powerful Breaker talents known to Seattle tinker with a witch's cauldron. She pored over the rest of the cauldron, presumably inspecting it for weaknesses. Roxy was a Breaker, one who would surely be even more powerful than her father had been. She'd sent O'Malley fleeing and yet here she was laboring over a menial task. His dossiers told him that before she'd been inked as a Slayer she'd taken a number of odd jobs for the coven. Still, it bothered him to see her doing this when she was meant for much greater things.

As a vampire, he did not need to breathe and he was used to

being in the shadows. For now, it gave him the luxury of studying Roxy as he wished, so he did.

Her long hair was tied back and she had a smudge of dirt on her cheek. Her skin glowed from the heat of the cauldron and she looked energetic and vital. Crackling with life. Even like she this, that energy of hers drew him in. Made him want to get closer.

She hadn't come to the bakery and though he knew Eloise saw her socially, he hadn't seen her since that fateful night in the Wilds. He'd waited for their paths to cross but she wasn't a woman who visited the Pleasure District and he rarely had cause to go to Market himself. He had people for that. But now he was done waiting.

When Roxy seemed satisfied with the cauldron she stood. A shorter woman with riotously curly hair also appeared from behind the cauldron. It was Laila, an enchantress of some caliber. Her dark eyes widened when she saw him.

Typically, his people conducted their business with the Blue Rowan Coven at their Market location, but on occasion his matters required more privacy and so he and Eloise came directly to the enchantress. But today he had arrived without an appointment, not to see the witch, but to chase down more interesting quarry.

Roxy merely wiped her hands with a rag she pulled from her pocket, and without turning to him she said, "Can you give us a moment, Laila?"

Laila's eyes darted back and forth between them. "Sure." She drew the word out. "I'll be in the back. Call if you need anything." She winked at Roxy before walking through a door in the back of the workshop.

Roxy didn't move, instead concentrating on cleaning her fingernails. "What do you want, Tyee?"

"I'm flattered you knew I was here."

Now she did turn but before she retorted she clamped her

mouth shut. Clever. Learning to hold her secrets. "Just like any woman, I have eyes in the back of my head. What do you want?"

She was prickly today, but he'd expected that. The Slayers that she had valued so highly had abandoned her. He took another step into the workshop, ducking under a row of hanging pots and brushing aside the trailing vines that clutched at him.

"Just checking up on...an acquaintance. I wanted to see how you were doing."

Roxy sighed and knelt to put away her tools. "I'm doing fine, Tyee. I'm busy, in fact, so if you could skip the pleasantries, I would appreciate it."

When she swept aside her coat, he noted that she wasn't carrying her hammers in their usual places on her belt. That felt oddly out of character for her.

Tyee waved his hand around the workshop. "This is a waste of your talents, *ma bichette*."

Her lips flattened. "You really came here to tell me that? Talents like mine were best used with the Slayers. Now that's not an option for me."

She should have sounded bitter, but mostly she sounded hurt. He didn't like that at all.

"They were wrong to let you go, but your talents would be highly valued by others." He paused, then added. "By me."

It took her a moment to register, then she threw the rest of her tools into her bag. "No. Not just no, but hells no. I already told you we can't be friends, Tyee, I won't work for you."

He knelt so that he could look her in the eye and dropped his voice to a whisper. Laila's heartbeat was far to the rear of the building, and he was reasonably sure she wouldn't hear them.

"O'Malley is still out there, Roxy. You saw what he was doing. Do you really think Bev's ranch was his only operation?"

Her eyes went distant.

Long moments went by with only the sound of the bubbling cauldron behind her. Finally, Roxy said softly, "No, I think he's planning a lot more."

Tyee thought so too.

Tyee knew the Slayers weren't going to move on O'Malley. Not if he wasn't making himself an overt threat to the city or the Pact. Typical Slayer shortsightedness. His people had been tracking O'Malley, but the slippery fish had managed to wriggle away and Tyee was again playing catch up.

He hated playing catch up. But he was sure Roxy was critical in his quest to pin down O'Malley. They had unfinished business and Roxy was the key.

Tyee wanted to push her, but Eloise had cautioned against it. So instead of pressing his case he pulled off his totem, a wood Chinook carving in the shape of a leaping salmon. It was precious to him but he knew he could trust her with it.

"If you change your mind. Come find me at my mother's court." He pressed the totem into her hand and she stared at him, speechless for once.

He stood and turned to leave, and paused at the door. "Get back in the game, Roxy. Something big is coming. We can't have you repairing cauldrons when it happens."

Outside, Tyee walked briskly across the street and headed back towards the Fangs. Three blocks from the coven workshop a dark shadow pulled away from an alley and fell in step beside him.

Eloise said, "That went well."

"I think so as well. Perhaps having her off the board for a while will be good."

"Oh?"

"The Slayers just culled their strongest candidate in years. If they appear weak, someone will make a move."

"This path is more dangerous."

Tyee smiled. "Nothing worth having was ever won without a little risk."

It was Eloise's turn for a crooked little smile. "What exactly are we talking about winning, again?"

Tyee's thoughts went to the feel of Roxy's calloused palm under his fingers as he'd passed his totem to her. The first time he'd given it to her, he'd assumed the rush he'd felt had been the risk of losing the totem. Now that he trusted her, the rush of sensation was even more visceral, and he wanted more.

"The only thing worth winning, *ma chère*. Everything."

~

AFTERWORD

Roxy has a lot to learn. Between Stakes and Bones and Bricks and Murder, she gets assigned troll duty. Of course, nothing goes as planned.

"I moved to Seattle to get my dream job with the Slayers. So far my work duties risk getting my throat ripped out on a daily basis. My sensei at the Slayers is sending me out on a job to deal with a rampaging stone troll. Even better, my backup is the new kid from Ireland who doesn't know which is the pointy end of the knife. If we fail, the Caravan can't cross the bridge and the citizens of Seattle who are counting on the life-saving medicine on the Caravan will suffer.

I'll get the job done, no matter what it takes, because I haven't come this far to wash out of Slayers now."

Thank you for supporting creatives and buying your copy of Roxy's Adventure direct from us!

Sign up for our Newsletter here and get your Slayer gifts exclusive to subscribers and Patreon backers.

THE FANGS

To read Tyee's perspective when seeing Roxy in the Fangs, scan below to get your complimentary copy of The Fangs:

To read an excerpt of Blood and Blades, Book 3 in the Seattle Slayers series, turn the page.

BLOOD AND BLADES

BLOOD and BLADES coming soon in early 2023! Pre-order now!

~

Blue Rowan Coven

I pulled out Big Bertha and tightened the faucet nut. I'd picked up the new parts for the coven and thanks to my handy skills, the witches would have running water in their market basin again.

Laila clapped her hands when I turned the faucet smoothly. "Thanks, Roxy!"

"Any time." And I meant it. Because right now the Blue Rowan Coven was my best paying customer. It was amazing how much repair work these witches need to keep their marketplace going and their personal workshops.

I'd had other offers for work but I'd turned them all down. I kept saying yes to the work the Blue Rowan Coven requested because I liked being able to eat and pay rent, and because their work didn't make me feel like I was doing something that would take me too far away from my Slayer vows.

Not that my Slayer vows mattered much right now.

I wiped down Big Bertha and put her away in my toolbox. I didn't carry Thor and Loki anymore but I did carry an ordinary hammer in the toolbox. It wasn't the same.

Loud cooing came from above us and we looked up. It was a carrier pigeon with an orange band. A message from Slayers.

I frowned.

Laila pointed. "You going to keep ignoring it?"

I'd been avoiding my uncle's pigeons all week. There didn't seem any point to opening the messages. What could they possibly say? For my entire life, Samuel had been a distant figure on the other side of the Veil while I'd been scraping by in Boston. But that had all changed after my dad died.

Samuel had sent us funds that helped pay for my mom's medical treatments. He'd encouraged me to cross the Veil and go through the Slayers Trials. I'd told myself that I had done all that to fulfill a promise to my dad and for the promise of a cure for my mom. But the last few months had given me more clarity on that and I could finally admit to myself that I had done it for myself.

To prove that I had been as good as my dad. That I had what it took to be a Slayer. The money had been nice too. Slayers paid a lot of silver and it had made my mom more comfortable. Bought us all some time.

Getting on the Slayers roster had also given me a lot of things I hadn't known I'd needed and one of them was Samuel's approval. Much like my dad, Samuel's approval had been rare and I'd found myself seeking it out at every turn.

If I trained harder at the Dojo, it was because I hoped Samuel would see that I was good. That I was worthy. And also so that Kotori wouldn't rub my face into the mat so often. When Samuel had given me a blade he'd crafted himself, his Maker magic wrought on the fine workmanship of the karambit, I'd taken it as a sign at last that he thought I would be a good Slayer.

But then he'd almost let Aislinn and Kotori kick me out of the Trials after a bad mission. I'd rescued Tyee from a peril of rogues and the Night Queen had sent the Slayers a chest of Tarim crystal as thanks. I hadn't gotten any thanks though. Samuel had almost booted me out then and would have if Kotori hadn't relented.

When I'd finally gotten through the Trials, my relationship with Samuel had warmed and I thought the uncertainty was behind us. That my uncle was starting to care for me and take an interest in my training.

Yes, I had disobeyed a senior member but Samuel hadn't given me the benefit of the doubt. He'd kicked me off the Slayers and now months later, he kept sending pigeons.

I would keep ignoring them.

"Yes. I don't need to hear it."

Laila squinted up at the pigeon. "I don't know, Roxy. You should at least read it. I mean, it's not like you have to respond."

She was being reasonable and I didn't feel reasonable. Which made me a little mad. I wasn't over the hurt and shame I'd felt, kneeling on the floor of the Dojo while they all condemned me. Samuel hadn't said the right things then. Now it was too late.

But maybe the Slayers wanted me back. Or would give me a chance to redeem myself. A small flame of hope that had never truly extinguished flared up and I found myself wondering if it was even possible. Could I live with myself if I didn't take the chance?

The carrier pigeon dove at us and Laila ducked. "Roxy! Do something!"

"Fine."

I raised my forearm and the pigeon swooped over Laila to perch gently on my wrist. I opened the little canister and pulled out the small scroll. There was one line of text in tight, precise letters.

"Roxy, we need to talk. Noodle Cat 2 bells. ~Samuel"

I frowned.

That told me nothing. And we had nothing to talk about. His conduct had spoken louder than his words. But the niggling ember of hope in my chest just would not die. Maybe Samuel was being monitored, and this was the only way he could reach out. That would explain why he wanted to meet at a neutral location. Certainly, no one else from the Slayers' leadership had tried to contact me, not even Tanner, who had taken an inordinate interest in me, just prior to my expulsion.

Laila waved her hand in front of my eyes, disrupting my navel-gazing. "Hello? Is it good news or bad news?"

"It's not news. But my uncle wants to see me."

"So are you going to go?"

As much as I wanted to stew in my anger, I had to admit

that it wasn't productive. If there was any chance I could get back in the Slayers' good graces, I had to take it. All the silver in the world was only going to buy my mom a little more time. I had to find a way to get some Cure across the Veil to her. For my mom's sake, I had to swallow my pride and see what my uncle wanted.

"Yeah. I guess it's been long enough."

I dug out a stub of a pencil from my pocket and scribbled, "Yes" before rolling the paper back into the canister. The pigeon waited gamely until the canister was secured before taking wing from my forearm.

Noodle Cat was a luxury that I could no longer justify. Kotori had taken me there after patrol and I'd become a fan of the nabeyaki udon. Just thinking about the dense chewy noodles and the rich broth was enough to make me salivate.

The shop was small and crowded as usual. A fat white cat waved at me from the cash register. The unctuous aroma of hearty broth and roasted pork enveloped me like a hug as I entered. If I managed to get back into the Slayers, this place was definitely going back on my rotation. I looked around and didn't see any other Slayers. Then a big hand pushed aside the indigo noren panels and Samuel poked his head out, gesturing for me to step into the back room.

My uncle was built tall, like me, but broad across the chest and shoulders, unlike me. I was used to seeing him in armor that broadened his already wide shoulders, along with a katana that added even more menace to his imposing frame.

What I wasn't used to seeing, was him dressed in a formal tangzhuang, with a snug collar and intricate embroidery along the right side of his chest. A row of frog closures held the jacket closed. I suddenly felt very underdressed, my shirt and pants still grubby from working on Laila's plumbing.

I edged my way between the tightly set tables, my emotions a distasteful mix of confusion and disappointment. Even the steaming bowls of noodles looked dull and lifeless now. I didn't know why my uncle had asked to see me, but dressed the way he was, I assumed it wasn't for anything related to the Slayers.

The whole situation only got more confusing as I neared the rear of the restaurant, as I noted my uncle's eyes darting back and forth, and sweat beading across his forehead. My uncle, one of the famed Seven Freaks of Seattle, was as nervous as a trainee heading out for his first exsanguination run.

When I stopped at the noren panels, his shoulders relaxed a touch. "Roxy. Thank you for coming."

My uncle's tension put me completely off my game and I forgot to be mad at him for a moment. "What's going on?"

Samuel paused for a moment and looked over his shoulder quickly as if for help. He turned back to me and actually wrung his hands as he spoke. "I know we haven't talked in a while, and things haven't gone smoothly at the Dojo. I'm...sorry I haven't been able to help you."

Someone in the room behind him cleared their throat. Loudly.

Samuel flinched. "I'm...sorry I haven't been here for you. As your uncle."

This was getting weird. Who was behind him?

I pitched my voice low, only for Samuel's ears. "Are you being threatened?"

My uncle coughed and I jumped forward, thinking he was choking, only to realize he was actually laughing. I stepped back, irritated that I was apparently not in on the joke. When Samuel got control of himself he wiped a tear from his eye.

I had to admit, it was nice to see my normally stoic uncle laughing.

He straightened up and cleared his throat. "I'm not doing this well. Maybe you should just come in." He stepped back and invited me into the back room.

The private room was cozy, a small space that held only one low table laid out with three place settings. The table had been set with a pristine white table cloth and to the side of the table lay a wrapped bouquet of red roses.

Paper lanterns set in the four walls filled the room with warm light and the place felt intimate, totally unlike the busy restaurant on the other side of the curtain.

A petite woman sat in one of the chairs.

Wait, was that Aanya?

I was used to seeing Aanya at the Dojo, or on duty at the Market, her talwar at her side. Today she wore her usual sari, this one in a vivid coral, and her long, black hair was pulled back into a coiled braid. Her deep-set eyes twinkled with amusement and she stood to hug me. She smelled of botanicals and roses. I leaned in and hugged her back reflexively but I remained confused. I mean, she could have asked me to eat noodles with her anytime. Also, why was my uncle so dressed up?

Then a weird thought hit me. Were they on a date?

If so, why was I here?

I must have been staring because Aanya said my name, as if she were repeating herself.

"Uh, hi Aanya. Really nice to see you."

Wow, this was awkward.

"Your uncle and I wanted to see you outside of work."

"Yeah, sure."

"We have something to tell you, don't we, Samuel."

I turned to look at my uncle. He ran a finger over the high collar of his jacket. "Roxy, Aanya and I are getting married. We wanted to invite you to the wedding."

I stared at him, stunned.

He stepped over to Aanya and put his arm around her shoulders. "You're my closest family and it would mean a lot to me if you were there."

Aanya put a hand over his. "It would mean a lot to both of us."

My gaze went back and forth between them, to the way they leaned in to each other, my behemoth of an uncle and Aanya's dainty frame. It looked strange and right at the same time. A rush of emotion tightened my throat, to be here and to have them telling me they wanted me at their wedding.

My uncle and I had never so much as had a pot of tea together and to leapfrog to this family event was a lot to take in. And I realized I wanted it more than anything. To be included in something. Even if it had no affiliation to Slayers. Or maybe especially because it was not related to Slayers. Where the only reason Samuel was asking me to do something was because we were family.

"I wouldn't miss it for the world."

Pre-order your copy of Blood and Blades today! Patrons receive chapters weekly on our Patreon:

EBONY GATE

Julia Vee and Ken Bebelle bring you a female *John Wick* story with dragon magic set in contemporary San Francisco's Chinatown

Emiko Soong belongs to one of the eight premier magical families of the world. But Emiko never needed any magic. Because she is the Blade of the Soong Clan.

Or was. Until she's drenched in blood in the middle of a market in China, surrounded by bodies and the scent of blood and human waste as a lethal perfume.

The Butcher of Beijing now lives a quiet life in San Francisco, importing antiques. But when a shinigami, a god of death itself, calls in a family blood debt, Emiko must recover the Ebony Gate that holds back the hungry ghosts of the Yomi underworld.

Or forfeit her soul as the anchor.

What's a retired assassin to do but save the City By The Bay from an army of the dead?

Pre-order your copy of Ebony Gate Today!

ACKNOWLEDGMENTS

~

Big thanks to our early readers, Penny and Michelle, who read this in record time and gave us their insights on things we could add to make this story really sing. Special thanks to Cisca, who gave Roxy's story lots of love. This is the fuel that keeps us writing.

~ Ken and Julia

ABOUT THE AUTHORS

Ken Bebelle

Ken turned his childhood love for reading sci-fi and fantasy into a career in prosthetics. After twenty years he came back to books, writing about plucky underdogs and ancient magical artifacts with deadly secrets. He grew up in northern California and now lives in southern California with his wife, two kids, and too many tomato plants.

Julia Vee

Julia likes stories about monsters, money, and good food. Julia was born in Macao and grew up in Northern California, where she studied at UC Berkeley and majored in Asian Studies. She is a graduate of the Viable Paradise workshop.

Ken and Julia have written together since middle school. Their forthcoming trilogy has been acquired by Tor and debuts with Ebony Gate in the Spring of 2023. Ebony Gate is a contemporary fantasy with Asian elements and mythology set in the Pacific Rim.

KEN BEBELLE AND JULIA VEE

SEATTLE SLAYERS:

Stakes and Bones

Bricks and Murder

Blood and Blades

PHOENIX HOARD

Ebony Gate

Blood Jade

Tiger Eye

Made in the USA
Columbia, SC
29 January 2023